SUPERMAN™

DAWNBREAKER

—DC ICONS—

SUPERMAN
DAWNBREAKER

— DC ICONS —

MATT DE LA PEÑA

Random House 🏠 New York

**Superman created by Jerry Siegel and Joe Shuster.
By special arrangement with the Jerry Siegel family.**

Copyright © 2019 DC Comics.
SUPERMAN and all related characters and elements © & ™ DC Comics.
WB SHIELD: ™ & © WBEI. (s19)
RHUS38089

Jacket art used under license from Shutterstock.com
Logo by Stuart Wade

All rights reserved. Published in the United States by Random House Children's Books, a division of Penguin Random House LLC, New York.

Random House and the colophon are registered trademarks of Penguin Random House LLC.

Visit us on the Web! GetUnderlined.com

Educators and librarians, for a variety of teaching tools, visit us at RHTeachersLibrarians.com

Library of Congress Cataloging-in-Publication Data
Names: de la Peña, Matt, author.
Title: Superman: dawnbreaker / Matt de la Peña.
Other titles: Dawnbreaker | Dawn breaker
Description: First edition. | New York: Random House, [2019] |
Series: DC icons series
Identifiers: LCCN 2018042230 | ISBN 978-0-399-54965-6 (hardback) |
ISBN 978-0-399-54966-3 (lib. bdg.) | ISBN 978-1-9848-5194-9 (int'l) |
ISBN 978-0-399-54967-0 (ebook)
Classification: LCC PZ7.P3725 Sup 2019 | DDC [Fic]—dc23

Printed in the United States of America
10 9 8 7 6 5 4 3 2 1
First Edition

TO OUTSIDERS EVERYWHERE
AND TO THE TEACHERS WHO SEE US

CHAPTER 1

The storm came with little warning. A flash of lightning lit up Clark's glasses as he huddled beneath the Java Depot awning with three former football teammates, all of them watching the sudden deluge pound the streets of downtown Smallville. The whipping rain had forced them elbow to elbow, and if Clark exercised a little amnesia, it almost felt like old times, back when he and the football squad were thick as thieves.

He doubted they would ever be close like that again.

Not after he had quit on them.

Clark had always marveled at the power of thunderstorms, which put even his own mysterious strength into perspective. For others, the storm was nothing more than a nuisance. An older businessman, holding a briefcase over his head, sprinted toward a silver SUV, where he beeped open his door and dove inside. A drenched calico slunk beneath an industrial trash bin, looking for a dry place to wait out the downpour.

"We can't just stand here all day," Paul shouted over the roar of the rain. "Come on, let's make a run for the library."

Kyle crossed his arms and rocked back on his heels. "Dude, this shit is, like, biblical. I'm not going *anywhere*."

"I guess we could just do this here." Tommy glanced back at the closed door of the coffee shop before turning to Clark. "Cool with you, big guy?"

Clark shrugged, still wondering what "this" was.

And why no one else could be within earshot.

He had been more than a little surprised when Tommy Jones, a lumbering offensive lineman, approached him at school wanting to "hang out." He'd been equally surprised when Tommy then showed up at the coffee shop with star running back Paul Molina and full-back Kyle Turner. After all, they'd wanted nothing to do with Clark for the better part of two years—since the day he abruptly left the freshman team midseason.

Now here they all were, kicking it on Main Street again.

Like nothing had ever happened.

But Clark knew there had to be a catch.

Tommy raised the brim of his baseball cap and cleared his throat. "I'm guessing you know our record this past season," he began. "We sort of . . . underachieved."

"That's one way of putting it," Kyle said, and Paul shook his head in disgust.

Clark should have known. This meetup was about football. Because when it came to Tommy, Kyle, and Paul, *everything* was about football.

"Anyway, us three have been talking." Tommy slapped a big, meaty hand onto Clark's shoulder. "We'll all be seniors next year. And we wanna go out with a bang."

A massive clap of thunder echoed overhead, causing the three football players to flinch. Clark had never understood that reaction. How even the bravest people he knew could get so spooked by a little thunder. It was yet another example of how different he was from his peers. The guys tried to play off their jumpiness by checking their phones and studying their drinks.

That's when Clark noticed something odd.

About thirty yards to his right, a wire-thin man in his early twenties was standing in the middle of the road, holding out his arms and staring up into the pouring rain. He had a tight buzz cut, and he was dressed head to toe in brown. Brown long-sleeved shirt. Brown pants. Brown combat boots. Clark had an uneasy feeling about the guy.

"Look at *this* freak," Paul said, noticing him, too.

"Who?" Tommy asked.

"Over there." Paul pointed, but a slow big rig rumbled by, blocking their view. When it had passed, the man was gone.

Paul frowned, scratching the back of his shaved head and scanning the empty street. "He was standing out there a second ago. I swear."

Clark searched for the man, too. Random strangers dressed in all brown didn't just appear on the streets of Smallville, only to disappear seconds later. Who *was* he? Clark glanced back through the Java Depot window, where a dozen or so people he recognized were sitting at little round tables, drinking coffee and talking. Doing homework. Taking refuge from the storm.

He wondered if any of them had seen the guy.

As swiftly as the storm had begun, it now slowed to a quiet sprinkle. Steam rose off a drenched Main Street. Heavy drops fell from the trees. They streaked down the windshields of parked cars and zigzagged down street signs. The road was a sea of puddles.

"Let's walk," Tommy said, and they set off toward the public square, Clark still looking for the man dressed in brown.

The four of them had to veer around a series of orange cones blocking off yet another construction zone. A surging local economy had led to a serious transformation of downtown Smallville over the past several years. Gone were all the boarded-up storefronts and dilapidated buildings of Clark's youth. In their place were trendy restaurants, real estate offices, a luxury condo development, and two shiny new bank branches. Multiple construction projects seemed to always be under way now, including the future headquarters for the powerful Mankins Corporation. But there was no work being done this afternoon. The storm had turned Main Street into a ghost town.

"Look, Clark," Tommy said, attempting to pick up where he'd left off, "we all know how much better we would be with you in the backfield. I mean, there's a reason we were undefeated in the games you played freshman year."

"Yeah, before he bailed on us," Paul scoffed.

Tommy shot Paul a dirty look. "What'd we talk about earlier, man? This is about moving forward. It's about second chances."

Clark shrank into himself.

Two years later and he still couldn't stomach the idea that he'd let the team down. And then lied to them. He hadn't quit football to concentrate on school, like he told everyone at the time. He quit because he could have scored on just about every play from scrimmage. And the urge to dominate—wrong as it seemed—grew stronger with each passing game. Until one day he ran over Miles Loften during a tackling drill, sending him to the hospital with fractured ribs. And Clark had only been going about 50 percent. After practice, he'd climbed the bleachers and sat alone, long into the night, contemplating what was no longer possible for him to overlook—just how drastically different he was. And how bad it would be if anyone found out.

Before leaving that night, he'd decided to hang up his cleats.

He hadn't played an organized sport since.

When Tommy stopped walking, everyone else did, too. "I'm just gonna come right out and say it." He glanced at Kyle and Paul before turning back to Clark. "We *need* you."

Kyle nodded. "Come back soon and you'll be able to reestablish yourself before summer workouts. Shit, Coach would probably even make you a captain."

"What do you say, Clark?" Tommy play-punched him in the arm. "Can we count on you?"

Clark wanted so badly to come through for these guys. To put on the pads and get back to work. To feel like he was a part of something again, something bigger than himself. But it was impossible. Injuring teammates and scoring seven touchdowns a game was bad enough when he was a freshman. Imagine if things like that happened on *varsity*. With everyone watching. He just couldn't risk it. His parents had warned him how dangerous it could be if the world were to discover the depths of his mysterious abilities. And the last thing he wanted to do was bring trouble to the family. Kids at school already teased him about being too good. Too perfect. It was the reason he'd started wearing glasses he didn't actually need. And mixing in a couple of Bs on his report card.

Clark adjusted his glasses, looking at the sidewalk. "I really wish I could," he told Tommy in a lifeless voice. "But I can't. I'm sorry."

"See?" Paul said. "Told you he didn't give a shit about us."

"Unbelievable," Kyle added, shaking his head.

Tommy turned away from Clark. "Easy, fellas. We can't *force* the guy to be loyal—"

The man in brown turned a corner and cut right through the four of them. He forcefully bumped shoulders with Tommy, causing him to fumble his iced coffee to the ground.

Clark and his ex-teammates were struck silent for several seconds, until Kyle kicked the plastic cup across the sidewalk and called after the guy, "Hey, asshole! You need to watch where the hell you're going!"

The man spun around and shouted something back at Kyle in Spanish. Then he spit on the sidewalk and held up a small blade, as if daring them to say anything else.

"Yo, he's got a knife!" Paul shouted.

When Clark stepped in front of his friends, he saw how jittery the man's bloodshot eyes were. And he was mumbling under his breath.

"What's he saying?" Kyle asked Paul, who was Mexican and spoke Spanish at home.

Paul shook his head. "I don't know. Something about getting back to Metropolis."

Clark wondered if the guy might be on drugs. What else could explain his bloodshot eyes and the way he'd been standing in the pouring rain? And he wasn't just staring at Clark now. He was staring *through* Clark. "Let's leave him alone," Clark said, focusing on the knife in the man's left hand. "There's something off about the way he's acting."

"Screw that," Kyle said, elbowing past Clark. He pointed at the man, shouting, "Nobody slams into my teammate like that without apologizing. You think I'm scared of that little bullshit switch-blade?"

The man lunged, swinging the knife violently, the blade grazing Kyle's forearm, before quickly retreating.

Kyle looked at the blood trickling down his arm. He looked at the man.

Then all hell broke loose.

Clark bounded forward to kick the knife out of the guy's hand, sending it skittering under a parked car. Tommy and Paul threw their backpacks into the street and charged. They tackled the man onto the hard, wet pavement, but he managed to scurry out of their grasp, leap to his feet, and retreat.

Kyle made a move to join the fray, but Clark pulled him back. "Hang on!"

"Oh, hell no! He just cut my ass!" Kyle took a wider angle this time and joined Tommy and Paul as the three of them stalked the guy, backing him into a row of parked cars.

Clark knew how lopsided the fight would be. The man was wild-eyed and showed no fear, but he was clearly no match for three hulking football players.

Clark's instinct was to rush in and break everything up before anyone got seriously hurt. But things had gone horribly wrong the last time he'd used his powers in public. It had been winter. He'd been walking to the library when he spotted a big rig careening across a large ice patch on Highway 22. Without thinking, he'd sprinted over and used his strength to grab hold of the massive truck before it could flatten the Alvarez Fruits and Vegetables stand at the side of the road. Only he'd somehow overcorrected the big rig's momentum, toppling the heavy trailer, spilling dozens of oil drums out onto the two-lane highway. Oil had gushed everywhere.

Clark would never forget helping the driver from the wreckage. The man's face had been as white as a sheet, his leg twisted grotesquely. Would he have even been hurt if Clark hadn't stuck his nose in things? The question haunted Clark, and he'd promised himself to stop and think before physically intervening like that again.

But he could use his voice.

"Let him go, guys!" he shouted at his ex-teammates. "It's not worth it!"

The man in brown backed right into an old truck before slipping between parked cars and running away.

Tommy turned to Kyle, grabbing his bloody arm and studying the cut. Paul huffed into the middle of the street to retrieve his backpack.

Clark cautiously followed the man in brown down the next block. He had to make sure he was really leaving, so no one got hurt. He stopped in his tracks when the guy began pounding his bare fists against the side of a beat-up white pickup truck while the driver cowered at the wheel. Clark stood there watching, absolutely baffled. What was wrong with this guy? And why was he beating on this one particular truck? It had just been innocently idling there at the side of the road. And the man was attacking it with a shocking ferocity, bloodying his fists in the process.

He turned suddenly and stalked back the other way, in the direction of Clark and the football players. Clark made a move to cut him off, but the man lunged toward the silver SUV instead, the one where the gray-haired businessman was waiting out the storm. The man in brown flung open the driver's-side door, threw the businessman onto the street, and climbed in to start the engine.

Clark's eyes widened with panic when the SUV lurched out of its parking spot and then sped forward, heading directly toward Paul, who was still kneeling in the street, zipping up his backpack.

"Look out!" Clark shouted.

Paul froze when he heard the screaming engine.

He was just kneeling there, a sitting duck.

Clark felt the familiar weightlessness of reaching warp speed.

His skin tingling and raw.

His throat closing as he bolted soundlessly into the street, eyes fixed on the SUV barreling down on Paul.

Clark instinctively calculated his angle, the speed of the SUV, and the potential for destruction. He dove at the last possible second. And as he tore through the air, he peered up into the crazed eyes of the man gripping the steering wheel, and he saw how lost the man was, how bewildered. In that instant, Clark understood this was an act that ran far deeper than he or anyone else could know.

Then came the bone-crushing impact.

CHAPTER 2

As Mrs. Sovak droned on about the history of American labor at the front of the classroom, Clark watched Paul's futile attempt to take notes left-handed. The poor guy's entire right side was out of commission. His right arm was in an elaborate sling designed to help heal his dislocated shoulder and partially torn labrum.

Clark replayed the scene in his head for the hundredth time. How he'd collided with Paul at full speed. How they'd skidded across the wet pavement and into the tire of a parked van. For the past week he'd been trying to decide if there was a way he could've saved his ex-teammate without injury. But each time he thought about it, he came to the same conclusion: the violent tackle was unavoidable.

Wasn't it?

The football team didn't see it that way. Kyle and Tommy hadn't spotted the SUV until it crashed into a retaining wall built to protect the new Mankins headquarters construction zone. And

Clark hit Paul with such force that they had ended up clear on the other side of the street. So the other players didn't understand how Paul could have been in any real danger in the first place. Especially when the police believed the Mankins construction site had been the man in brown's intended target. Not that they could have asked the man himself. He was in a coma. And doctors didn't expect him to survive.

Now some guys on the football team thought Clark had blasted Paul on purpose, out of jealousy. And maybe they were right. Not about the jealousy part, but it was possible the SUV wasn't going to run over Paul.

Maybe Clark had miscalculated.

It felt like every time he tried to help, someone got hurt. And he came out looking like the bad guy.

As if the universe were trying to mock him, Clark now heard the faint crying sound of someone else who might need help. It was coming from a girl, he was pretty sure. But none of the female faces around him seemed the least bit upset.

Bored to tears, maybe, but not upset.

Mary Baker was smacking gum and covertly texting beneath her desk.

Olivia Goodman was biting her fingernails while staring longingly out the classroom window.

Sherry Miller was sketching some kind of dark unicorn scene in the margins of her poli sci textbook.

"Clark," Lana Lang whispered beside him.

The crying sound reminded Clark of Paul's quiet whimpering as the four of them watched a rescue crew use the Jaws of Life to free the man from the mangled SUV. Not only was Paul's shoulder in bad shape, but the skin on his arm and the side of his face had been badly scraped up when he and Clark slid across the wet pavement.

Clark, of course, didn't have a scratch.

Even his glasses, which had fallen off in the collision, had come out unscathed.

"Earth to Clark Kent," Lana whispered more forcefully. "Dude, what's your deal?"

This time he turned to look at his best friend. She was wearing the oval moonstone necklace her mom had given her on her sixteenth birthday and a T-shirt that read THE FUTURE IS FEMALE. Her red hair was pulled back into a ponytail, like it always was at school, and the closest thing to makeup she had on was lip balm.

Who, me? Clark mouthed to her.

"You're, like, all over the place today," she whispered.

More crying. He wondered if Lana could hear it, too. Or . . . maybe it was coming from somewhere *outside* the classroom?

Lana motioned toward Paul. "He's going to be fine," she whispered. "If it wasn't for you, he wouldn't even *be* here."

Clark shrugged and turned back to their teacher, trying to focus on Mrs. Sovak's marathon lecture. She was breaking down the evolution of migratory work in America. "Agricultural migrant work started as far back as the 1600s," she explained. "These were the indentured servants coming from England. Of course we can never forget the monstrosities of slavery, when African people were brought to this country against their will. And in the 1840s, tens of thousands of Mexican workers began coming across the border to take labor jobs. This particular group, as I mentioned earlier, will be the focus of our final unit. . . ."

It wasn't that Clark was uninterested. His problem was that he couldn't stop staring at Paul's sling. Replaying the incident downtown, thinking about the man with the knife. And now he was also fixated on the subtle crying he kept hearing.

Mrs. Sovak stopped and eyed the class. "I'm not telling you all this for my health, you know. It'll be on our final."

Clark sat up straight as her gaze briefly fell upon him.

"I'm sure you're aware of the protests downtown," she went on. "This stuff is as relevant as ever. How we choose to address the situation today will significantly impact the future of your town and family farms. . . ."

Clark tried to isolate on the crying sound, but everything else was getting in the way. Jessica Napier was whispering to a friend in the back of the class. "Tommy's party next weekend is gonna be huge. Everyone's gonna be there. . . ."

Out in the hallway, a student walked by with headphones, listening to an old country song Clark vaguely recognized.

Clear across campus, Kyle made a joke about bulldozing right over Willie Moore during yesterday's spring scrimmage. One of Kyle's cronies snickered loudly, and then a locker slammed shut.

Clark could even hear a small plane somewhere in the sky. A single-engine prop plane, to be exact. He could tell by the whipping sound of the front propeller. The plane was flying somewhere over a neighboring community. Like Noonan, maybe—

No, that was impossible. Noonan was the nearest town, but it was still more than thirty miles away.

Great, now his mind was playing tricks on him.

He rubbed his ears with the heels of his hands and stared at Mrs. Sovak.

It wasn't just his hearing ability that was changing. *All* his powers seemed to be getting stronger. Two days ago he'd seen right through a wall, into the classroom next door. He'd watched a freshman girl pass a note to another girl, who laughed without sound. These new abilities both thrilled him and scared him to death.

But it was his hearing that he was focused on now.

Somewhere on campus, a girl was crying.

Her soft sobs sounded so broken and desperate that they eventually drowned out everything else in Clark's head.

He needed to find out who she was. And why she was so sad.

"Clark," Lana's hushed voice interrupted again.

This time Clark waited until Mrs. Sovak was writing on the board to turn to Lana. He found her staring at him, her large green eyes narrowed with concern.

"You've been acting really weird lately," she said. "Even for *you*."

Clark shrugged, ignoring the dig. Lana had a sixth sense when it came to reading people. It's what made her such a good reporter. And it's what made Clark sometimes feel anxious around her. There was so much he needed to keep hidden.

"Honestly, though, is everything okay? I'm here if you need to talk."

"Thanks," he told her. "But I'm good. I just—"

The final bell rang, saving him from having to finish the thought. He smiled at Lana instead, doing his best to look normal. Anyway, it's not like he could confide in her that he heard someone crying on the other side of campus.

She wouldn't understand.

Nobody would.

As they filed out of the classroom, Lana reached up to brush something off Clark's collar, saying, "Oh, get this. The inequity within the athletics department runs even deeper than I first thought. I just found proof of an attempted cover-up last summer."

"Like, in the accounting?" Clark asked.

"You got it." Lana was already the editor of the school paper as a junior. She was good at asking questions. And even better at getting answers. "Can you believe something like this could be happening right here under our noses? At Smallville High?"

Lana's current story centered on how much of the school budget was spent on athletics. More specifically, male athletics. Even *more* specifically, football.

This was the way it had always worked between Clark and his best friend; whatever story she was currently working on became a big part of their conversations. Lana liked using Clark as a sounding board, and Clark enjoyed being part of her investigative whirlwinds.

"Is Rice cooperating?" Clark asked, referring to their principal.

"Oh, yes, she is." Lana waved her phone in front of his face. "She's sent me three emails over the last two periods."

Clark grinned. No one could make a powerful adult sweat quite like Lana Lang could.

The hallways were filled with students excited for the weekend. Clark and Lana swerved around a group of JV defensive linemen doing some kind of pre-practice chant Clark vaguely remembered from freshman year. They ducked past a group of loud pom-pom-wielding cheerleaders. After a while he was able to filter out all the peripheral noise and focus solely on the crying girl.

What was wrong? he wondered. Was she hurt?

"Listen, Lana," Clark said as they neared the front doors, "there's something I gotta do real fast."

"Sounds mildly intriguing. What's up?"

"It's not a big deal. Just have to check if I, uh, left my—"

"Lana?" Speak of the devil, Principal Rice was standing in the doorway of the front office, wearing her usual gray power suit. "Can I have a quick word?"

Clark and Lana shared a knowing glance, and Clark whispered, "Meet you at the front steps in ten?"

Lana nodded and turned to Principal Rice. "Of course, ma'am. Would you like to speak in your office?"

Clark watched Principal Rice and Lana start toward the office, then turned his attention back to the crying. He followed the sound through the freshman locker hall and past the gym, where the women's basketball team was warming up. The sound eventually led him to an empty classroom halfway across the school.

He recognized the girl right away.

Gloria Alvarez.

A senior he'd always admired from afar. She was one of the few people at Smallville High who were able to navigate effortlessly across multiple social groups. One day she'd be eating lunch in the library with the Latinx Book Club. The next day Clark would see her laughing in the halls with a group of white cheerleaders. He also knew she was one of the smartest kids in the school and so good with computers that she codes.

Gloria sat at a desk in the front row, hunched over, wiping tears with a bundled tissue. At first she didn't notice Clark in the doorway, so he simply stood there and watched her, feeling awkward. She clearly wasn't in any danger. But the depth of her sadness was so gut-wrenching that he couldn't pull himself away. He wondered if he'd ever felt *anything* so intensely.

Was he even capable?

In a way, he actually *envied* her sadness.

He took a tentative step forward and cleared his throat. "Excuse me, but . . . are you okay?"

Gloria looked up at Clark, startled. Her eyes red, cheeks streaked with tears.

"Sorry," Clark mumbled, averting his gaze. "I just—I was passing by or whatever and . . ." He studied her again. "What's wrong?"

"Everything." Gloria stood up, then froze, staring at him. "People are disappearing," she snapped, "and no one in this town even *cares.*"

Her words caught Clark completely off guard. "Who?"

She shook her head and pushed past him, out the door. Watching her hurry into the crowded hallway, Clark felt confused.

And helpless.

People were disappearing from Smallville?

CHAPTER 3

After school that day, a small helicopter whirred above the field of the Kents' rural farm, just a few miles south of Smallville. Clark and his dad watched it pass overhead yet again. Third time in the past twenty minutes.

This didn't sit well with Clark.

He'd always felt protective of the farm. And his aging parents. The feeling had only intensified as he'd gotten older.

Helicopters were a rare sight in the area. Most farmers no longer dusted crops by air. But what really bothered Clark was the way the chopper weaved across the gray sky in a distinct pattern—flying over their small farmhouse, past the pond and the cornfields and the chicken coop, and then dipping lower near the large crater that butted up against their old barn.

Whoever was up there was looking for something.

But what?

When Clark had brought up his concern earlier, his dad

shrugged it off. "Can't say I appreciate it either, Clark. But there's no law against flying over someone's property."

So Clark stuck with the other law-related subject they'd been discussing: the controversial new stop-and-search issue on the ballot in Smallville. It had already been passed into law in a couple of neighboring towns, but Clark refused to believe the residents of Smallville would support it. Would they? "So the police would be able to stop anyone?" he asked his dad. Clark was thinking about what Gloria had said about people disappearing. "At any time? With no cause?"

Wiping his brow on the shoulder of his flannel shirt, Jonathan Kent turned to Clark. Clark thought his dad had been looking older lately. There was more gray in his hair. More puffiness under his eyes. All the years of backbreaking farmwork were catching up to him. "The population's changing, son. And some communities . . . I think they're scared about where this change might leave them."

"But it's racist."

His dad studied him for several seconds before saying, "Well, it's probably a little more complicated than that. But still, I'm voting no on the issue."

Clark nodded and drove his shovel back into the ground. Even in his annoyance, he was careful not to use *too* much force. He'd already snapped a half dozen shovels this spring. And his folks didn't have money for that kind of extra expense. But it seriously depressed him to think that *anyone* in Smallville could vote for a law that allowed police to make traffic stops based solely on the color of someone's skin.

And what happened if the people in the car didn't have documentation? Could the police just throw them into the back of a squad car and whisk them away?

"That storm's closer than it looks," Jonathan said, peering into the sky again. "This really isn't a great time to be flying."

"What do you think they're looking for?"

Jonathan repositioned a loose fence post in one of the holes Clark had dug. "Whatever it is, they should think about heading in soon. Especially after what happened with that plane today."

Clark froze. "Plane?"

Jonathan paused, too. "A small plane crash-landed out by Noonan this afternoon. The pilot stalled it somehow and couldn't regain control."

Clark stared at his dad in shock. The plane he'd heard in class . . . it was real. His mind *hadn't* been playing tricks on him after all.

A drizzle began falling, and the sky swiftly grew more sinister.

"What about the pilot?" Clark asked. "Everyone okay?"

His dad nodded, glancing up at the helicopter again. "She broke several bones. But from what I hear, she should eventually recover."

"Dad, I . . ." Clark paused to think about what he wanted to say.

"Yes, son?"

Clark shook his head, imagining how absurd it would sound.

"You can tell me anything," his dad said. "You know that."

"It's just . . . I *heard* that plane today." Clark had to speak up, to make sure his dad could hear him over the sound of the helicopter as it passed overhead again. "How's that even *possible*?"

Jonathan stared at Clark. "All the way in Noonan? From school?"

Clark nodded. He'd never tried to hide his powers from his parents—not that he could have if he'd tried. He'd been showing signs since he was a toddler. One summer, when Clark was eight, their closest neighbor, Mr. Peterman, had rolled his four-wheeler on their property. Clark had been playing in a nearby field when he heard the screams for help. He raced over to the scene and, without even considering the impossibility of the task, began hoisting the thousand-pound vehicle, an inch at a time, every muscle in his body straining, until the trapped man could scurry out from beneath it, where he promptly passed out. It was easy to convince the man later that he'd crawled out himself and Clark had merely found him there.

Another time he'd accidentally touched an electrified wire on the Kents' steer pen. Sparks flew. The air crackled. His skin trembled and buzzed, and his palm grew warm, but he didn't feel pain. He wasn't even sure what pain was exactly. He understood it conceptually. He'd seen his dad wince and shake his hand out after slamming his thumb with a hammer. And he'd never forget watching Miles Loften writhe in pain at the twenty-yard line after Clark had accidentally busted his ribs. But pain for Clark was different. It was more of a minor irritant than anything else. Which he knew wasn't normal.

The point was, Clark's parents already knew he was special. They'd seen him go around the farm as a kid, trying to lift everything that wasn't nailed down. They'd seen him running at the speed of light. But these new powers were different. They seemed almost . . . otherworldly.

His dad kept a poker face as he studied Clark.

The helicopter overhead looped away from a dark cloud, then came back around for yet another pass as the rain picked up. Clark kept expecting his dad to hurry them toward shelter. But Jonathan didn't. Maybe he considered the conversation too important to interrupt.

"Well," Jonathan finally began, "I don't know *how* it's possible, but . . ."

The whir of the helicopter blades was drowned out by a loud

clap of thunder. The sudden silence that followed made them both look up. Helicopters weren't supposed to just stop making noise. Clark thought of the plane in Noonan.

They spotted the helicopter at the same time.

It was plunging toward the ground near the old barn.

Swirling unnaturally in some kind of death spiral.

Clark resisted the urge to intervene. After the incident with Paul and the SUV, he'd vowed to keep his nose out of places it didn't belong. He'd only make things worse. He cringed as an instinctive energy surged through his body with such ferocity that he accidentally snapped the shovel in two.

The helicopter was just seconds away from crashing into the Kents' field when Clark tossed away the shovel pieces and took off.

"Clark!" his dad called after him. "Wait!"

Clark tore across the field, hyperaware of everything around him: the thick drops of rain suspended like teardrops in the sky, the deafening silence cocooning his body, the breath suspended in his lungs. In instances like this one, when his powers took hold and his thoughts receded, Earth felt smaller and more fragile, as if its rules no longer applied. Yet Clark knew this was only an illusion. Gravity would still yank down the chopper. The collision with the ground would still be catastrophic. The people inside would die.

He was the one somehow breaking the rules.

But could he break them in time?

With a desperate leap, he made it just before impact, grabbing hold of the landing skids a fraction of a second before they slammed into the ground. He clutched the thick steel in his hands and braced himself with his feet. But Clark's knees buckled under the tremendous weight of the chopper's momentum as he attempted to absorb it with his back and shoulders. His muscles screamed, his neck tweaked so far forward that his chin was nearly flush against his chest.

It took all Clark's strength to kneel in the mud as the massive machine jolted and twisted in his grasp. Spinning out of his control, it landed on its side with a tremendous crash, blades digging into the soft earth with a wet thwacking sound, shrapnel flying everywhere.

The chopper settled only inches from the side of the old barn, at the lip of the crater that had always marked this part of the Kent farm. Clark stared in shock at the helicopter's battered underbelly, smoke and steam spewing out of the wreckage.

"Hey!" he shouted, scooping his glasses off the ground and putting them back on. "Anyone need help?"

No answer.

He thought maybe he'd failed again, but in a few seconds the smoke had thinned and he spotted someone hanging halfway out the cracked back window.

Clark hurried over and pulled the limp body down from the vessel. Just in time, as the remainder of the window fell from the frame in a single sheet, shattering against the side of the chopper. Clark held the guy in his arms, looking him over. It was a kid he recognized from school. Bryan Something. He must've been thrown from the cockpit when the blades smacked against the ground. His head had punctured the window.

Bryan's eyes were closed, and his pale arms hung lifelessly.

"Son!" Clark's dad was calling for him in the distance. "You all right?"

A sick feeling spread through Clark's stomach the longer Bryan stayed still. But eventually the boy groaned weakly and blindly reached a hand up toward the raw scrape on his forehead.

Breathing a sigh of relief, Clark set him on the ground.

Bryan tested his arms and legs as if trying to confirm that he was still alive.

Clark studied his dark, scraggly hair. His deep-set eyes and stooped shoulders. He was thin, like one of the fence posts Clark and his dad had just been repairing. Yet there was a fire in his eyes. Then Clark remembered how he knew Bryan. He was new at school, having started just before the end of the year.

"What . . . *happened?*" Bryan managed to say.

"There's been an accident." Clark motioned toward the ground near the helicopter. "You're lucky you landed *here*. In the mud."

Bryan scrambled to his feet. "Corey!" he shouted, hurrying around to the battered cockpit.

Two other people were now cautiously climbing out of the wreckage. They each had several cuts and bruises, but miraculously none of their injuries appeared to be serious. One was a middle-aged, balding man. He wore thin glasses that were slightly bent, and he was holding a cell phone in his right hand. He stood in the mud, looking back and forth between the helicopter and Clark, something unsettling in his gaze.

The other passenger wasn't much older than Bryan. He was taller, though. And broader. They looked like brothers.

"Thank God you're okay, Corey," Bryan said.

His brother marched right up to Bryan and jabbed an angry finger into his chest. "What were you thinking up there! You could've *killed* us!"

"I just looped back around like you—"

"This is the *one* thing you're supposed to be good at, Bryan! But you suck as a pilot, too, don't you? God, no wonder Mom and Dad think you're such a loser!"

Clark watched Bryan turn away silently.

Jonathan showed up, breathing heavily after sprinting across the field. Mercifully, he stepped between the brothers, saying, "Easy, guys. I've already called for help. What matters is that everyone's okay."

Clark marveled at how quickly Bryan's older brother's demeanor shifted. Two seconds ago, he'd been berating his brother. Now he was smiling at Clark's dad like some kind of overcaffeinated tractor salesman. He held out his hand, saying, "I was just explaining that to my brother, sir. The main thing is we're all okay."

Clark's dad tentatively shook the guy's hand.

"I'm Corey Mankins," he said through an artificial grin. "This your farm?"

Jonathan nodded.

Clark realized these weren't just any brothers. They were the sole heirs to the powerful Mankins Corporation. But what were they doing in a helicopter above his farm? He glanced at the middle-aged man with the bent glasses, who appeared to be discreetly snapping pictures with his phone. He aimed it at the wrecked helicopter, and the barn, and the crater, before slipping it back into his pocket. Clark watched the man suspiciously.

When the rain picked up again the man pointed to the old barn and said, "Why don't we duck inside here, wait for this to pass—"

"Unfortunately, I don't have the key with me." Clark's dad looped around the wrecked chopper so that he was in front of the barn doors. He grabbed hold of the rusted padlock and looked up at the dilapidated building. "Roof's pretty much shot, anyway. We can duck under the eaves here."

All of them crowded under the part of the roof that extended over the ground. It was broken in several places, but it gave some relief from the rain.

Jonathan had always been oddly protective of the most run-down structure on the Kent farm. He'd told Clark it was dangerous. That the whole thing could come crashing down at any moment. Clark had never really given it much thought. But now, watching Corey and the man in glasses share a curious glance, he wondered if there wasn't more to it.

"Where are my manners?" Corey said to Jonathan. "This is Dr. Paul Wesley, a renowned scientist from Metropolis. And you've already met my brother, Bryan. The three of us were out here taking atmospheric measurements to help inform our harvest schedule."

Jonathan gave his name and shook hands with them.

Clark did the same. The scientist's handshake was especially aggressive, like he was trying to establish some kind of unspoken dominance. Clark fought the urge to show the guy what a tight grip could *really* feel like.

"Listen, I'm sorry about your field," Corey went on. "My father would be happy to pay any damages—"

"No, no, that won't be necessary," Clark's dad said, cutting him off. "Just a bunch of mud and dirt out here. And a barn on its last legs. I'm more concerned about *you* fellas." He turned to the scientist. "So . . . atmospheric measurements."

"That's right," the man said, pushing up his glasses. "My company specializes in agricultural gene editing and environmental strategies."

"Future of farming," Corey added. "By tracking weather patterns, we can better predict when to plant, what to plant, and where to plant. It's like crop disease and pest scouting on a whole new level. The more science we bring to farming, the more efficient we'll be. And efficiency, as I'm sure you know . . . It was Mr. Kent, wasn't it?"

"That's right."

"Efficiency, Mr. Kent, brings prices down and production up. Everyone wins."

Jonathan nodded politely, but Clark could tell his dad was just as skeptical as he was. Corey was a smooth talker. Clark and his dad had never liked people who pretended to have all the answers. No matter *how* rich they were.

Soon a couple of fire trucks arrived at the scene.

Then an ambulance. And the county deputy sheriff.

Deputy Rogers had a long yellow raincoat on, and he peered out from underneath the oversized hood after each question. Corey did most of the talking, while Clark tried to stay out of it, standing beside his father and occasionally glancing at a dejected-looking Bryan.

EMTs took the three crash victims to the back of the ambulance to check their injuries, and Deputy Rogers followed with a notepad and pen, occasionally barking directions into his crackling radio.

By the time a special flatbed tow truck had arrived, the rain was a full-on downpour. Clark and his dad huddled under a worn-out umbrella Deputy Rogers had given them while the crew worked to load the wrecked helicopter awkwardly onto the truck, Corey insisting they do it according to his special instructions.

Before the truck pulled away, Dr. Wesley climbed up onto the bed and reached into the helicopter cockpit to retrieve some kind of small briefcase. Clark kept expecting Deputy Rogers to ask about that, too, but the rain was so heavy now, everyone seemed focused on finishing things up so they could get back to their vehicles, where it was dry.

Clark pulled Bryan aside. The kid's arm was now in a sling similar to the one Paul had been wearing at school, and a fresh butterfly bandage covered the cut on his forehead. "You okay?" Clark asked, motioning toward his arm.

"It's nothing," Bryan said, forcing a smile. "Just a precaution until they can do X-rays."

Clark's eyes widened as he stared at Bryan's arm. Suddenly, he could see right through the sling. Through the skin and muscle and cartilage. He found himself staring at Bryan Mankins's bones—as clear as if they were outside his body. Seeing all the stuff inside a human arm didn't bother him. He was mostly curious. Fortunately, all the bones he saw were intact. There were no cracks or breaks or dislocations of any kind.

"You pulled me out the window before it came down on me," Bryan said, rubbing the back of his neck. "You're like . . . you're a hero, man. I could've been seriously hurt."

Clark scoffed, adjusting his glasses. "I'm definitely not a hero. Just in the right place at the right time, I guess."

"Well . . ." Bryan turned to look at the battered helicopter lying on its side on the truck. "Can't believe I lost control like that. I'm not even sure what went wrong exactly."

"Had to be the storm," Clark told him. "It got bad really fast."

"But it's not like the wind was that strong. A little rain shouldn't have thrown me off like that." Bryan turned back to Clark, shaking his head. Lightning flashed, illuminating the concerned look on his face.

A powerful roar of thunder followed.

"Bryan!" Corey called out from beside the ambulance. "Come on. Let's go."

After Bryan turned to leave, Clark glanced over at his dad.

He'd been watching the entire exchange.

So had Dr. Wesley.

CHAPTER 4

Clark stood in the shower, running through everything that had just happened out near the old barn. How he'd darted clear across the farm in a matter of seconds. How he'd grabbed the plummeting helicopter in his bare hands and somehow wrestled it to the ground without anyone incurring serious injuries. But the part Clark kept circling back to was his conversation with Bryan.

He'd called Clark a hero.

No one had ever done that before.

Clark knew he wasn't supposed to use his powers in public, yet he couldn't deny the exhilaration of being referred to as a hero. It made him feel important. It made him want to go out there and save someone else.

As the warm water continued pelting the back of his head, Clark found himself thinking about his rapidly changing powers. As he'd raced toward the falling chopper in the rain, he'd had the sudden urge to just . . . leap into the sky. To soar up toward the two-ton machine and *catch* it. In midair. Which was ridiculous, he knew. Humans couldn't fly. But the instinct had been incredibly powerful.

"Clark!" his mother called from downstairs, breaking the spell of his daydream. "Dinner's ready!"

Clark cranked off the water and toweled dry and went to his room to get dressed. On his way downstairs, he imagined what it would be like to play football now. He pictured himself taking a handoff from the quarterback, juking left, then soaring into the air to avoid a wall of converging defenders. Not coming down until he'd crossed the goal line some forty yards later. Spiking the ball from up near the goalpost as the opposing defense stared in awe.

He pictured Lana cheering wildly from behind the bench.

Pictured Gloria cheering.

Tommy, Paul, and Kyle hoisting him up onto their shoulders and carrying him into the locker room to celebrate.

When Clark sat down at the table with his parents, his dad passed him the bowl of green beans, saying, "I was just telling your mother what happened." He shook his head. "I've never seen anything like it, son. You saved three lives out there today."

Clark beamed, thinking of that word again: *hero*.

Martha Kent eyed him as she buttered a roll. "As long as you're being careful."

"I just reacted." Clark scooped himself a healthy serving of beans to go along with his chicken and mashed potatoes. His mom had always longed for a simpler, more peaceful life for him. A happy life. And she worried that the burden of his gifts would one day become more than he could bear.

"Your mother's right, Clark." Jonathan set down his fork. "What you did today . . . ," he began. "It really was a wonderful thing. I'm sure Montgomery Mankins would see to it that you're set for life if he knew you saved his sons."

Clark took a big bite of potatoes, mumbling, "But . . ."

"But we don't want you taking any unnecessary risks. Like I was telling you earlier, some people in this world . . . they don't appreciate anyone who's different."

"It could make things really difficult on you," his mom added.

Clark glanced out the window. He knew his parents were only trying to protect him, but was it really fair to ask him to change who he was in order to appease closed-minded people? He turned back to them. "I understand what you guys are saying, but if I have an opportunity to help someone . . . I mean, shouldn't I help them?"

"Of course," his dad said. "We're not asking you to turn your back on someone in danger."

"But *our* main concern is *you*," his mom said.

Jonathan nodded. "There's a quote that comes to mind, son. From the Bible. 'To whom much is given, of him will much be required.' It's a good thing for you to remember."

They ate in silence for several minutes, Clark thinking about what his parents were trying to tell him. It was obvious his powers were intensifying. And he had a feeling that, as his dad's quote said, more power would somehow lead to more responsibility. Would there ever come a time when he'd have to go against his parents' wishes? When he'd have to step out of the shadows and reveal to the world who he really was?

He snuck a glance at his mom and dad, then closed his eyes briefly and listened to the muted sounds of his home. Forks clinking against plates. Rain pelting the thin roof above their small kitchen. Mice scurrying inside the walls of the attic and bugs burrowing holes into the wet soil outside.

This house.

The farm.

His parents.

If anything ever happened to any of them . . .

Clark opened his eyes, recalling Dr. Wesley's cold stare. And the pictures he'd been taking with his phone. What had he been looking for? And why had he been looking for it on the Kents' farm?

Deep down, Clark knew his parents were right. Being called a hero was nice, but he could never let anyone find out the truth about his powers. Not if it meant putting his family, and the farm, in jeopardy.

CHAPTER 5

The following afternoon, as Clark was walking to the public library to meet Lana—their long-standing, post-chore ritual on Saturday afternoons—a bright red sports car came speeding down the highway toward him. When it got close, the driver swerved directly at Clark, as if trying to run him off the road.

Clark didn't budge.

He stood his ground, staring right at the tinted windshield as the car whizzed past, missing him by a fraction of an inch.

"I'm right here!" he shouted after the car as it continued down the road.

Clark had never seen anyone drive so recklessly on Highway 22, the narrow two-lane road that connected many rural farms to downtown Smallville. The driver had to have been going a hundred at least. Nearly double the speed limit. And who was it, anyway? Clark had lived in Smallville his entire life and knew pretty much every car in town, which family owned it, and who might be driving. There were a ton of pickups, of course. And old sedans. And minivans. But *nobody* in Smallville owned a bright red sports car with tinted windows.

Had to be an outsider.

He readjusted the straps of his backpack and continued until he reached Alvarez Fruits and Vegetables, the covered produce stand run by Carlos Alvarez and his son, Cruz. It had been a staple of Highway 22 for as long as Clark could remember, and the Kents stopped by every weekend. He'd seen Cruz go from a shy elementary school kid handing out plastic bags, to a confident middle schooler who managed the cash box and translated whenever his dad needed help communicating with customers. Cruz was tall for his age. Almost as tall as Clark. So most people assumed he was in high school—until he opened his mouth, that is.

Clark found the two of them in front of their stand, staring down the road. "You guys saw that, too?"

Carlos put his hands on his hips, shaking his head. "Is very dangerous."

"Do you know what kind of car it was?" Cruz asked Clark. "It wasn't shaped like a Lamborghini. Maybe an Aston Martin? Or a Maserati?"

Clark shrugged. "It wasn't a Ford F-150, that's for sure."

"I heard a Maserati can go one-eighty, easy. Do you know how sick that is? I'd probably get a speeding ticket every day." Cruz was in awe of anything flashy and American. Fancy cars. Big, gaudy houses. Blockbuster movies and celebrity gossip. Clark knew from talking to the kid over the years that he longed to one day leave the fruit and vegetable stand behind. To get out of Kansas and pursue a career that would give him a shot at some sort of fame.

Carlos flicked his son's ear good-naturedly and motioned for him to get back to work. Cruz rolled his eyes, then went over to a table of green apples and began rearranging them.

Seeing Carlos and Cruz made Clark think of Gloria. They were related. She'd even spent the summer after her freshman year working at the stand. "I'm curious," he said, recalling what Gloria had told him at school. "Do you guys know anything about . . . people disappearing?"

Carlos picked a dead leaf off a tomato. "Oh, yes, of course," he said, nodding. "But some young people . . ." He turned to his son and said something in Spanish.

Cruz listened to his dad before turning to Clark. "My dad says people are making high wages with the Mankins Corporation. More money than they've ever had. And some of them go to Metropolis to gamble and buy things. He says it's a very bad idea." Cruz grinned and said in a quieter voice, "Personally, I don't see how making a little cash is so wrong. I've been thinking about working for Mankins myself."

Carlos said something else to Cruz, who then turned to Clark, adding, "He's keeping his eyes open, though. He's not sure how safe it is for us in Smallville right now." Cruz glanced at his dad before telling Clark, "Me, though? I'm not scared of *anyone*. I say, 'Bring it.'"

Clark appreciated the kid's audacity. "What about the police?" he asked, thinking of the proposed law. "They're not randomly stopping anyone, are they?"

Carlos looked genuinely bewildered. "No, no. It is the same as before with them."

This assurance made Clark feel relieved. "All right, then." He saluted his friends. "See you guys around."

The three of them smiled and waved, and Clark continued down the open road.

About a half mile later, just as Clark was passing the big white church that stood alongside the highway, he heard the hum of the red sports car coming up behind him. He stopped and turned around, readying himself for more static. But when it got close to Clark this time, the driver hit the brakes, and the car screeched to a stop beside him.

It sat there idling for several seconds, smoke rising up off the tires.

Clark tried to peer through the passenger-side window, but the tint was so dark that he couldn't see a thing. And when he tried to use his newfound X-ray vision, nothing happened. He knew that a normal person would feel fear at this point, but he'd never been very good at fear. He was mostly just curious. The car definitely looked expensive. He didn't even recognize the logo on the front grille. Whoever was inside had to be rich—and wanted everyone to know it.

"You just gonna hide in there all day?" Clark shouted.

The passenger-side window began slowly motoring down, and Bryan Mankins poked his head out. "Clark," he called. "You okay? I tried to tell Lex not to buzz you like that."

"Bryan?" Clark looked past him, to the driver's side and this Lex guy. But he couldn't get a good view. "You almost ran me over."

Bryan smiled uncomfortably. "Sorry, man. He thinks shit like that's funny. But I made him come back so we could offer you a ride."

"I'm fine walking," Clark said, irritated.

Bryan mumbled something to the driver before turning back to Clark. "Seriously, hop in. We'll take you wherever you want to go."

Clark hesitated at first. He didn't even know Bryan. Or this Lex joker. And he definitely didn't appreciate the stunt they'd pulled earlier. On the other hand, he *was* a little curious about the car. "I'm going to the library downtown," he said.

"Shit, man, we're headed in that direction anyway. Come on."

Clark climbed past Bryan, into the cramped back seat. He took off his backpack and set it in his lap and latched his seat belt. Then he glanced at the driver, Lex, by way of the rearview mirror. He was a young white guy, not much older than Clark and Bryan, but he was dressed like some kind of important businessman. A sport coat and collared shirt. He had wavy hair and wore a pair of expensive-looking designer sunglasses.

He was the kind of guy Lana might describe as good-looking.

He was the kind of guy Clark would describe as soft.

The inside of the car was every bit as showy as the outside. Leather seats. Digital everything. A massive touch screen that took up more than half the dash. It was the nicest ride Clark had ever seen. Actually, it seemed more like a spaceship than anything else. He wondered if it was one of those cars that could drive themselves.

"This the guy who saved you?" Lex asked, nudging Bryan. He clearly owned the car. He seemed totally at home behind the wheel of such an expensive-looking vehicle.

"This is him." Bryan turned to Clark. "What's your last name again?"

"Kent. Clark Kent."

Bryan nodded. "That's right. Clark Kent, I'd like you to meet my buddy Lex Luthor." He tapped the driver on the arm. "Lex, meet Clark."

Lex hit the gas.

The three of them were thrown back into their seats as the car accelerated at an insane rate. Bryan spun around wide-eyed and looked at Clark. "You ever felt that kind of power?" he shouted over the wind whipping through his open window.

"It's pretty fast," Clark said, marveling at the quiet engine. He'd reached speeds like this on foot, but never as the passenger in a car. It felt strange to relinquish control.

Lex took his foot off the gas and let the car slowly decelerate. "The library, you said?"

"If it's cool," Clark told him.

Lex motioned toward Bryan. "You save this guy's life, you earn a free ride."

"Thanks," Clark said. "But I didn't actually save *anyone*."

"I already told you," Bryan said to Lex. "Guy refuses to take credit."

Lex glanced at Clark in the rearview again. "So what happened?"

Clark knew he had to set the record straight before any rumors got started. "I was just working the farm with my dad, and . . . we both saw the helicopter coming down, so we took off." He tapped Bryan on the shoulder. "Is everyone okay?"

Bryan nodded. "Didn't even have to keep that sling on my arm."

Clark sat back, relieved. "I guess we were all pretty lucky."

"Luck. Yeah, that's probably it." Lex accelerated around a rumbling big rig. "Kind of like you got lucky on the football field during your freshman year, right? From what I read, you scored thirty-three touchdowns in *six games*? I guess you're, like, blessed with luck."

Clark was shocked that some fancy-car-driving rich dude could quote his football stats.

Bryan turned to face Clark. "Jesus, is that true?"

Clark shrugged. "I guess I didn't like getting tackled. So I ran. Fast as I could. Anyway, it was only freshman football."

"Why aren't you still playing? The team was bad this year, right? And aren't they usually pretty good?"

"Yeah." Clark tapped his backpack. "But I'm better off hitting the books. That whole concussion thing's pretty scary."

Bryan turned back to Lex. "How'd you know his stats?"

Lex grinned. "There's this new thing out there called the internet, Bry. You should try it sometime."

Bryan grinned. "Dude, you must have a lot of time on your hands if you're browsing freshman football stats from two years ago."

Lex cracked a smile but never took his eyes off the road. "Eh, I Google everyone. When you told me what Clark did, of course I looked him up."

Bryan looked over his shoulder at Clark and rolled his eyes. "That's not creepy at all. Anyway, Clark, you gotta be pretty strong to punch it into the end zone that many times. What was your secret? Just lifting weights every day? Shoveling cow shit on the farm?"

Clark shrugged. He knew Bryan was just messing around, but he'd never really loved farm jokes. At least from outsiders, that is. Actual farm kids could make as many country-bumpkin jokes as they wanted. That's just how it worked. "I went to the gym a few times, I guess," Clark said. "But mostly it's my mom's home cooking. She's all about meat and potatoes."

"I need to change my diet," Bryan said, squeezing his right bicep through his shirt. "Tuna tartare isn't doing me any favors."

Truth was, Clark had stopped lifting back in ninth grade. Once he realized it wasn't necessary. Back then he was fairly thin, too. But his strength had always far exceeded his appearance.

Bryan started messing with the touch screen on the dash. When he found a hip-hop song on the satellite radio, he turned it up.

Lex immediately turned it back down. "When we're in your plane, we can listen to that stuff. But when we're in my ride, it's all about hard-core." He switched stations, and a thrashing rock song came on. He turned the volume low enough so that they could still talk. "You know this guy doesn't even have a driver's license, right?" Lex said, glancing at Clark in the rearview.

"Most people don't drive in Metropolis," Bryan said.

"I drive," Lex said.

"Yeah, so you can show off your car." Bryan turned to Clark. "Normal people take the subway. Or call a car. Or walk. Also, I have a *pilot's* license."

Clark had heard that Bryan was at a fancy boarding school in Metropolis before finishing the year at Smallville High. Rumor had it that Bryan's brother, Corey, had graduated from a school in Switzerland, where their dad had gone, too. "So how come you left Metropolis?" Clark asked. It was the question many people had been asking since Bryan showed up so late in the school year. Once they found out who he was.

Bryan was quiet for several seconds, his face serious.

Lex glanced at him, as if curious about how he would handle the question.

"There weren't many opportunities to fly out there," Bryan finally said, without looking back at Clark. "Not like there are here. And that's all I really want to do lately."

Clark could tell by Lex's expression that Bryan hadn't told the whole truth. But Clark decided not to push it.

Lex slowed a little as he turned off Highway 22 and onto Main Street. They passed a string of Smallville institutions—Howe's

Coffeehouse, Randy's Hardware, the Old Winter Saloon—before coming to a stretch of new businesses. The grocery store and pharmacy that had opened during the winter. Java Depot. A Thai restaurant Lana had been wanting to get Clark to try for weeks. A large toy store that was so new it didn't even have a sign up yet.

As they passed the large construction site across the street from city hall, Bryan pointed. "There it is," he said sarcastically. "Home, sweet home."

Every time Clark set eyes on the future home of the Mankins Corporation, he was reminded of the man dressed in all brown who had carjacked the SUV and driven it right at Paul. The retaining wall the vehicle had ultimately crashed into was still badly damaged. But now Clark noticed another detail. There were no tire marks in front of that part of the wall. The guy had never hit the brakes. Maybe the wall in front of the new Mankins headquarters really *had* been his target all along.

But why?

"Gotta be almost done now, right?" Lex asked.

Bryan nodded. "I think they're gonna do some kind of grand-opening festival in the next week or so. I'm sure it'll be some big spectacle, but whatever."

When Lex pulled the sports car up to the steps, the three of them glanced across the street at city hall, where a dozen or so Mexican men and women were picketing. "What do you guys think about that new law being proposed?" Clark asked. It was definitely a loaded question, but the way these two responded seemed important to him.

"The stop-and-search thing?" Bryan asked. "It's brutal. I'll say this: if something like that can pass here, I know Smallville's not the town for me."

"Yeah, nothing like that would even be *proposed* in Metropolis," Lex added. "It's a small-town thing."

Normally Clark felt defensive when someone criticized his hometown, but this was different. Bryan was right; if a law like that could pass in Smallville, it would be embarrassing. So Clark just sat there watching people march silently while holding up their signs. He recognized one of the men from the cattle feed and tractor supply company just outside of town. One woman was a new student teacher at Smallville High. The guy who seemed to be the leader wasn't much older than Lex. He had a goatee and spiky black hair, and seemed to be directing all their movements.

"We'll vote it down," Clark said, feeling a surge of confidence. "I believe in the people of Smallville."

An older white man who was wearing a suit and carrying a shopping bag approached the protesters from across the street. Clark was surprised when he began handing out bottles of water.

"One of yours?" Lex asked.

Bryan nodded. "My dad has food sent to them, too. And he's the one funding that new 'get out and vote' campaign."

Clark was genuinely impressed that a rich guy like Montgomery Mankins would take an interest in how people less fortunate were being treated. Seemed like it would be easy for the guy to just sit in his ivory tower, counting his money.

Bryan stepped out of the car and folded down the seat. After Clark climbed out with his backpack, Bryan nudged him in the arm. "Hey, I was thinking. Why don't you meet up with us tomorrow night at the All-American Diner?"

Clark was taken aback. "Sure," he said. "What time?"

"Seven-thirty?"

"Okay, cool. See you there." Clark turned and started toward the library.

"Hey, Clark!" Bryan called out.

He turned back around.

"Try not to pull a muscle in there studying, all right?" Bryan climbed back into his seat and closed the door, and the red sports car sped away.

Clark watched it rip through the nearest intersection, Lex's music now blaring out his open window. Bryan hadn't told Clark why he'd really left Metropolis, and Clark realized he had no idea why Lex was in Smallville either. He definitely didn't seem like a small-town kind of guy. It seemed like the more he got to know these two, the more questions he had.

CHAPTER 6

Clark took the stairs two at a time up to the library, where he found Lana waiting for him just inside the front doors. Before he could say anything, she whisked him into an empty quiet room and closed the door. "Okay, spill it," she said, sitting down at the long conference-style table. She had on a blue sundress Clark didn't recognize, and she was wearing her hair down. She put away her headphones, saying, "I wanna know *everything*, Clark."

He set his backpack on the table and sat across from her. "About what?"

She shot him a dirty look.

For the past couple of years, the library had been Clark and Lana's spot. It had started soon after Clark quit the football team. Lana had noticed (because Lana noticed *everything*) that Clark was feeling lost. Maybe a little lonely. Possibly depressed. So she showed up at his farmhouse one Saturday and said, "Clark Kent, you're coming with me." He did. And they'd been here almost every weekend since. He knew the library wasn't the hippest hangout in the world, but it's not like they were always doing homework. Sometimes they'd sneak food into a quiet room and gossip while they ate lunch. Or Lana would run news story ideas past him. Or they'd watch random videos on Lana's tablet.

But today was no ordinary Saturday. Clark had been involved in the biggest news story of the day, and Lana hated being out of the loop.

"I take it you heard about the helicopter crash," he said.

"Of *course* I heard about the helicopter crash," she told him. "I hear about *everything* that happens in this town. You know that."

Clark did. If some freshman kid cheated on his girlfriend at a party, Lana knew. If a herd of hogs got loose on a local farm, Lana knew. Once she even found out that Clark's dad had been invited to be a panelist at an agriculture and livestock conference at Kansas State before *he* did.

"Okay, but first," he told her, "you won't believe how I got here today."

She narrowed her eyes at him. "You didn't walk?"

He shook his head. "This guy named Lex drove me here in a fancy red sports car. Bryan Mankins was with him."

"Bryan Mankins?" Lana shouted. "The kid who's barely said two words to anyone since he showed up last month?"

Clark nodded, putting a finger to his lips. Two older ladies were frowning at them from the stacks just outside their quiet room. But his gesture didn't do much to stifle Lana's enthusiasm.

"You know he got kicked out of his boarding school, right?" she went on at the same volume.

"Really? What'd he do?"

"Nobody knows." Lana shook her head. "And it's not like he's a willing source."

Clark wondered what Bryan could have done. Maybe it was something really serious. "Bryan was the one piloting the helicopter that crashed on our farm," Clark said in a softer voice, hoping Lana would take the hint. "I think the storm caused him to lose control or something. Luckily, they landed in the mud and nobody was hurt."

"The article I read didn't give any names." Lana had lowered her voice. "I bet his dad made some calls to keep his son's name out of the paper. Anyone with him?"

"Bryan's older brother, Corey. And some scientist named Dr. Wesley."

"Dr. Wesley," Lana muttered to herself. "Dr. Wesley. Why does that name sound so familiar?" She leaned toward Clark. "And why were they flying over your property in the first place?"

Clark shrugged. "They claimed to be taking atmospheric measurements."

Lana laughed out loud. "Likely story."

"You don't buy it." Clark knew it was a little odd. But the Mankins Corporation had made a fortune by being on the cutting edge of modern-day farming. The company had recently developed a top-secret "miracle" mineral that radically affected crop growth. And all the family-owned farms that were using Mankins's genetically engineered seeds were reporting record harvests. So it didn't seem implausible that Mankins might be taking atmospheric measurements of some kind.

Lana sat back. "Look, I get it. Mankins has done a lot of good in this community."

"But . . ."

Lana stared at the table for a few seconds before looking up at Clark. "Do you ever wonder if the company is, like, a little *too* good to be true? I mean, Mankins *is* buying up a shit ton of family farms. Shouldn't we be asking why?"

Clark leaned back in his chair. "You sound like my dad. He wonders what kind of chemicals Mankins might be dumping into our water."

"A good reporter doesn't take *anything* for granted." Lana began pulling textbooks out of her bag, but Clark knew this conversation was far from over. "Now, let's hear about this crash," she said.

Clark gave Lana a play-by-play of the entire incident, leaving out, of course, the part where he'd caught the chopper with his bare hands and wrestled it to the ground. When he'd finished talking, she asked, "So, you basically rescued these guys from a burning helicopter?"

"I helped Bryan out of the cockpit, but that's about it. Nothing was burning. Just a little smoke."

"Work with me, Clark. This would make such a great lead story for the last paper of the school year: 'Local Heartthrob Saves Three from Exploding Chopper.'"

Clark laughed to mask his embarrassment. Lana had a knack for coming up with silly headlines like that. But did she really think of him as a "heartthrob"?

"You're getting dangerously close to fake news," he told her. "Honestly, I was just in the right place at the right time. Or the wrong place. However you wanna see it. The point is, me and my dad were able to call in the crash, and they sent out Deputy Rogers and an ambulance and this special tow truck. Luckily, everyone was okay."

Lana was shaking her head in disbelief. "I can't believe you saved Bryan Mankins. You probably have a job waiting for you when you graduate."

Clark laughed. "My dad said that, too." Clark shook his head as he pulled his psychology book out of his bag and set it in front of him. He didn't open it. "Anyway, me and Bryan *are* hanging out tomorrow."

"Wait, *what?*"

His eyes met Lana's. "Yeah. We're going to All-American. The two of us and that guy Lex, who drove me here."

"You're going to dinner with Bryan? Clark, you buried the lede. We have so many questions for him."

"'We'?" Clark couldn't help smiling.

"Listen, after we get a little work done, I'm going to teach you everything I know about the art of the interview. By the end of dinner, we'll know all about this kid and his mysterious family. Once you report back to me, that is." Lana rearranged the textbooks on the table in front of her so that her math book was closest. She looked up at Clark. "You know, for a tiny little town, we sure do have a lot of strangers hanging around lately. This Lex guy with the sports car. Dr. Wesley. I even met a cute stranger at the coffee shop this morning."

Clark was surprised to hear Lana describe someone as "cute." Most of the time she hardly even noticed when someone was flirting with her. "So, who's this coffee shop guy?" Clark asked.

"He was ahead of me in line, and when I got up to the counter, the barista said, 'The customer ahead of you is covering your order as well.' And when I turned around, he gave me this little wave and came over and told me he liked my dress." She mimed the little wave with a smile. "We only talked for a few seconds before he got a call on his cell and said he had to go. He seemed a tad 'business smarmy,' but he was definitely cute."

Clark felt oddly protective all of a sudden, and he wasn't sure why. A part of him wanted to head straight to the coffee shop and conduct an interview of his own. He couldn't have a smarmy guy messing with his best friend. "You didn't even get his name? What kind of reporter—?"

"We didn't have time to introduce ourselves," Lana interrupted. "My point is, what's up with all the mystery men in Smallville lately? Seems kind of odd, don't you think?"

"Speaking of odd," Clark said, eager to steer their conversation someplace else, "have you heard anything about people in Small-ville . . . disappearing?"

"Disappearing?" She was back to her loud voice.

"I'll take that as a no. Someone mentioned it to me in passing, and I thought—"

"If anyone in Smallville disappeared," she said, hastily putting her hair in a ponytail, "I'm pretty sure I'd know about it."

Clark gave a sarcastic nod. "Right. Kind of like you knew Bryan Mankins was the one piloting the helicopter that crash-landed on my farm."

She shot him a playful glare. "Whatever, Clark. That's differ-ent." She opened her math book and began flipping through the pages. "I mean, we can definitely look into any kind of possible disappearance. I just haven't heard anything."

Clark grinned as he opened his math book, too. Any chance he had to give Lana a hard time, he took it. It was often the other way around.

"Interview strategies to come," Lana said, looking up at Clark. "But first . . . what should we start with today? Extreme Value Theorem or Newton's Method?"

Clark pulled a folded homework sheet from his math book and flattened it out. With everything going on in Smallville, it was a relief to be temporarily turning to math.

CHAPTER 7

The All-American Diner was famous for two things: cheap, massive portions of french fries and a generous owner who never seemed to stop smiling. The owner, however, was not as all-American as the name of his restaurant might suggest. David Baez was one of Smallville's first-ever Mexican immigrants. He'd moved to town in the 1960s, from Oaxaca, and never left. He eventually married a local woman and had a large family and became a citizen. Dave's constant jokes, his tendency to give away free milkshakes, and the restaurant's proximity to Smallville High School meant that the place was almost always busy. Especially after school and on weekends.

Tonight was no exception.

The first thing Clark noticed as he walked through the front door was that every single table was taken.

And then he noticed Gloria Alvarez.

She was serving a table at the far end of the loud diner, smiling brightly at a group of football players. Most of them were Clark's former teammates, including Tommy, Paul, and Kyle. If he were still on the team, he thought, he'd be sitting right there in the middle of their booth. Joking with everyone. Talking to Gloria.

But he couldn't play anymore, so here he was, on the outside looking in.

Like always.

Clark successfully focused his super-hearing on their conversation for a few seconds, and sure enough, they were vying for Gloria's attention. She snapped something right back at them that made the whole table of football players burst out laughing.

He felt a tinge of jealousy watching her laugh along with his ex-teammates. But at least she seemed happy. The last time he'd seen her, she was wiping away tears.

Gloria picked up a couple of empty plates, then turned and hurried off toward the kitchen. Clark must have stared just a little too long, because now Tommy was waving him over. Clark headed to their table reluctantly.

He noticed that Paul was wearing a much lighter shoulder sling. That was a good sign. His condition was improving.

"Clark," Tommy said, "wanna join us?"

"Or can you not even sit with us anymore?" Paul joked.

A couple of the players chuckled.

Clark smiled good-naturedly and looked around the crammed booth. Even if he'd wanted to join them, there was nowhere for him to sit. The booth was designed to hold five normal-sized humans, but it was currently stuffed with four hulking varsity offensive linemen, a fullback, a six-four quarterback, and a pit bull of a running back. They all had big pops in front of them. "I would," Clark said, "but I'm meeting a friend."

"Someone from the debate team?" Kyle quipped humorlessly.

"Careful," Paul said, glancing down at his shoulder sling, "or he'll blindside your ass, too."

The football players all nodded in agreement, and a right tackle named Bobby Hanson said, "It's all good if you don't wanna play, Clark. But did you really have to take Paulie out like that? All we got is a damn freshman in the backfield right now."

"I'll be back soon," Paul said. "Trust me."

"Guys, can we give Clark a break?" Tommy said. "He's only apologized, like, a hundred times for what happened to Paul."

As the guys grumbled a little, Clark looked at his former friend. He and Tommy used to be close in freshman year. Back when Tommy was opening up holes in the opposing defense for Clark to pummel through. Back when they used to sit around after practice talking about how hard it was to balance football and farmwork. Tommy wanted to be a vet; Clark, a farmer, like his dad. They used to have so much in common. It amazed Clark how quickly things could change.

He glanced around the diner, looking for his escape. It wasn't that he didn't like these guys. He liked them a lot, actually. And deep down he knew they liked him, too. But this was the way it worked with a team. When you were in the trenches together, fighting for a common goal, you were brothers. But as soon as you left the team, they dropped you. It was even worse in Clark's case, because he'd been their best player. And it's not like he'd gotten hurt or been ruled academically ineligible. The way they saw it, he'd simply walked out on them.

Clark spotted Bryan at a table at the other end of the diner. Just as he was about to head there, quarterback Curtis Baker spoke up for the first time. "Clark, you're gonna swing by Tommy's on Friday night, right? His family sold their farm, so we're throwing one last rager for old times' sake. Giving the place a proper funeral."

Clark knew all about the party. Everyone did. But he'd never expected any kind of special invitation. And because it was the starting quarterback who had offered it, everyone else was now nodding in agreement. "Yeah," he said. "I'll probably stop by."

"Just let us know what you need," Paul added. "Whole milk. Two percent. Skim. We got you covered, Clark."

Everyone cracked up.

The "milk drinker" dig didn't bother Clark. If anything, it made him feel nostalgic. He missed the team parties Tommy's parents threw at their farm after every home game. All the pizza they could eat. And all the pop they wanted. But because Clark had never really liked pop, he always asked for milk instead. It quickly became a running joke with the team.

Clark slapped hands with Tommy and a few of the other guys and moved on.

He was happy to see he'd have to pass Gloria on the way to Bryan's table. She looked up as he approached, their eyes locking for two or three butterfly-inducing seconds before she turned back to a table of old-timers. He watched her interaction with the Kellers and the Smiths, two couples who met at the diner nearly every night to eat pie and drink coffee and play cards. Most restaurant owners wouldn't let a table sit occupied for hours like that, but David Baez loved these guests. He'd sometimes even join them for a hand or two and would occasionally pick up their check.

Clark swallowed hard as he passed Gloria, close enough to catch the faint scent of her flowery shampoo. She pulled a pencil from behind her ear, which was lined with piercings. She wrote down the old folks' orders—as if she didn't already know—and placed the pencil back behind her ear as she moved toward the kitchen. The whole thing made Clark's stomach tighten. Was he really getting flustered by the way someone took an order? And stuck a pencil behind her ear?

"Clark," Bryan called out as he stood up. "Glad you could make it."

Clark slapped hands with him and sat down on the opposite side of the table. "Where's Lex?"

"Canceled on me last minute. He tends to do that." Bryan pointed to the menu sitting in front of Clark. "Guess he doesn't appreciate the utter genius of the rubbery diner steak."

"You ever had one here?" Clark asked. "They're really good."

"I've only had the burger. And the fries. You're right, though— food's not bad." Bryan's face grew serious as he set down his menu. "Hey, I wanted to say . . . I appreciate you helping me out after we crashed onto your farm. Not everyone would have reacted so quickly. So thank you."

Clark smiled as he nodded. "You're welcome," he said, feeling a warmth rise up to his scalp. He picked up his own menu.

As Bryan went back to quietly studying the food options, Clark glanced across the diner at Gloria. She was picking up an order at the food pass. He watched her spin gracefully and somehow carry four heaping plates to a family, then set them down without dropping so much as a leaf of lettuce. She gave the family a genuine smile before heading over to another table.

When Clark turned back to his menu, he found Bryan staring at him. "What?"

Bryan motioned toward the front of the restaurant, near the table where Gloria was now refilling someone's coffee mug. "Don't tell me you have a crush on that hostess, too."

Clark shifted his eyes slightly toward the hostess stand, where Moira DeMeyer, a tall, blond junior, was wiping down menus. She and Lana used to be close friends back in middle school, but they didn't hang out anymore. Clark knew Moira was one of the most popular girls at school, and a few years back she'd abruptly dropped Lana as a friend in favor of a group of "mean girls." And that didn't sit well with Clark.

"Not even close," he answered. "I was just thinking about how crowded this place is. Every single table is taken."

Bryan laughed. "Good. It's a little irritating watching every guy follow her around at school like a little puppy dog."

"Exactly," Clark said. He set down his menu and attempted to change the subject. "So, Lex cancels on you a lot?"

"He had some kind of emergency conference call he had to take. I don't know. Honestly, that guy's always wheeling and dealing, looking for a new way to take over the world."

Clark studied Bryan, thinking back to Lana's tutorial on how she thought Clark should approach this dinner. Now that it was just him and Bryan, though, the dynamic seemed different. So he simply went with his gut. "He doesn't live here, does he?"

"Lex?" Bryan laughed out loud. "That's a good one. No, Lex would *never* live in a place like Smallville. No offense." Bryan leaned in closer. "To be honest, he got into a little trouble back in Metropolis. Nothing major, I don't think. But his dad thought he should stay out of the city until stuff blew over. And he suggested our place." Bryan leaned back. "Our dads went to college together."

Clark was surprised how much Bryan was telling him. At school he mostly kept to himself. People assumed he was super private because of who his dad was. Clark pressed on. "Is he working for you guys while he's here?"

"Lex doesn't work for my dad, no. But neither do I." Bryan picked up his menu, then immediately set it back down. "I'm not like my brother, who's being groomed to take over at some point."

"What about that scientist guy who was with you?"

"Dr. Wesley? My dad would *never* hire him." Bryan looked around, making sure no one else was within earshot. "He's pretty creepy. Before coming to Smallville, he spent a couple years in prison."

This revelation surprised Clark. "For what?"

"I guess he had ties to some pretty shady mobsters back in Metropolis. They funded everything he did." Bryan shook his head and picked up his menu again. "Anyway, he has his own company. Corey's the one who insists on bringing him onto certain side projects. He has to do it on his own dime, though, because my dad would be pissed if he knew they were collaborating."

The conversation was flowing, and Clark felt like he was learning a ton of information about Lex and the Mankins Corporation. But it was time to focus on Bryan. "So, why *don't* you work for your dad? I mean, now that you're back from Metropolis—"

"Look, Clark," Bryan said, cutting him off, "I need to be upfront about something."

"I'm prying too much," Clark told him. "I'm sorry."

"It's not that." Bryan folded his arms and leaned back into the plush padding of the booth. "It's just . . . when it comes to my dad's company—"

Bryan was interrupted by a food server, who stepped up to their table and asked, "You two ready to order?"

Clark looked up at the woman with mild disappointment. He'd been hoping they were in Gloria's station. They both ordered steak with fries. And Bryan asked for a cherry cola. The server wrote these things down and said, "I'll get this started for you right away."

"Anyway, where was I?" Bryan said after the woman had left. "Oh, right. The family business."

Clark felt bad and waved him off. "If it's too personal—"

"No, let me get this out," Bryan interrupted. He stared at Clark for several seconds, his deep-set eyes filled with something that seemed oddly familiar to Clark. Loneliness, maybe? Confusion? "My dad's company . . . Honestly, it has nothing to do with me. That's *his* thing. My brother's always been desperate to be a part of it. But I'm, like, my own person, you know? I want to do *my* thing."

Clark nodded. But this seemed like wishful thinking. The Mankins Corporation had made Bryan's dad rich and powerful. And Clark was sure the company's success directly affected every part of Bryan's life. It had to.

"Here's the thing." Bryan scooted forward in his seat a little and leaned his elbows on the table. "We don't get to choose where we're born, right? Or when we're born. Or what family we're born into. It all just sort of happens to us. And because of that, people shouldn't judge us for it, good or bad. I mean, Smallville really respects my dad's company, all the charity work he does and the advancements he's made in farming. And I'm genuinely proud of the good it's doing in this community. It'd be real easy for me to just jump on that wagon and ride the family name. But I wanna make my own path, find my own success. Does that make sense?"

"It really does." Clark knew his mom and dad would love for him to take over the family farm one day. And he believed farming was an honorable path in life. But was it *his* path?

Bryan got a strange, faraway look in his eyes. "It's weird, Clark. Sometimes I feel . . . I don't even know. It's like I'm a foreigner in my own house. You probably wouldn't understand. Your family seems great."

"They are," Clark said. "But I still get what you're saying."

"Really?"

Clark nodded. Something about what Bryan had just said really hit home for Clark. His secret powers made him feel like a freak sometimes. Not just in his family, but in all of Smallville. No one else he knew could lift a truck with their bare hands. Or outrun an SUV. Or hear airplanes flying an entire county away. He wished he could open up to Bryan about that part of himself, too. Have a real conversation for once in his life.

"I don't know," Bryan said. "We all have our struggles. And I'm aware that most people's are a lot more complicated than mine."

"Yeah. Same here," Clark said.

The food runner arrived with their dinner. He set down their plates and drinks and asked if they needed anything else. When they said they didn't, he took off.

Their conversation seemed effortless. Bryan talked about his boarding school. How the pressure to be the best was overwhelming. Some of his closest friends would sink into a deep depression if they got a B in a class. He talked about what it was like to get sent away from home at such a young age. And then to come back. And how he was still trying to find his footing at a public high school. Clark talked about his life on the farm. How he had to get up long before school to do chores. He used to resent it. He'd imagine what it would be like to sleep in until seven every morning, like some of his friends did. But now early morning was his favorite part of the day. Sometimes he'd lie at the lip of the crater on his farm as the sun came up in front of him, and he'd feel a powerful connection to the universe. One that he could never truly put into words.

Clark felt like he could mostly be himself with Bryan. And it wasn't awkward. Clark felt the same way with Lana, but that was

Lana. He'd known her all his life. This was the first time he'd felt comfortable with someone he'd just met. Clark's default state with new people was to be guarded. To protect his secrets. But maybe being guarded was part of what kept him from feeling like he belonged.

As Clark finished up, he caught Gloria's eyes across the room. She quickly looked away and went back to pouring water at a table of Smallville sophomores Clark recognized. It was the cast of the new school play, which Lana had just reviewed for the Smallville High paper. They were probably getting dinner after a show.

Bryan set his fork down. "Wait, you weren't looking at that girl Moira earlier. You were looking at the Mexican waitress."

Clark's first instinct was to pretend it wasn't true. But why should he lie? "Her name's Gloria," he said. "She goes to school with us."

"I know her." Bryan studied Gloria. "Well, I don't *know* her know her, but I know who she is. She seems really cool. And I heard she's the best coder in the school."

A busboy came to refill their water glasses. After he left, Bryan said, "Why don't you go talk to her?"

Clark shook his head. "Nah, I can't."

"What do you mean, you can't?" Bryan asked. "Why not?"

A wave of butterflies passed through Clark's stomach. "I don't know. She just seems super busy."

"Clark." Bryan slapped both palms on the table in front of him. "We can't be spectators our whole lives, right? At some point we have to take a risk. Step into the action."

Clark saw that Gloria was coming toward their table on her way to the food pass. "You know what?" he said, feeling a sudden surge of courage. He stood up. "Maybe I should."

Bryan nodded his approval. "Just be yourself, and it'll be all good."

Gloria slowed several feet past their table, almost like she was waiting for him.

Clark swallowed down hard on his butterflies and took a deep breath. *Too late to back out now*, he thought, awkwardly beginning his approach.

When she noticed him coming, she looked up from her order pad and said, "You guys need anything over there?"

"We're good." Clark was surprised by the shakiness of his voice. Could she tell? "I just wanted to say . . . the other day at school— I'm sorry for disturbing you like that."

At first Gloria looked sort of confused, but then her big brown eyes flashed with recognition and she smiled. "Wanna know something weird?" she said. "I've been hoping to run into you."

"Me? *Really?*" Clark's heart was beating faster now.

Gloria nodded. "I feel like *I'm* the one who should be apologizing."

He frowned and shook his head.

"I don't know why I rushed out like that. It was nice of you to check on me." She tucked her pad into her apron and slipped her pencil behind her ear again. "You're Clark, right? Clark Kent?"

"Yeah." He'd never heard anything quite so perfect as the way she said his name. "And you're Gloria."

She brushed a few strands of hair out of her face. "Anyway, it's nice to run into you again," she said, glancing toward the kitchen. "But I probably have an order up."

"Oh, for sure," Clark said. "I'll let you get back to work." He could tell she was about to go, and he wanted just a few more seconds. "But . . . make sure to come get me if you need help with that *one* table."

Gloria looked at him, confused. "Help?"

Clark motioned toward the Kellers and the Smiths, who were consumed by their card game. "They look kind of rough. I'm just saying . . . I'm here for you if things get out of hand."

Gloria looked over her shoulder at them. "Ooh, I see what you mean." She turned back to Clark, pretending to take him seriously. "They do look a little dangerous. If one of them acts up, I'll definitely flag you down."

"I'll be right over here." He pointed back at his table.

"You're a real gentleman, Clark."

He shot her his best gentlemanly grin. It made her laugh a little before she turned away and hurried over to the food pass, where an annoyed cook in the back was trying to squeeze another order onto the crowded hot plate.

Clark felt like he was walking on air as he headed back to his table. He plopped down in the booth across from Bryan in a kind of daze. He'd had minor crushes on other girls over the years. Even dated a few briefly. But he'd never felt anything like *this*.

Bryan was grinning from ear to ear. "You were great, man."

"Really?" Clark asked. "I felt like I should have talked more."

"No way," Bryan said. "That's part of your charm, Clark."

"Well, I appreciate the pep talk. I probably never would have spoken to her." Clark noticed that Bryan had only managed to eat a few bites of his steak. And it looked like he'd already thrown in the towel.

As if reading Clark's mind, Bryan looked down at his plate and said, "Guess my eyes were bigger than my stomach. But I saw a guy sleeping in the alley on the way over here. Let's pack this to go and hook him up."

Clark glanced at his own plate, which was empty, and wished he had something to contribute.

Bryan looked around for their server, saying, "When you grow up in my family, charity's sort of in your blood. My dad's horrified that anyone in Smallville is living below the poverty line. I don't know if you heard, but he's opening a food bank slash homeless shelter slash treatment center downtown."

"Really?" Clark thought about this. "Is Smallville even big enough for that kind of thing?"

"That's the beauty of it. It's not just for Smallville residents," Bryan said, shaking his head. "The plan is to have people coming from as far off as Metropolis to get help." He nudged his plate away. "That's one thing I really respect about my dad. He doesn't do things like that for the attention. In fact, he thinks publicity can sometimes take away from the cause itself."

Clark was impressed. He made a mental note to tell Lana about the shelter next time he saw her. It'd be tough for her to question Mongomery Mankins's character after learning that he wasn't even taking credit for some of the charity work he was doing.

CHAPTER 8

On Monday night, after doing all his chores around the farm after school, Clark sat down at his desk to study. But he was having a difficult time concentrating. He kept reading the same passage in his applied physics textbook over and over, but the material wasn't sinking in. He'd get halfway through the second sentence and his mind would drift to his conversation with Gloria at the diner. He was staring at the words, but all he could see was her sliding her pencil behind her ear. And her smile. The way her eyes had lit up when she laughed at his joke.

Clark rubbed his temples, trying to concentrate on the pages of his textbook. To stare intently at the information, which had something to do with electromagnetic propulsion. He forced himself to absorb each word, one at a time, trying to make sense of it in the context of the chapter.

But then a strange buzzing filled his head.

A warmth rose up through his legs and chest and into his arms and fingertips. And his whole body became strangely rigid as a terrifying flash of bright red filled his vision.

He pinched his eyelids closed, leaping out of his chair and tumbling over a laundry basket full of clean clothes that he'd forgotten to put away. He clawed at his eyes as he scrambled to his feet, yelling. His back slammed against the wall.

Was he going blind?

The backs of his eyelids were on fire, and when he first opened them he couldn't see a thing.

The world had gone black.

In a few seconds, though, the burning subsided. And he could see shapes. And then colors. As he slowly regained his vision, he sat back down at his desk, trying to catch his breath. He'd never felt so relieved in his life.

That's when he realized his textbook was on fire.

He panicked, thinking his bedroom might go up in flames. The whole farmhouse. And his parents weren't home to help control the blaze. He pounced on the crackling textbook, tamping down the flames with his bare hands. The heat from the fire pressed into his palms, but it didn't hurt exactly. At least he didn't think so. It felt more like tiny needles pricking his skin, like when his arm would fall asleep in bed and he'd wake up, turn over, and feel the blood slowly spreading back through his veins.

Once he'd smothered the flames in his textbook, he stamped out a few embers that had fallen onto the rug next to his small desk. Smoke rose up near the ceiling, setting off the fire alarm in the hall. It wailed and wailed until he raced out of his room and leapt up to disarm it. The piercing sound of the alarm quickly subsided, but now Clark heard something else.

The revving of an engine outside the house.

His parents were at a town hall meeting about the proposed stop-and-search law, and he didn't expect them back for hours. Alarmed, Clark hurried back into his bedroom to look out the window, but he didn't see anything in the darkness.

Weird, he thought, staring out at the still farm.

When he finally turned away from the window, he looked at his applied physics textbook. It was ruined. He turned one of the charred, blackened pages, and it broke off in his hand.

Had he really just started his textbook on fire with his stare?

Clark shook his head, trying to will away this possible new power. Being able to see through walls seemed mostly like a good thing. Same with his super-hearing. And his speed and strength.

But shooting lasers out of his eyes?

So much for studying, he thought, looking down at the scorched rug near his desk. And how was he going to explain these burn marks to his mom?

She was going to *kill* him.

He picked up his cell to call Lana. She was in the same applied physics class. Maybe he could borrow *her* book tomorrow after school. He knew that the information in this chapter would be on the final, and he needed to ace it in order to secure an A in the class. Clark was just about to call Lana when he heard voices outside.

He set down his phone and went to the window again.

Nothing but darkness.

His super-hearing was picking up a conversation a good distance from the house. He slipped on his shoes and hurried outside to investigate.

When he was halfway across the farm, he spotted a man

dressed in jeans and a cowboy shirt moving toward the old barn with an ax.

Clark froze. "Hey!" he shouted. "What are you doing here?"

Now he saw two more men, dressed similarly, emerging from the crater in front of the old barn. One was carrying a metal-detector wand. The men looked at Clark, and he looked at them, and for several pregnant seconds, no one moved. Clark felt his heart pounding in his chest.

Intruders were on his property.

And one had an ax.

For the first time in his life, he felt a flicker of legitimate fear. It wasn't a fear of the men, exactly. That they might hurt him. No, he feared for his parents. What if he were across town right now and his *parents* were home? What would they do? How would they protect themselves?

An anger swelled inside Clark, and he shouted, "Get off our property! Now!"

As the men scurried, Clark felt another buzzing in his head. A warmth rising, quicker this time. A flash of red filling his vision.

Just as he went to turn his head, another laser shot out from Clark's eyes, torching the dry grass to his right. A small fire sprang up, and Clark quickly stamped it out.

His powers were out of control at the worst possible time.

Clark jogged toward the hay shed, where his dad kept many of the farm tools, and rummaged around, looking for something to scare the men off with. He emerged with an old, rusty scythe. He perched it on his shoulder and began marching toward them. One of the men was backing up in an old white pickup truck that looked vaguely familiar. The front grille was badly dented, and the driver's-side door was painted gray.

These guys were burglars, Clark reasoned. They'd come here to steal farm equipment. It was something that occasionally happened in Smallville.

But no one had ever tried to steal from the Kent farm.

"You hear me?" Clark shouted across the dark farm as he closed in on the men. "Get out of here! Before I call the cops!"

One of the men emerged from behind the old barn on a dirt bike and darted directly at Clark, the lone headlight nearly blinding him.

Clark quickly retreated into the hay shed to run through his options. His powers had gone haywire, so he didn't feel safe using them. Besides, he didn't want to give himself away. But it was clear these men weren't going anywhere if he didn't do *something*. The one driving the pickup seemed ready for a quick getaway. A second was now hacking at the padlock on the front door of the old barn with an ax. And the man on the dirt bike was waving around a bat as he zipped across the farm. He was clearly trying to buy the other burglars time to steal what they could.

Clark had to think of something fast.

After the guy on the dirt bike had passed by the hay shed a second time, Clark quickly gathered three freshly rolled bales of hay and sent them rolling in the direction of the truck and the man hacking at the lock on the old barn door. As the large bales bore down on Clark's targets, he raced across the farm toward the small front-end loader his dad had recently purchased.

In a fraction of a second, he had the loader roaring to life and was driving it directly at the man on the dirt bike. The first hay bale exploded against the pickup truck, nearly tipping the vehicle on its side. The second narrowly missed the man with the ax just as he broke through the padlock.

The man panicked and dove into the bed of the truck, which ground into reverse, then shifted forward, *clunk*ing over a long, uneven stretch of dead grass and off the Kent property.

The man on the dirt bike noticed the others retreating and swerved back toward the main road. Clark stopped the front-end loader and hopped down to watch the battered pickup and dirt bike speed down the road, out of sight.

The burglars hadn't been able to steal anything from the farm, but Clark knew something far more important had been lost.

All his life this place had been his escape.

His safe space.

But now he knew that was only an illusion.

CHAPTER 9

The next day after school, Clark and Lana were sitting across from each other in their usual quiet room at the library. "Okay, now explain again what happened to your textbook?" Lana said, sliding her copy across the table. "You weren't exactly clear about that on the phone."

"Long story," Clark said.

He hadn't told Lana about the attempted burglary yet. He would eventually, of course, but first he needed to process it himself. Figure out if it was really just a simple robbery or if someone was targeting the Kents specifically.

And if so, why?

Lots of strange stuff had been happening in Smallville over the past several days, starting with the appearance of the man in brown, and Clark was beginning to wonder if it would get worse before it got better. He knew this: he no longer took his safety for granted in his hometown. Even on his own property. And there was no way he was going to just sit around waiting for the intruders to come back and try it again.

He was going to *do* something.

"I've got nothing else going on," Lana said, waiting for the full story. "Why are you being so sketchy about a stupid physics text-book?"

"Forget the textbook for a second," he told her. "Don't you want to hear about my dinner with Bryan? I couldn't really get into it at school with so many people around."

She grinned and scooted her chair closer to the table. "Did you use the interview tactics I taught you?"

"Sort of." Clark set his backpack on the floor and rolled up his sleeves. "He was pretty easy to talk to, though. I didn't really need 'tactics.'"

"Oh, you naive junior reporter," Lana said. "This entire industry is built upon the proper execution of one's tactics."

Clark shook his head. "My main takeaway was this: I think you're officially wrong about the Mankins Corporation. From everything Bryan was saying, his dad is a genuinely decent guy. He's even opening a food bank and homeless shelter down here. For people from all over Kansas. And he's doing it *anonymously*."

Lana seemed genuinely taken aback. "That's a Mankins proj-ect?" She folded her hands and looked at the table in front of her. "Interesting. I'd heard it was linked to some big church in Metropolis."

"Apparently Bryan's dad does all kinds of charitable work on the down low. So you know it's not just a publicity play."

Lana furrowed her brow. "When was the last time you heard of a major corporation 'hiding' its charitable work?"

Clark shrugged. "According to Bryan, his dad thinks publicity can undermine an actual cause."

"Yeah, okay." Lana leaned back in her chair.

She was quiet for a long stretch, just staring at Clark with a blank look on her face. He knew this version of Lana well. She was moving chess pieces around in her head. But this time, he was, too. He suddenly remembered where he'd seen the beat-up white pickup truck. That day the football players had brawled with the man dressed in all brown. Just before the guy had carjacked the SUV and driven it into the retaining wall, he'd attacked the pickup with his bare fists while the driver cowered at the wheel inside.

Could these two incidents be related somehow?

Or was it just a coincidence?

Lana leaned forward, slapping her palms against the table. "I have an idea!"

Clark knew this excitement, too. And it usually required him to do something he didn't want to do.

"We go ask him," she said.

Clark frowned. "Who?"

"Montgomery Mankins."

"You're kidding, right?" But Clark knew she wasn't. Lana had that look in her eyes that he knew all too well. It was the same look she'd gotten when she decided to investigate what percentage of the school budget was spent on the football program. Clark tried to reason with her. "Look, Lana, I'm pretty sure we can't just waltz into the Mankins corporate headquarters and interview the most powerful man in Smallville."

"Why not?"

"Because . . . well, he's probably busy, for one thing." Clark shook his head, trying to come up with other reasons. "He's not gonna grant two random high school kids an interview right there on the spot."

Lana started packing up her backpack with a sly grin on her face. "Clark, I'm insulted," she said. "It's as if you've never seen your best friend in action."

"I bet they don't even let us in the front door."

"Watch and learn, Mr. Kent."

Not fifteen minutes later an executive assistant—a young, clean-cut guy in a gray suit—emerged from a back room. Wearing a fake plastic smile, he said, "Montgomery will see you now."

"I stand corrected," Clark whispered as he and Lana hoisted themselves off the plush couch in the waiting room.

Lana had a cocky grin. "You never get answers if you don't ask questions."

Clark and Lana followed the guy into a huge corner office with floor-to-ceiling glass walls. It overlooked all of downtown Smallville. Clark had never seen such an amazing view of his hometown. The office was relatively spare, with a small seating area off to the side and a massive wooden desk in the center. It was obvious this setup was only temporary, until the company moved into its new facility.

A large man stood up from his chair, smiling, and held out his hand. "Montgomery Mankins. Pleased to meet you both."

Lana shook his hand first, saying, "I'm Lana Lang. And this is my associate, Clark Kent."

Clark shook hands with the man, too, noting his flimsy grip. Clark had seen Montgomery Mankins on TV several times, giving interviews. And on billboards. And Clark had been at the speech the man gave at the grand reopening of the library. Up close like this, Clark recognized some of Bryan's features in his father's face.

Aside from having a fancy office, he wasn't what you'd expect from the CEO of a major corporation. He wasn't wearing an expensive-looking suit or a Rolex. He didn't have slicked-back hair or designer glasses. Montgomery Mankins looked more like an English professor than a financial bigwig. He wore jeans, a T-shirt, and a brown button-down sweater. His hair was long and unruly and almost entirely gray. His small wire-framed glasses seemed like they might slide off his nose at any moment.

What struck Clark most was the man's air of supreme confidence.

"Welcome!" he said, motioning for Clark and Lana to sit in the two chairs on the other side of his desk. "Sorry I don't have a lot of time this afternoon, but we'll do our best."

"We appreciate you giving us any time at all," Lana told him as she and Clark settled into the chairs. "I'm sure you're a busy man, Mr. Mankins."

"Call me Montgomery, please." He sat and reached into his right-hand desk drawer, pulling out a checkbook. "Before we get started here . . . Clark, I understand you've met my boys."

Clark nodded. "Yes, sir."

"Well, I need to thank you for being so gracious after their little debacle. Bryan told me you and your father rushed to help them. I know there weren't any property damages per se, but I'd like to offer some compensation just the same."

"No, thank you, sir," Clark interjected. "My father won't take a penny, trust me."

The man closed his checkbook and leaned back in his chair. "Now, you're sure about this?"

"They landed in an empty, muddy field." Mentioning the field made Clark flash back to the attempted robbery. The white pickup careening across the farm, toward the road. The man on the dirt bike waving around the bat.

Montgomery shifted in his chair. "In that case, let's get on with your questions, shall we?"

Lana riffled through her notepad. "As we all know," she said, looking up at Montgomery, "your corporation has done a lot of great things for Smallville. The economy is stronger, our town's infrastructure is vastly improved—"

"Well, not everything we've done is so great," Montgomery interrupted. He leaned forward in his chair and folded his hands in front of him. "For instance, purchasing local land from generational farmers . . . Sometimes I worry we're stripping this community of its very identity."

"Huh," Lana said, flipping to the next page of her pad. "That's what I was going to ask about next."

Clark was surprised. He'd been expecting some kind of political nonanswer. But here the guy was, pointing out his company's flaws before Lana could even bring them up.

"We also have to take into account the rising rents here in town," Montgomery went on. "I'm afraid this is an unfortunate by-product of a surging local economy. And what about the high wages we offer for fieldworker positions? It's great for a certain population, yes, but it certainly makes it harder for small farms to find and afford good help."

Lana was frantically scribbling in her notebook now, wearing her best poker face. But Clark knew she was as impressed by Montgomery as he was. She looked up. "Is that why you donate so much to local causes? To sort of square your net effect?"

As Montgomery answered, Clark found himself bombarded by all the sounds around him. The subtle creaking of Montgomery's chair as the man changed position. The scratch of Lana's pen across the page. Someone in the office next door speaking quietly on the phone, calling the person on the other line "sweetheart." Her kid, maybe. The cranking sound of someone's parking brake. A woman out on the sidewalk saying in an irritated voice, "But there *is* no more Project Dawn, okay? Not here. Now, if you'll excuse me, I have to go." And a man saying back, "Please, ma'am, it's a matter of life and death. I need to find him *now*."

Clark sat up in his chair, and as soon as he did, his super-hearing cut out. He tried to concentrate, to learn more about this "life and death" situation, but the only voice he could hear now was Lana's.

"And what about supporting the protests over the rights of undocumented workers?" she asked.

Montgomery adjusted his glasses. "This company and I universally condemn any form of bigotry. And I'm confident Smallville will do the same when it comes time to vote." Montgomery pushed back his chair and stood up. "Now I'm afraid we're out of time. Please email my assistant any additional questions you might have." He held out a business card.

Lana took it and stood up, too, slipping the card into the front pocket of her jeans.

"Last thing," Clark said. "Do you know anything about a . . . Project Dawn?"

Clark watched Montgomery's eyes grow wide as he stood frozen for several awkward seconds. Then his smile returned, and he shook his head. "Can't say I do." He extended his hand to Clark. "But like I said, email any more questions. I'll try to respond within a few days."

Clark shook the man's hand. "Thanks for your time."

After shaking Lana's hand, too, Montgomery hit a button on his desk, and the executive assistant came back into the room to show Clark and Lana out. Just before they went through the double doors, Clark glanced back and saw Montgomery still standing near his desk, smiling and waving at them.

"Well, that was an odd goodbye," Lana said in a low voice as they headed back through the lobby and toward the exit.

Clark nodded. "Tell me about it."

"What the hell is Project Dawn, anyway?" she asked.

"No clue. I overheard someone say it on the way into the building, and I was curious."

"I have to say, overall I was pretty impressed. Of course, people like him don't get where they are without being able to turn on the charm—" Lana stopped in her tracks and grabbed Clark by the wrist. "Shit, it's him," she said in a much quieter voice.

Clark stopped, too. "Who?"

"The guy from the coffee shop." Her gaze slid meaningfully toward the front door.

Clark saw a tall, muscular guy heading for the exit in a hurry, like he was late for a meeting or something. Clark recognized him immediately. "Wait, *that's* who was hitting on you?"

She grinned. "Cute, right?"

"That's Corey Mankins, Lana. Montgomery's older son."

Lana turned to Clark. "So he's cute *and* rich?"

"Yeah," Clark said. "And according to Bryan, he's also a punk."

Lana ignored this comment, saying, "Let's follow him."

"What?" Clark didn't understand what was happening. *"Why?"*

But Lana was already pulling him through the lobby.

Once they were outside, Clark saw Corey walking across the street toward an old commercial building with several FOR LEASE signs posted in the storefront windows. The building he entered was in bad shape. It was as if the surging Smallville economy had missed a spot. Few of the storefronts still had company banners above the doors or OPEN signs. The door Corey went through displayed a small sign with a generic-looking sunrise logo and a company name: WESCO SCIENTIFIC RESEARCH INDUSTRIES.

Lana looked to Clark.

He didn't know what she expected to find in a place like this. But then again, he was sort of curious about Bryan's brother, too. For a very different reason. He motioned across the street. "After you."

They crossed and Lana opened the door and they went inside.

This Wesco company clearly wasn't anticipating any new clients. The front lobby of the small commercial space was empty aside from a dusty plastic plant hanging in a corner of the room. The reception desk was stacked with uneven piles of takeout menus, coupons, flyers, and other solicitations that had probably been slipped under the front door over the past several months.

Corey stood leaning against the far wall with his arms crossed. "Can I help you?" After focusing on Lana a few more seconds, he uncrossed his arms and pushed off the wall. "Wait," he said. "Do I know you?"

Lana smiled. "You may have bought my coffee the other day."

"Oh, that's *right*. Cool. You're . . ."

"Lana."

"Lana. Cool. I'm Corey." He glanced over his shoulder at an open door just inside a hallway. "What are you doing here?"

"I'm working on a news story for school, and I saw you outside, and . . . I don't know. I thought I'd come say hi." Lana tilted her head and looked up at Corey.

Clark felt like she was dangerously close to batting her eyelashes. He stepped up beside her, telling Corey, "You know me, too."

Corey looked Clark up and down. "You're that Kent kid. From the farm." He turned to Lana. "You two *know* each other?"

Lana shrugged. "Sort of."

"Wait, you're not, like . . ."

Lana laughed and shook her head. "Not even close. We're just friends."

Clark bristled at how dismissive Lana had sounded. What did she mean, "not even close"?

"Man, small world," Corey said. He walked over to the open door and gently pulled it closed while saying over his shoulder to Lana, "Anyway, if you wanna hang out or something, we should go back to the coffee shop. This place isn't great for socializing." He motioned around the empty room.

Lana took out her notepad and pen. "The story I'm doing is on your dad's company. Would it be okay if I just interviewed you real quick? I promise it'll only take a few minutes."

"Wait, you want to *interview* me?" Corey looked anxious. "So you're, like, a reporter?"

Lana shook her head. "Not a real one. It's just for class. My teacher assigned an article about charities, and I know how much your family gives back."

"They're definitely not wasting their money on decor," Clark said under his breath as he looked around the room.

"This place has nothing to do with my dad's business," Corey said, sounding a little irritated. "It's my friend's research firm." He turned back to Lana. "Anyway, we can talk philanthropy if you want."

"You sure?" Lana said. "I know you're probably *impossibly* busy."

Clark was impressed by how seamlessly Lana had transformed herself into a ditz. It always struck him how often her interviews involved some form of acting.

Corey looked toward the hall again, then back at Lana. "Fine, we can do it here. But only if you give me your number this time. In case, you know, I think of something later that I forgot to tell you."

"Of course," Lana said in an overly excited voice.

"Cool. Hang on." Corey hurried into the hall, past the door he'd pulled closed.

As soon as he was out of sight, Clark turned to Lana and said, "I think Ditzy Lana's working. Make sure you ask him the Dawn Project question, too. I think there's something there."

She shushed him.

Just then Corey returned with two metal folding chairs. "Sorry," he told Clark. "Only have these two."

"No, you guys go ahead," Clark said. "I'll just . . . do my own thing."

"Don't touch anything," Corey snapped. "Like I said, this isn't my office. And my friend's super particular about his things."

Clark linked his hands behind his back while looking around the room. "You have my word."

Corey placed the chairs side by side on the opposite side of the room from Clark, and he and Lana sat down, awkwardly close, and began talking.

Now it was time for Clark to get some answers of his own.

He'd noticed how concerned Corey had been with the door he'd closed in the hall. What was he hiding? Clark inched toward it nonchalantly, occasionally glancing back at Lana and Corey to make sure they were still caught up in their conversation. When Clark made it to the wall nearest the closed door, he stared at it intently, trying to get his X-ray vision to punch through.

Every other time he'd tried to do this on command, he had failed, but to his great relief, this time it actually worked. He was now looking through the thin wall, into the small office on the other side, where a man he recognized immediately was sitting at a tiny wooden desk, working on a laptop.

Dr. Wesley.

So *he* was the "friend" who was "particular" about his things.

Clark stared at the back of the scientist's head, recalling the way Bryan had cringed when describing the man. He'd said Wesley was creepy and connected to bad people. Clark looked around the small office: the ugly brown rug, the motionless ceiling fan, the hodgepodge of coffee mugs lined up along the bookshelf to the right of the desk. The wall on the opposite side of the office was covered with large photographs that had been tacked up. The photos were mostly of farm fields. And farmhouses. A few barns and grain elevators. Clark recognized Smallville landmarks in a few of the photographs. These were *local* farms. The angle of the shots suggested that the photos had been taken from a helicopter.

One of the photos that had been circled with a marker showed a deep crater on Tommy Jones's family farm—the farm they'd just sold. Which struck Clark as odd. Some of the other photos were taken with a strange filter, too, with the objects in the photos a variety of bright colors, almost like infrared.

Clark blinked, momentarily losing his view. He stared at the wall again, concentrating even harder this time, and eventually his vision penetrated the wall. This time he found himself staring at a particular cluster of photos that made his skin crawl.

It was *his* farm.

There was a photo of their farmhouse. And one of the pond. And *several* of the crater near the old barn. He flashed back to last night, recalling the trespasser with the metal detector. But the photo that triggered a sick feeling in Clark was the picture of the old barn itself. The photo was blown up and had been taken with the strange filter. The barn was lit up in different shades of green and yellow. And there was a handwritten black arrow pointing from the crater to the barn.

Dr. Wesley got up from his desk, walked over to the wall, and stared at the photo of the crater at the Joneses' farm. He pulled out the tack and took it down and examined it closely before putting it back up. When Dr. Wesley turned toward the door, Clark spun around and started for the lobby, only to have someone grab his arm.

It was Lana. "Clark, you okay?"

"Can we leave? Like, now?"

Lana turned to Corey just as the door in the hall opened. "My friend's sick," she said. "Gotta go. Sorry!" She pulled Clark toward the front door and opened it just as Dr. Wesley emerged from his office.

"Wait!" Corey shouted. "I didn't get your number!"

"See you Friday night!" Lana called to him through the closing door.

The two of them walked casually past the window of the building, then took off in a brisk jog. They didn't stop until they had made it all the way back up the library steps. The pair ducked inside the front doors, and Lana leaned over, out of breath, saying, "What was *that* all about?"

Clark pretended to breathe hard, too.

He wanted to tell her exactly what he'd seen in Dr. Wesley's office, but he wasn't sure how to go about it. He couldn't tell the truth, that he'd seen some suspicious-looking photos through the wall using his X-ray vision. He'd have to tell it slant. "When that guy opened the door of his office, I saw pictures of farms hanging on the wall. *Smallville* farms, Lana."

"Really? *Why?*"

He shook his head. "No clue."

She stood up straighter and patted him on the shoulder. "Clark, you seem seriously spooked."

Clark *was* spooked. Because now he believed the burglary wasn't random at all. They'd targeted his house. And he no longer believed they were there to steal farm equipment. They'd come for something else. But what did they want with the crater and the old barn? He couldn't answer these questions yet, but seeing photos of his property tacked up to Wesley's wall like that . . . he couldn't help feeling that his family was in legitimate danger.

"One of the photos," he told Lana, "I think it was of *our* farm. Why would our property be on the wall of some run-down scientific research office?"

"I have no idea, Clark. But we're going to find out. I promise."

Clark nodded.

There were pictures of a lot of farms, he kept telling himself. But he came back again and again to that blown-up photo of the old barn, taken with some kind of infrared camera. And he kept replaying the man in the cowboy shirt hacking at the lock on the door with an ax.

It was time to look inside the old barn.

CHAPTER 10

That night, well after his mom and dad had gone to sleep, Clark snuck down the stairs and out of the house. The moon hung so low in the sky that it muted the stars. For the first time since fall, the night air was warm and slightly damp, and the bugs whined around his ears as he cut across the farm. Clark followed the faint tire tracks from the old pickup, feeling a profound sense of violation.

He walked down the long, subtle decline toward the pond, wondering why anyone would be interested in the seemingly ordinary farm. Eventually he found himself staring down into the crater. It looked as if the very center had been dug up. What could those men possibly have been looking for?

As a kid he used to come here all the time. He'd take summer naps under the large maple tree near the old barn. Or he'd rest his head against the lip of the crater when he needed to think about something. But now he tried to see it from Dr. Wesley's point of view. It was fifteen yards across and maybe twenty feet deep. But other than the fact that it was so close to the old barn, Clark didn't see what was so special about it.

Clark stood in front of the old barn next. The large wooden doors loomed over him. The padlock was badly scuffed and hanging wide open, and in his head he could still see the man hacking at it with the ax.

Clark remembered how strange his dad had always been about this place. For the first time in Clark's life, he wondered if Jonathan was hiding something from him.

Clark tossed aside the busted padlock. The doors creaked as he slowly pulled them open, prompting him to glance up the hill at the dark farmhouse, where his parents slept. How disappointed would they be if they knew what he was up to right now? Behind their backs.

The air inside the barn was musty and stale, and the dust he kicked up swirled all around. He picked his way past heaps of old junk, moving blocks of rotting wood, old tractor parts, scrap metal, toys from his childhood. Rusty toolboxes sat on the workbench along the wall, likely filled with random screws and nuts and bolts. On a small family farm like theirs, if something broke, buying a new one wasn't an option. Clark had become quite adept at doing makeshift repairs on pretty much anything.

He worked his way to the back, toward the corner that had shown the most color on Dr. Wesley's photo. Could it have been highlighting all this random stuff? he wondered. It was piled nearly to the ceiling. He climbed up the heap, grabbing a few broken two-by-fours and tossing them aside. He chucked away an old oilcan, a rusted motorcycle muffler. As he continued to make his way through all the junk and garbage, an uneasy feeling came over him. Like he knew there was something important beneath all this clutter, but did he really want to find out what it was?

He pressed on until he had removed enough of the old junk to see that there was a large object under an old tarp. It was roughly the size of a small car. He froze. What if this was something Jonathan and Martha had hidden for a reason? What if it was something personal?

Did he really have a right to be snooping around like this?

While his parents slept?

A wave of guilt overtook him, and he ended up leaving the barn without digging any further. Instead, he would try a more forthright approach.

It was nearly three in the morning when Clark reached a hand through the dark to shake Jonathan awake. His dad slowly stirred, then opened his eyes. When he saw Clark standing over him, he bolted upright and swung his legs off the side of the bed. "Clark? What's wrong, son?"

Martha didn't stir.

Clark motioned with his head for his dad to follow.

They went down the stairs quietly and cut through the living room. Clark grabbed a flashlight out of a drawer on the other side of the living room. Jonathan pulled his tattered robe on over his pajamas as they walked out the front door. "What's this about, son?" he asked Clark nervously. "Is everything okay?"

"I want to show you something." Clark led him up to the edge of the crater and shined the flashlight on the part that had been dug up. "After you left last night, I found some men on our property. One was messing around inside here with some kind of metal detector. Another was trying to break into the old barn."

"Oh, God, Clark," Jonathan said, visibly upset. "Why didn't you tell me right away? Did you call the police?"

"I wanted to talk to you first."

His dad whirled around, looking all over the farm. "I noticed something odd about the hay rolls this morning. And the hogs seemed on edge. But I never suspected—" He grabbed Clark by the elbows. "Are you all right? Did they try and harm you?"

Clark shrugged. "I managed to scare them off."

Jonathan let go of Clark and turned toward the barn. "They broke the padlock. Were they able to get inside?"

"They never made it inside," Clark said. He knew his dad would react this way to the intrusion. But he hadn't dragged Jonathan out here in the middle of the night just to tell him about the trespassing. Clark wanted to get answers about the barn. And what was hidden in there. But now that he was standing here with his dad, he wasn't sure he was *ready* for the truth. Not if it was something major that he'd be forced to deal with. He had so many other things on his plate right now. Like all his finals at school. And the new powers he seemed to have very little control over.

"How'd you get them to leave?" his dad asked.

"I came at them with the front-end loader." Clark paused, staring at his dad through the darkness. "Is there anything I should know about the barn?" he asked vaguely.

Jonathan stared at Clark for a long, awkward stretch. At one point he nodded to himself. But seconds later he sighed and began shaking his head in an exaggerated manner. "Son, your mom and I . . . ," he began. "All we've ever wanted is what's best for you."

Clark turned away, filled with trepidation. "I know that."

Jonathan got quiet again. He glanced over at the barn, then turned to Clark and opened his mouth, like he was going to say something.

"I'm sorry, Dad," Clark said, beating him to the punch. This whole conversation was a mistake, he now realized. "It's the middle of the night. I shouldn't have pulled you all the way out here to tell you what happened."

"You wanted to show me how they were digging inside the crater," his dad said, seemingly happy to back out of some deeper conversation they'd been skirting around.

Clark nodded. "Yeah, I just . . . I never imagined seeing thieves on our property like that."

Jonathan nodded and patted Clark on the shoulder. "Let's go on back to the house. Get some sleep. I'll call the police first thing in the morning. Once we get to the bottom of that part, we can talk about anything else on your mind. That sound okay?"

Clark nodded. "You go ahead. I'm gonna stay out here a little longer."

"You sure?" His dad looked at him like he wanted to say more, but he didn't. He just stood there awkwardly, a pained expression on his face. "Okay," he said. Then he turned and started back to the farmhouse, leaving Clark alone in the dark.

CHAPTER 11

Clark managed to avoid any heavy conversations with his dad over the next few days. There were so many other things to focus on. He spent his free time studying for his finals and racking his brain about Dr. Wesley and his wall of photos. And how those photos might relate to the men he'd caught trespassing on his farm. And the interview he and Lana had had with Montgomery Mankins.

He considered going back into the barn on his own. But every time the thought crossed his mind, he found a reason to put it off. He didn't even understand why.

On Friday night, Lana picked Clark up at the end of his long driveway just after dark and drove them across town. After taking several narrow roads, they pulled down the uneven dirt path that led to the Joneses' farm, one of the oldest farms in Smallville. They parked among a sea of other cars.

Clark stepped out of Lana's car wearing his only black button-down shirt and a freshly washed pair of jeans. Lana wore a black sundress with a pair of faded skinny jeans underneath. Throughout

the week, the party had been the focus of every school conversation Clark had been part of. The Jones Farm Funeral, everyone was calling it. Half the junior and senior classes were expected to be there, and everyone was supposed to wear black, as if they were attending an actual funeral.

Clark was hit with a sudden bout of nerves as he spied the bonfire blazing high above the heads of his classmates, partying near the cornfields. Music spilled from the nearby farmhouse, and he could see several silhouettes through the thin white curtains. It had been a while since Clark had gone to a party like this. Way back during freshman year, when his teammates would drag him out. He hoped he'd remember how to act.

"Clark!" someone shouted from behind them.

He turned and found Bryan and Lex closing the doors of Lex's red sports car, parked a few rows back in the field. They jogged over to catch up to Lana and Clark.

"Nice look," Bryan said, motioning toward Clark's black button-down.

"This is all the black I own," Clark said.

"I figured." Bryan wasn't very dressed up himself. He had on a faded black sweatshirt and black jeans. Lex, on the other hand, was dressed to impress. He was wearing a pair of black designer jeans and a dark gray button-down tucked in under a black blazer. Black aviator sunglasses—even though it was night.

"This is my best friend, Lana," Clark said. "Lana, meet Bryan and Lex."

They all shook hands, and Lex said to Lana, "Bryan tells me you write for the school paper."

"Are you kidding?" Bryan said. "She *is* the school paper."

"It's true," Clark said.

Lana beamed. "I don't know if I'd go *that* far."

Lex took off his sunglasses. He pulled a business card from his jacket pocket and handed it to Lana. "When you graduate, look me up. My company in Metropolis is always looking to bring on talented writers."

"Thanks," Lana said, taking the card. She was clearly flattered, but Clark still didn't know how he felt about Lex. The guy was just so slick. Like a smarter and more sophisticated version of Corey. And it struck Clark as odd that Lex wanted to be at a high school party.

Clark squashed these thoughts as the four of them started toward the farmhouse. He was flooded with a sudden sense of nostalgia. How many times had he been here during his freshman year? Ten? Fifteen? The place was almost exactly as he remembered it. A long dirt path led up to a faded white two-story house. There was a large, grassy side yard, where they used to have barbecues. And a large backyard that sloped down toward a vast stretch of farmland.

The Joneses' property was unique in that it was extremely long and had several rows of tall trees breaking up the vast acreage. Tommy's grandfather had planted them with the intention of creating several different plots with family houses for each of his children. But he'd never had enough money to build anything, and Tommy's father was the only one still living in Smallville.

Inside the house, country music blared as dozens of people dressed in black milled about, laughing. Dancing. Shouting to one another over the music and drinking from red cups. Two large speakers were perched on a folding table, next to a spread of chips and pretzels and half-empty pizza boxes. Three big coolers on the ground were filled with melting ice and floating cans.

Aside from all the partyers, the house was virtually empty.

There was no furniture besides a few folding tables and cheap plastic chairs.

When Lana spotted several friends from the school paper huddled together in the living room, she walked over to talk to them.

Lex scooped up three cold cans of beer and went to hand them out. Bryan took one, but Clark shook Lex off, saying, "I don't really drink." Lex shrugged and tossed the extra can back into the cooler. Then the three of them strolled out to the backyard, where another large crowd of people dressed mostly in black stood around a massive, crackling bonfire, talking and laughing.

Clark assumed he'd know everyone at this end-of-the-school-year party, but he didn't. A few wore letterman jackets from a neighboring county high school. Others seemed slightly older, like Lex. College kids, maybe, back for summer break.

Clark stood a little straighter when he spotted Gloria standing in a small group of Mexican kids he recognized from school. She was wearing black overalls and a light blue T-shirt, and her long, thick hair was pulled back into a ponytail. She looked at him over her shoulder and gave a slight wave, then took a sip from the red cup she was holding.

He waved back, the butterflies hitting him hard as she started walking over. "I was hoping I'd see you here," she said.

"Same with me."

They were both quiet for a few seconds, and then she said, "No drink?"

He shook his head. "It's not really my thing."

"Yeah, me neither," she said. When Clark glanced at her red cup, she held it out so he could see what was inside. "Water. I hate feeling like I'm out of control."

Clark grinned. "To be honest," he told her, "I haven't been to a party like this in a long time."

Gloria glanced toward the crowded bonfire area. "Yeah, I'll take the neighborhood barbecues any day. I only came to keep an eye on my little brother. Do you know Marco?"

"Yeah. He plays soccer, right?"

She nodded and looked back at her group of friends. "Great," she said. "Looks like he's already ditched me."

"I can help you find him," Clark said.

"It's okay." Gloria glanced around before turning back to Clark. "I'm not usually the overprotective type. It's just . . ." He saw fear flicker in her eyes. "Three more people from my community have disappeared. One of them—this guy Danny Lopez—was good friends with my uncle Rene. He went to work at a local farm and never came home. That's six total, Clark. All young guys. And I'm not trying to lose my baby brother."

"Whoa," Clark said. *"Three more?* What's happening?"

Gloria shook her head and sipped her water. "There are a lot of rumors flying around, but the bottom line is, we don't know. Not yet, anyway. And I don't place a whole lot of faith in our local police force these days. Not when it comes to stuff like this."

Clark hated that Gloria had to second-guess local authorities, when so many of the white kids partying out here tonight—even *poor* whites—would never know that kind of anxiety.

Including him.

"Anyway, let me go track him down," Gloria said. "Catch up with you later."

Clark watched her walk back toward her group of friends, wishing he could ease her fear about her brother. He realized that since catching those men trespassing on his property, he'd been entirely consumed with what was happening in *his* world. From now on he would try to focus on the big picture. Starting with these mysterious disappearances.

He drifted back over to Lex and Bryan, feeling guilty about being at a party when there were so many more important things happening in Smallville. He and Lana had work to do. And he didn't see why that work shouldn't start right away.

"Clark?" Lex snapped his fingers in front of Clark's face. "Hello? Anyone home?"

Clark left his thoughts to focus on Lex. "What happened?"

"I just asked you a question. Are you going to be Bryan's gym partner?"

"It's no big deal," Bryan said. "I just started this new workout routine and nutritional plan. And Lex is giving me shit."

"Not even," Lex said, grinning. "I'm your biggest supporter. I just think you need a workout buddy. It's too easy to backslide if you don't have someone holding you accountable. And you know *I'm* not a gym guy."

"I'll go with you," Clark said.

"See?" Lex said. "Told you Clark would come through."

When Lex got pulled into a conversation about Metropolis a few seconds later, Clark nudged Bryan. "So, you've been going to the gym?"

Bryan shrugged. "Remember how I urged you to talk to Gloria at All-American? And said you needed to step into the action? Well, it's time for me to practice what I preach."

Clark nodded. "How's it going so far?"

Bryan shoved his hands into his pockets. "I've been working

pretty hard. And Corey, of all people, hooked me up with this supplement that's been helping me recuperate. Honestly, I never thought of myself as a gym guy either. But I feel good."

"That's what matters," Clark said.

They both went quiet for a little while. Clark was tempted to tell Bryan about the people disappearing from Smallville and how he was determined to find out what was going on. But he didn't know if they had that kind of friendship. They were still just getting to know each other.

"It's weird," Bryan said. "I want so badly to *be* someone, you know? A person who makes an actual difference. But I have no idea how to do it. I mean, I love flying, but my dad doesn't really think it's the best future for me. He says the real money's in finance. Or law. And since I came back from my boarding school . . . I don't know. He's just different."

"I'm not really sure what my calling is either," Clark said. "I know that sounds dramatic, but you get what I'm saying."

"Totally."

"It's like you have all this pent-up energy," Clark said, "but you can't figure out where exactly to put it."

Bryan nodded excitedly. "And you can't just ignore it or else you'll explode."

"Exactly." Ever since Clark was a kid, he'd wondered what his purpose was. When he was younger, he told himself it was farming. Tending to the land. Caring for animals. And those things were still important to him. But lately he'd been wondering if there was something greater he was put on this earth to do.

Like helping people.

Before Clark could say anything else, Tanya Davis, a star pitcher on the Smallville softball squad, took him by the elbow, saying, "Sorry to bother you, Clark. But I need you to step into this game of beer pong we got going."

"What?" Clark said, caught off guard.

"We each get a lifeline," she said, "and you're mine."

"You're picking Clark?" a baseball player named Jules asked. He turned to one of his teammates, Beau, laughing, and the two of them slapped hands. "I know we're good now, 'cause this dude doesn't even drink."

A couple of other baseball players laughed.

"You guys are ignorant," Tanya said. "I've seen Clark break about fifty tackles on a single run. You think he can't figure out how to throw a damn Ping-Pong ball into a cup of beer?"

"We'll see."

"Go on, Clark," Bryan said, nudging him forward. "Let's see what you got."

Clark shrugged, took the Ping-Pong ball, and looked at the triangle of cups at the other end of the long table. "What do I do? Toss it into one of those cups?"

"Whichever one you want," Tanya said. "And those assholes have to drink."

A few people nearby started paying attention to the game as Clark lined up his toss. He estimated the velocity he'd need, based on the weight and tension of the Ping-Pong ball, taking into account the slight breeze. He aimed for the very point of the triangle and watched his toss arc toward the cup, landing right inside.

"Ha!" Tanya said. "Drink up, suckers!"

"Lucky shot," Beau said after he'd downed the contents of the cup in one go. His own shot bounced away.

"Let's see if you can double down," Jules said.

Clark took the Ping-Pong ball again, lined it up, and made his second toss. The ball went straight into the next cup in line. He felt Bryan slap him on the shoulder. "Maybe *this* is your calling, Clark!" he joked. "You're a natural."

It was just a silly game, but Clark was getting a thrill out of it. Having a small crowd watching him perform. Competing against the two baseball players on the other side of the table. He made four more throws, sinking all of them in a clear pattern and working the small crowd into a frenzy. As they urged him to go on, though, he began to wonder if he was revealing his powers.

He missed the next toss on purpose and thanked Tanya for letting him have a turn.

"Come on, Clark!" she shouted. "I need you for the next round."

"I would, but I have to go find someone," Clark told her. He slapped hands with all of them and made his way back into the house.

Bryan followed, saying, "Damn, Clark, that was impressive."

Clark laughed him off. "I just got lucky."

"Whatever you say."

They joined Lex in the living room. He was talking to twins named Jenny and Laura about the haunted old theater that had been demolished downtown to make way for the brand-new Mankins facility. "Here's the man himself," Lex said, motioning toward Bryan. "But don't ask him about any of this, because he wants nothing to do with his dad's business. Isn't that right, Bry?"

Bryan had an irritated look on his face as he stared at Lex. "Can I get you another beer?" he said sarcastically. "Because, clearly, you haven't had enough."

Lex ignored the dig. "It's just weird, Bryan. Whenever I ask you something about the family business, you say you don't know. When are you gonna pull your weight?"

Sensing that things were quickly escalating, the girls discreetly backed away.

Clark nudged Bryan. "You okay?"

"Yeah, I just wish Lex would tell us why he's really here in Smallville. He claims it's to lie low and hang out. Yet he seems pretty obsessed with my dad, if you ask me." Bryan turned to Lex. "Seriously, like, ninety percent of the times we're hanging out, you're digging for info about my dad's company."

Clark sensed this was more of a private conversation between Bryan and Lex, and he began searching for an exit strategy. When he spotted a group of ex-teammates through the window, he said, "I'm gonna go say hi to some people. Be right back."

But Bryan and Lex were too caught up in their bickering to even acknowledge him.

Clark walked out to the back porch, where Paul, Tommy, Reggie, Willie, and Kyle were hanging out. "You showed up," Paul said. "Tommy, let's take Clark to the cows. See if he'll drink straight from the tap."

The guys chuckled as Paul drank from his cup. It was clear he was drunk.

"I'll pass," Clark said. Despite the jab, he was happy to see that Paul was no longer wearing his sling.

"We sold them all, anyway," Tommy said.

"Still can't believe this is our last party here," Kyle said. "*Ever.* What are we supposed to do now?"

"I'm glad you're focused on the parties," Tommy said, leaning against the wooden staircase. "Meanwhile, me and my family are thinking about all the meals we shared here. And all the work we did in those fields. The animals we raised."

Kyle waved him off dismissively. "Dude, you know what I'm saying."

"Why'd your folks end up selling?" Clark asked. "I thought you guys loved this place."

"They had no choice," Tommy answered. "A local buyer came in with an all-cash offer that was too good to pass up. Gave us enough to buy a new house in town *and* get a winter home in Arizona."

Clark nodded, making a mental note to share this information with Lana. He could think of only one local buyer who'd be able to lay down that kind of money up front: Montgomery Mankins.

Coincidentally, Corey walked by just then with a few of his boys, all of them looking a little old to be at a high school party. Corey had on an expensive-looking black suit, with a black shirt and tie underneath. His two friends wore black blazers and jeans. When Corey noticed Clark, he stopped and asked, "Where's your friend?"

"Lana?" Clark feigned glancing around. "She's here somewhere."

Corey looked at the football players, then muttered something under his breath to his friends, who laughed. He said to Clark, "If you see her, tell her I'm looking for her."

After they left, Paul said what everyone was thinking: "Who invited *that* douche?"

"I heard they showed up in a hearse, though," Kyle said. "With a chauffeur. Which, you gotta admit, is pretty sick."

"He's a Mankins boy," Reggie said. "So you know he's got that disposable income."

The rest of the guys agreed.

"I guess technically he doesn't need to be invited, though, right, Tommy?" Willie asked. "As of midnight his dad *owns* this place."

Tommy shook his head. "It wasn't Mankins who bought the place. It was some company called Wesco. And according to my old man, they're not even using the place for farming. He thinks they're gonna turn it into vineyards. I guess the soil all around the crater out back is especially rich and good for vines."

"A winery in Smallville?" Kyle asked. "That shit doesn't even sound right."

The guys all went quiet, shaking their heads. But Clark was still stuck on the buyer, Wesco. Now he was more confused than ever. He thought of all the crater photographs on Dr. Wesley's walls, including those of the crater on the Kents' farm. Did the guy really want to make wine out here? And how could someone with such a crappy-looking office buy the Jones farm with cash?

Clark needed to find Lana. She'd want to hear about this.

Tommy slapped a big mitt onto Clark's shoulder. "Were your ears burning earlier?"

"Why?" Clark asked.

Reggie stood and brushed off the back of his black pants. "Kyle here made a pretty massive statement. He said if you would have stuck with football, you could've gone pro."

"Really?" Clark looked to Kyle, who nodded. It felt nice to hear that kind of compliment, but it also made Clark feel even guiltier for quitting. He knew a lot of these guys saw football as their ticket out. But without a winning record, college coaches would be less likely to scout their games.

"Shit, we all think that, Clark," Tommy said. "You were un-stoppable."

"Well, everyone except Paul," Kyle said, turning to him. "Paul?"

Now they were all focused on Paul, who was leaning against the railing, looking like he was about to be sick. Reggie pulled a half-empty bottle out of his friend's hand, and Kyle was quick to get Paul some water.

Clark made a move to help, too, but Tommy cut him off. "Don't worry about it, Clark. We got him."

Clark backed off a few steps, watching Paul slowly recover. In that moment, he saw the colossal distance that now existed between him and his former teammates. Talent didn't matter as much as trust. And they only trusted the guys on the team.

He turned and started back toward the farmhouse.

CHAPTER 12

An hour later, Lana was hastily pulling Clark outside, past the raging bonfire, to the edge of the backyard, where they would have more privacy. He was eager to tell her what he'd found out from Tommy, but she beat him to the punch. "I talked to Gloria Alvarez," she said.

He paused, wondering where she might be going with this. "Okay . . ."

"She told me about all the disappearances." Lana looked back at the crowd surrounding the towering bonfire. "You were right, Clark. Whatever's happening in Smallville, it's literally tearing families apart. And I'm starting to wonder . . ."

"What?" Clark said after she trailed off.

Lana looked around to make sure no one else was within earshot. "The people in town, the ones who are lobbying for this new stop-and-search law? Could they be taking things into their own hands?"

"What, like, *kidnapping* people?"

Lana shrugged, picking up a small rock and rolling it between her fingers. "It sounds absurd when you say it out loud like that. But there seems to be only one demographic being targeted, right?"

Clark thought about this. "But why wouldn't they just wait to see if the issue gets voted in? Then they wouldn't have to take such a huge personal risk."

Lana shook her head. "I don't know what to think anymore, Clark. This is all new territory for Smallville. Two years ago, immigration wasn't such a big thing. Not on a local level. Now it's all anyone talks about."

Something about that statement felt incomplete to Clark. Everyone he talked to believed the proposed law was wrong. They were actively fighting *against* it. He felt like he and Lana needed to consider the disappearances in the context of everything else that was happening in town. The men trying to break into his barn. The protesters marching outside city hall. The photos he'd seen on Dr. Wesley's wall. "So, I was talking to Tommy and them earlier," he told Lana. "Turns out Mankins didn't buy this place."

Lana narrowed her eyes at him. "Then, who did?"

"Wesco. Dr. Wesley's company. And he paid for it in cash."

"Really?" Lana pitched the rock into the grass. "Where the hell'd he get that kind of money? You saw his office downtown."

"That's exactly what I thought."

She stared at Clark for a few seconds and then smiled. "Maybe it's time for me and you to pay Dr. Wesley a little—"

Lana was interrupted by a loud crashing sound, followed by the rise of several voices. Clark spun toward the bonfire and saw the shattered sliding glass door. People were filing out of the house to see what all the commotion was about.

Lana grabbed Clark by the wrist. "Come on!" They both hurried toward the crowd.

On the other side of the bonfire, Paul and one of Corey's friends were standing chest to chest, shouting in each other's faces. "I'll talk to whoever I *want* to!" Corey's friend yelled. "And you aren't gonna do shit about it!"

"I said, back off," Paul growled, jabbing a finger inches from the other guy's face.

Corey rushed to the scene. "Hey!" he yelled. "Mikey! What the hell's going on?"

"This dude's drunk," Mikey answered with a cocky grin. "That's all."

"Nah," Paul said. "Tanya told you to back off, but you weren't hearing it." He scowled at Mikey, adding, "We don't play that shit here."

"Careful now," Mikey told Paul. "I could have you shipped out of the country by morning. Trust me."

Paul shoved Mikey. But when he did, he slipped and had to catch himself on the beer pong table. Paul was built like a tank and was as tough as nails, but he was also drunk. And he was still healing from his shoulder injury. Clark knew he was in no condition to fight.

Mikey returned the shove. And when Paul stumbled backward, Mikey pounced, throwing an awkward left hook that grazed Paul's jaw. Paul grasped Mikey's collar on the way down, pulling him into his fall, and everyone gasped as they twisted toward the roaring bonfire.

An electric charge shot through Clark's entire body, and in an instant he was hurling himself through the warm night air, teeth and fists clenched, eyes locked on the flames. In a fraction of a second he arrived, shoving Paul and Mikey away from the fire.

Mikey sprang to his feet and swung at Clark, missing badly.

Clark froze, afraid to swing back. Afraid he might do real damage. In front of everyone. So he just stood there as Mikey charged
and shoved him in the chest as hard as he could. It took Clark a second to realize he should be falling, like Paul had, so he threw himself backward. His fake fall turned real when he tripped over a small
pile of wood, launching himself directly into the searing flames.

The crowd around him gasped and screamed as the fire torched
Clark's clothes and hugged his skin, the smoldering red logs popping against his rigid back, giving off an odd warming sensation and
a smell like burned rubber.

Clark spun quickly out of the pit and into the glass-covered
grass, where he began frantically tamping down the flames leaping
off his shirt.

"Jesus, Mikey!" Corey shouted, racing to Clark's side. He helped
pat down Clark's shoulders, saying, "Shit, man, you okay?"

Clark nodded, scrambling to his feet. He reached down for his
glasses and put them back on.

His clothes were torched, and everyone was staring. He shoved
his hands, which should have been covered in burns and cuts, into
his pockets. "I'm fine. I was only in there for a second."

Corey pulled Mikey away.

Gloria hurried to Clark's side. "Oh my God, Clark! You fell
right into the fire."

"I'm okay," he insisted.

"Are you burned?"

He shook his head.

Bryan was there now, too. He held Clark's right arm as he
looked at his brother. "Corey, get that guy out of here! You see
what he just did?"

Several of the football players huddled around Clark. "You saved him," Tommy was saying. "You saved Paul from the fire."

Paul was still kneeling on the ground a few feet away from Clark, picking glass out of his elbow. "You had my back," he said.

Clark shook his head. "I just reacted."

The hum eventually died down once people saw that Clark wasn't seriously injured. In the dim light, it must have happened really fast for those watching. They probably assumed he had minor burns under his shirt. And little cuts from the glass, like Paul did. But Clark didn't have a mark anywhere. The flames had been warm against his skin. He'd *felt* them. But they'd caused him no harm.

"You have to go to the hospital, Clark," Gloria said, visibly shaken. "Have them check out your back."

"I'll take him," Lana said. "I'm his ride."

"I'm okay," Clark assured them both. "Honestly. I just want to get out of here."

"Of course." Lana turned toward a group of friends. "He's okay. I'm taking him home."

Corey was shouting at his friends as they headed out to the parking area with their chauffeur.

Bryan kept asking Clark if he was okay. Lex, too, and lots of people from school. Everyone wanted to talk to him, to see if he needed anything.

But all Clark wanted to do was disappear.

He'd shown a glimpse of his powers, right here in the open. Were they all secretly wondering about him now? Did they think he was a freak?

Lana was eventually able to lead Clark through the crowd, toward her car. "You really are a good guy," she said, opening his door. "Those football bros always give you shit. Yet you're the first one there when any of them is in trouble."

They were both quiet as she drove them to Clark's house.

He played back everything that had happened after they heard the shattering of the sliding glass door. Paul and Mikey falling toward the flames. The impossible speed he'd reached in getting to them. How he'd rolled out of the pit with his shirt on fire.

Had he revealed himself to his classmates?

Did they know?

Lana was in her own world, too. She stared straight ahead as her headlights cut through the dark night. Sometimes she would nod to herself. Other times she'd shake her head or tap the steering wheel as if emphasizing some unspoken point. It wasn't until she pulled up to the foot of Clark's long driveway that she spoke. "What are your plans for tomorrow morning?"

"Going back to the Joneses' farm," he told her. "With you."

She looked at him suspiciously. "How'd you know that's what I was going to say?"

"Because," he said, "there might be something there. And we both want answers."

She nodded.

As Clark went to get out of the car, he felt Lana's soft hand on his wrist. "Clark," she said. "Wait."

He turned to look at her.

"I agreed not to take you to the emergency room." She paused, looking him in the eye. "But at least let me make sure your back is okay."

Clark fell into his seat again, feeling anxious. How was he going to explain it to her? That the fire hadn't marked him. That the glass hadn't cut him.

But this was Lana.

So he turned away from her, giving her access to his back.

In a few seconds he felt her slowly lifting his shirt up his back. Then he felt her warm hands on his skin. And he listened to her breathing. And when she slowly slid her entire hand down the length of his back, his whole body tingled under her fingertips. And his breath caught. It was Lana's hand. His best friend. But at the same time it was the hand of a beautiful woman. The hand of someone he trusted. Someone he'd do anything for.

"Not even a single mark," she whispered in awe. "How's that possible?"

He turned to her, his heart thumping inside his chest. "I rolled out as quickly as I could."

"But your shirt—it's torched."

He didn't have an answer for that part, so he kept quiet.

She stared at him for several long seconds, their eyes locked. He wondered if she might lean forward and kiss him.

Or if he might kiss her.

And what would that feel like?

She released an audible breath and turned to look out the windshield. "I guess I'll see you in the morning, then," she said.

He pushed open his door, stepped out of the car, and closed the door behind him. He ducked to look through the passenger-side window, trying to think of something to say. But he didn't have words for what he felt. So he tapped the hood twice and turned around and started up his driveway.

CHAPTER 13

The sun had just begun to rise when Clark left the house the following morning. He started down his driveway, thinking that he was early, that he'd have to wait for Lana. But there she was, her little hand-me-down Honda idling at the foot of his long driveway, as if she'd never left the night before. As he made his way to her, he worried it might be weird between them. Nothing had happened last night, of course. But there were a few intense seconds where it felt like something *could* have.

Luckily, he had it all wrong.

When he opened the door, Lana greeted him with a big smile, saying, "You want the latte or the mocha?"

Clark looked down at the two large cups, one sitting in each drink holder. "Oh, wow," he said. "Maybe the latte?"

"Good. 'Cause I'll drink *any* kind of coffee."

He climbed in and picked up the latte and took a sip, feeling intensely grateful for their friendship. "You already stopped for coffee? What time'd you get up?"

"Early bird gets the blah, blah, blah." She put the car into drive and pulled out onto the quiet street. "To be honest, I didn't get much sleep last night. Just tossed and turned, thinking about my conversation with Gloria. And the fact that Wesco bought the Joneses' farm." She glanced at Clark. "And your run-in with that rich asshole, obviously."

Clark sipped his coffee, staring out the window at a flock of birds flying in a great *V* in the sky. He turned back to Lana. "You know what I realized after you dropped me off last night? I've never been in an actual fight in my life. I didn't even know what to do."

"Um, I consider that a *good* thing."

"No, I do, too," Clark said. "I'm just saying. In many ways we're lucky to be growing up in a place like Smallville. Some kids have to deal with stuff like that every day. I just wish . . ."

She followed Clark's gaze to the VOTE YES ON ISSUE 3 sign proudly planted in a neighbor's yard. "That we weren't also racist?"

"Well . . . yeah." Clark thought about this for a few seconds before amending his answer. "Though I truly believe that most people in Smallville are accepting of others."

Lana raised an eyebrow and shot Clark a skeptical look. "Let's let voter turnout be the judge of that." She refocused on the road. "If you're too busy to get out there and vote with your accepting little heart, guess what? You're complicit."

Clark nodded and took another sip of his latte. He couldn't argue with her there.

A minute or two later, she pulled the car over at the Alvarez Fruits and Vegetables stand, saying, "I don't know about you, Clark, but I could use a bagful of Honeycrisps right about now."

"Let's do it," Clark said, knowing they were really here to ask some questions.

As he and Lana got out of the car, he called to Carlos and Cruz. "Hey, guys!"

The father-son duo waved and continued organizing one of their stands. Clark could tell by Carlos's slumped shoulders that he wasn't his usual jovial self.

While Lana went to pick out apples, Clark sidled up to Cruz. "Everything okay?"

Cruz stopped stocking bananas. He glanced over at his dad before telling Clark in a quiet voice, "The cops were here yesterday morning, asking questions."

"Deputy Rogers?" Clark asked.

Cruz shook his head. "Two people I've never seen before."

"What'd they want?"

"They said if we want to stay in business, we'll have to submit a permit by the end of the month. My dad's been selling produce here for over ten years. He's never had to have a business permit before," Cruz scoffed.

The thought of this conversation pained Clark. "So what are you guys gonna do?"

"Sell off what we have left," Cruz said. "Then shut the stand down. Do something else."

Clark couldn't believe it. "I'm really sorry to hear that." It was one thing for Cruz to move beyond the fruit stand when he got older. It was another to have his family's livelihood taken away.

"Seems like there are more cops around now," Cruz said. "My dad's worried."

Lana and Carlos joined them near the register, and Clark could tell that Carlos was in no mood to talk. He gave Lana the price for the apples, took her money, and handed her a couple of dollars as change. Then he went back to stocking fruit.

Lana looked at Carlos before turning to Clark and Cruz. "I wish there was something we could do," she said.

"We'll be okay," Cruz said, forcing a smile. "I've got a plan, actually. We'll see."

They said their goodbyes, and then Clark and Lana climbed into her car and drove off in silence. After a few minutes, Lana shook her head. "What was that you were saying about Smallville?"

Clark sighed. "I don't even know anymore."

Lana eventually merged onto the same back road she'd taken the night before, on the way to the party at the Joneses' farm. "So now we have *two* different companies buying up Smallville farms," she said. "My question is this: Are they competing? If so, how does Corey fit into the equation? Is he some kind of interloper?"

"According to Tommy," Clark said, "Wesco didn't officially take ownership of the property until midnight last night. So I doubt we'll actually find much there."

"Most leads are dead ends, Clark. But we still have to follow them all."

Lana pulled into roughly the same spot she'd taken the night before. But this time her car was the only one around. She put it in park, removed the key, and turned to Clark. "Here's what I keep coming back to: Why would Wesco buy a farm they didn't intend to use for farming? I mean, doesn't that strike you as odd?"

Clark shook his head as he took off his jacket and tossed it onto the back seat. "Tommy's dad thinks they're going to transform the place into a vineyard. Apparently, the soil around the crater is super rich."

Lana pushed open her door. "So, that's why they're so interested in craters?"

"Maybe." Clark got out, too, and closed his car door.

As they walked toward the farmhouse, he expected to find empty beer cans and red cups strewn about. Overflowing trash cans. But the only reminder of last night's party was the charred remains of the bonfire, piled inside the makeshift fire pit he'd tumbled into. Otherwise the place was immaculate. Even the shards from the shattered glass door had been removed. Whoever Tommy had hired to help clean up had left the place in great shape.

"Pretty quiet out here," Clark said.

"Yeah. But this place *is* almost two hundred acres, according to the public property sales records I found online last night."

Clark nodded. *Of course* Lana had done research last night.

As if reading Clark's mind, she turned to him and said, "What? I told you—I couldn't sleep."

They walked past the fire pit and down the slight slope in the grass where they'd been hanging out when the fight started. Within a few minutes they'd crossed through a thin line of trees and reached the farm area. Aside from the fact that all the Joneses' farm animals were gone, Clark didn't see anything out of the ordinary. When he and Lana came upon a small, dilapidated shed, Clark opened the creaky door and looked inside. Nothing but old and broken tools covered in spiderwebs.

They passed an empty mud pen where the Jones family had kept their hogs. Then came a vast stretch of dirt that had once been a cornfield. As they neared the end of the long field, they came upon a second row of trees, which had been planted as a windbreak. This one was unusually dense. Clark estimated that it was eight to ten trees deep, and it stretched out on both sides as far as the eye could see. This must have broken up the land for one of the homes Tommy's grandfather never got around to building.

Clark stopped when he thought he heard voices in the distance.

Lana stopped, too, and looked at Clark. "What?"

He pointed beyond the line of trees before realizing she likely hadn't heard a thing. "Hang on," he said, turning his left ear in the direction of the sound.

There it was again. Human voices. Maybe a half mile away, which he assumed was still within the property.

"Do you see something, Clark?" Lana asked anxiously.

He shook his head. "I thought I heard something. I'm not sure, though."

Lana stared at the line of trees for a long time before saying, "We should keep going. Just . . . let me know if you hear anything else."

As they crept through the dense trees, Clark motioned for Lana to stop a second time. "You can hear it now, can't you?"

"No," Lana said. "What is it?"

Clark strained to determine where the sounds were coming from. He heard a male voice: "Mark it there." The words were as clear as day to him now, and he flashed back to the night he'd found the three men in cowboy shirts on his own property. He half expected to hear the sound of the beat-up white truck.

"Voices," he told Lana. "Someone giving instructions."

"Shit, Clark, someone really *is* here. What now?"

The distinct sound of an aerosol can in use was coming from beyond the third thick grove of trees, this one over a hundred yards ahead of them. Clark waved for Lana to follow, and they hurried through the clearing.

As they neared the third row of trees, they slowed to a walk and then crouched. Lana could hear it now, too.

"What's that sound?" she whispered.

"I think it's some kind of spray can." Clark turned to Lana. "Maybe this isn't such a great idea. Can't we get into trouble for trespassing?"

"It's not the police I'm worried about."

Creeping forward slowly, they exchanged a look as they neared the edge of the tree line. Then they proceeded into the thick grove, picking their way carefully and silently through the dense foliage. They got as close as they dared to a large clearing on the other side, stopping behind the trunk of a broad tree.

There were three men in the clearing, wearing unmarked black fatigues. Clark thought of the man downtown who'd attacked his teammates. But that guy had been wearing brown fatigues. And he was Mexican. These men were white. They looked like they were part of some kind of top-secret Special Forces unit. Two of the men were measuring something in the tall, weedy grass while another followed along behind them making marks with a can of white spray paint.

Whatever they were doing, it had nothing to do with traditional farming.

Or designing vineyards.

The clearing was large, nearly half the size of a football field. And it was well protected. Two thick groves of trees on opposite ends, to the north and south; a small hill to the east; and a shallow valley with a creek running perpendicular, to the west. And there was the crater. It was slightly larger than the one on Clark's property. There was some kind of machine inside it, digging into the center.

The area was obstructed from view by anyone nearby on the ground. It could only be seen from above. And Clark had a sneaking suspicion that this clearing, and the crater, were the reasons Wesco had purchased the farm.

A huge black truck with a row of runner lights mounted across the top of the cabin was parked behind the men. A fourth figure sat inside it, just a silhouette behind the glare of the sun off the windshield.

When Clark shifted his weight to try to get a better look at the truck, a large branch snapped under his feet. He and Lana cowered, wide-eyed, as the men stopped what they were doing and looked in their direction.

"Who's there?" a man wearing a black hat shouted.

A second man stepped forward, calling out, "Stay where you are!"

Clark watched the man in the hat reach behind his back and pull out a small, dark object that looked like a handgun. Clark's eyes widened even more as he looked at Lana. "Is that . . . ?"

"What?" Lana whispered anxiously. "What are you talking about?"

The man in the hat was pointing the object toward the ground as he advanced on them. Clark instinctively positioned himself between the man and Lana, saying quietly, "He's got a gun."

"Jesus!" She grabbed him by the arm. "Come on, Clark. Let's get out of here!"

The two of them spun around and took off running.

Lana led the way, tearing back through the line of trees, in the direction of the farmhouse. Clark raced after her at what he thought was a normal person's pace, keeping himself in a position to block Lana from view as much as possible. When he glanced back, he saw that three of the men were chasing them. The fourth had stayed behind with the vehicle.

"Stop!" the tallest of them shouted. "We just want to talk to you!"

Clark then heard a brief argument among the three men.

He and Lana were now halfway across the wide-open field. If they could just make it past the final line of trees, they could take cover on the other side of the farmhouse. And then he could go get Lana's car and bring it around so she wouldn't be out in the open for long.

Two gunshots cracked across the field, ripping through the trees ahead of them. Lana screamed and tripped. Clark dove on top of her to provide cover, terrified that she'd been hit. He could hear the men shouting at each other behind them.

"Were you hit?" he asked her, his voice trembling.

"I'm fine," she barked.

Clark lifted Lana up by the back of her shirt and shoved her forward, yelling, "Go!" Just then a third shot rang out, and Clark felt a slight stinging sensation in the small of his back, like someone had slapped him there with a bare hand.

He ran, making sure he stayed positioned between Lana and the source of the gunfire. But the shooting had ceased.

When Clark glanced over his shoulder, he saw the tall guy shoving the man in the hat to the ground and shouting him down. The third man was still moving in their direction, but more slowly. And he was unarmed.

When Clark and Lana finally reached the farmhouse, they raced around the corner, and Clark looked back again. The third man was walking now, shouting, "Go on! Get out of here! This is private property!" The other men were just two shapes in the distance, standing at the edge of the line of trees. And it appeared that they were still arguing.

As Lana knelt down, catching her breath, Clark tried to make sense of what had just happened. This was the first time in his life he'd ever been shot at. At least he *thought* they were shooting at him and Lana. Or had the shooter been aiming at the treetops, trying to scare them?

"Shit!" Lana barked between desperate breaths. "Do you see them anywhere? Are they still following us?"

Clark looked again. The third man was retreating now, heading back to the other two. And Clark heard one of them say, "It was just a couple stupid kids. Our orders were to use force as a last resort." Clark tried to determine if any of them had a good view of Lana's car, if they could have seen her license plate. He didn't think so.

"They're going back," he told her. "Let's get out of here."

They hurried to her car. Lana beeped open the doors and they climbed in. She started the engine and peeled out in reverse, and as they sped down the bumpy driveway, she shouted, "Who the hell were *they*?"

"No clue!" Clark answered. But even though these men looked completely different from the three who'd tried to break into the barn on his farm, he had to believe there was a connection. Both properties had a crater. There was no way the two incidents were completely unrelated.

Lana was gripping the steering wheel tightly with both hands. "Look at me, Clark. I'm, like, shaking. We have to go talk to the cops."

"I thought you didn't trust them."

"That guy just shot at us, Clark! Isn't that why the police exist? To protect ordinary citizens like us?"

Clark looked back one last time as Lana merged onto the empty road. He reached into the back for his jacket, thinking about how scared he'd been when he heard the shots. When Lana had fallen. He could have sworn she'd been hit. The thought completely wrecked him. He didn't know what he'd do if he ever saw Lana get hurt.

CHAPTER 14

"What do you mean, there's nothing else you can do?" Lana demanded.

Deputy Rogers set down his cell phone and leaned back in his worn leather chair. "I listened to your story, Miss Lang. And I sent two men out there to have a look around. But they just called in to say they didn't find a thing. No bullet casings. No spray-painted grass. No men in fatigues. I'm sorry."

"How far in did they go? That place is huge." Clark turned to Lana. "Maybe pull up the property sales records you found online."

Rogers shook his head. "Won't be necessary. My men are already on their way somewhere else."

Lana had warned Clark on the way to the County Sheriff's Office that the deputy didn't care much for her. He thought she asked too many questions. He thought she was always sniffing around in places she didn't belong. But this was different. A man had just shot at them. In Smallville. Clark and Lana had been sitting around the station for two hours now, and they weren't getting anywhere.

Deputy Rogers placed his hands on top of his desk, which was strewn with stacks of papers and file folders. It looked less like the desk of a high-ranking law enforcement agent and more like a place where important files went to die. "Now, if you two will excuse me . . . ," he said, pushing back his chair.

Clark wished there were something more he could say or do, but Deputy Rogers had always been a simple man. If there was proof, he'd pursue a lead to the end. If there wasn't, he'd move on. It was the way he'd always operated in Smallville.

"What about Wesco?" Lana asked. "Are you at least going to talk to Dr. Wesley?"

"I told you, Miss Lang, we'll look into it." Rogers wiped a hand down his face, softening a little. "Look, we're stretched real thin right now. Between these protests downtown and the upcoming Mankins festival, we've already had to bring in a few deputies from the next county. Just to keep us above water. And that's not to mention a slew of other problems the public's not even aware of yet." He gestured behind him at a pile of overstuffed folders stacked on top of a filing cabinet.

Clark read the names on the five files. He then thanked the deputy for his time—because he knew Lana wouldn't—and ushered her out of the man's office.

"What Mankins festival?" Lana mumbled as they started back toward the front lobby of the county wing of city hall.

"Bryan told me about that," Clark said. "The company is celebrating the grand opening of its new building. And I think they want to make it a big deal."

Lana was shaking her head. "What a colossal waste of time this was."

"I don't know about that," Clark said. "Did you read the labels on those files Rogers pointed at when he made that cryptic reference to stuff the public doesn't know yet?"

"No. What'd they say?"

"There were five Hispanic names. And I recognized one of them from talking to Gloria at the party. Danny Lopez."

Lana stopped. "The missing workers."

"Maybe the police are trying to find out where they are, too. Which would mean the police have nothing to do with their disappearances, right?"

Lana stared at the white stucco wall beside them for several seconds. "I guess so," she finally said, turning to Clark. "Unless it means they *do* know what happened to them. Like, they're keeping records of the people who get deported. It's too soon to rule anything out."

Clark nodded. "I guess you're right."

He noticed a restroom sign and said, "I'll catch up with you in a minute."

Lana nodded and sat on a nearby wooden bench and pulled out her phone.

As Clark stood in front of the mirror, he replayed what had happened on the Jones farm, for maybe the twentieth time since they'd arrived at city hall. What was the spray paint all about? he wondered. And what were they digging for inside those craters? He'd thought there could be a perfectly legitimate answer to these questions—until the man in the black hat had *shot* at him and Lana. The one thing Clark was sure of was that these men weren't random locals. They were outfitted like some kind of Special Forces team. But why would military men be on the property that Dr. Wesley, a scientist, had just purchased?

Clark splashed water on his face and washed his hands. Smallville had always been the kind of place where everyone knew everyone else, and no one locked their doors at night. Now people had gone missing, and men dressed in black fatigues were firing warning shots at unarmed high school kids.

Before Clark left, he took off his jacket and slung it over his shoulder. As he turned toward the door, something in the mirror caught his eye. He stepped back in front of the mirror and pulled off his shirt and held it in front of him.

His stomach dropped.

There was a single hole in the white fabric near the lower back.

He knew right away what he was looking at.

A bullet hole!

Clark spun around and looked at his bare skin in the mirror. He discovered a subtle red mark just above the small of his back. It matched the hole in his shirt exactly.

Clark's knees wobbled, and he grabbed the sink to keep his balance.

The armed man in the black fatigues hadn't been firing warning shots.

He'd been shooting to *kill*.

And what if he'd hit Lana instead?

Clark's first thought was to march right back into the deputy's office and offer up his bullet-hole shirt as evidence. That was what Rogers based everything on, wasn't it? Then maybe he'd actually *do* something.

But this wasn't the kind of evidence Clark could submit. The bullet hole might motivate the sheriff's department to get serious about his and Lana's accusations, yes. But eventually it would lead to both the deputy and Lana wanting to look at Clark's unharmed back. There was no way he could reveal to anyone that he was somehow . . . *bulletproof.*

Instead, Clark slipped his shirt back on, then his jacket, and went out to the lobby, choosing to keep his mouth shut. But whatever was happening in Smallville . . . he now knew it was life or death.

"Check this out, Clark," Lana said as soon as she saw him. She took him by the wrist and led him to the front door, which she pushed open slightly so that he could see.

The protest in front of city hall had increased dramatically since they'd entered the building a couple of hours earlier. No longer a handful of people marching with signs, there were now dozens. He recognized the leader from another time he'd watched them. He had a goatee and spiky black hair, and he lifted an electric megaphone and shouted in perfect English, "We belong, same as you. Smallville's our home, too!"

The crowd behind him echoed each sentence, one at a time.

The effect was powerful.

"The deputy was right about one thing," Lana said. "This is only going to get bigger before the vote. And I'm all for it."

CHAPTER 15

"Hope you don't mind that I invited Lex," Bryan said as they sat down across from Clark in a large corner booth at the All-American Diner. The place was packed again, even though it was only Wednesday. Gloria wasn't working tonight, but on his way in, Clark saw that she was here eating dinner with her brother, Marco. Unable to tear his eyes away from her, Clark had nearly knocked over a busboy carrying a tray full of dirty dishes.

"That's fine," Clark said with a shrug. But he had to admit, he was a little annoyed. It had been four days since the men in black fatigues shot at him and Lana, and they'd gotten nowhere on their own. Clark had asked Bryan to meet up with him to find out what he knew about Dr. Wesley's relationship with Corey and in what capacity they were working together. Lex's presence would only complicate matters—Bryan might not be as forthcoming.

"So you wanted to talk about my brother," Bryan said, picking up his menu.

Lex stared across the booth at Clark with a slight grin. He

125

seemed to always have that grin on his face, Clark realized. Even when he and Bryan were getting into it at the party. It was as if everything Lex encountered in Smallville was kind of a joke to him.

Clark glanced at both of them anxiously. He didn't know who he could trust anymore.

"Clark, relax," Bryan said. "Anything you say to me, you can say to Lex, too. He'd just find out anyway. He always does."

"You have my complete confidence," Lex added. "I'd never cross a guy who can take on a bonfire and actually *win*."

"So, you guys made up, then?" Clark asked, wanting to steer clear of any talk about his fall into the fire at the party.

Lex laughed. "When you're tight like us, sometimes you get into little . . . debates. But there's never any hard feelings, right, Bry?"

Bryan shook his head. "He and I both have rich, powerful fathers," he said. "We just approach things a little differently."

"I think Bryan should take more of an active role in the family business," Lex said. "Like I do. But ultimately it's his choice. And I respect that."

"Anyway, you can trust Lex," Bryan said. "He's on the level."

Clark looked at them both. Despite Bryan's confidence in Lex, Clark would be careful about how much he revealed in front of the guy. He pulled his phone out to see if Lana had texted. She was supposed to be here already, and he didn't want to get into the meat of this conversation without her.

He looked across the restaurant.

As if on cue, Lana suddenly burst through the front door. When she spotted them, she waved and hurried over. Clark stood, and Lana slid to the inside seat of the booth. "What'd I miss?"

Lex shot Clark a curious look.

"Relax, guys," Clark said with a smirk. "Anything you say to me, you can say to Lana, too. She'd just find out anyway. She always does."

Bryan and Lex grinned, and Bryan said, "Hey, no arguments here."

The server showed up just then. She was an older Mexican woman Clark recognized from previous visits. He glanced at her name tag: *Margie*. She wore her graying hair tied back in a ponytail, and a bulky cross hung from a silver chain around her neck. She described the pot roast special, then took their orders and left.

"Before we get into anything too heavy," Bryan said, looking at Lana, "you should probably know something. My brother seems to think you and him have a . . . thing."

Lana frowned. "Wait, *what?*"

Bryan nodded. "He only went to the fake funeral party because you were going to be there."

Lana shot Clark a look as she sipped her water. "Well, that's, uh . . . flattering?"

"Unless you actually know Corey," Lex said.

Clark didn't exactly love the direction of the conversation, but he also saw it as his opening. "Look, Lana's my best friend," he said, "so I need to know a few things."

Bryan nodded. "What's up?"

"So, he's not a good guy?"

Bryan set down his water glass. "My brother's a dick."

"I'll go ahead and confirm that," Lex added.

"Really," Lana said, playing along. "He's been nice the couple of times I've talked to him. Could it be that he's just misunderstood?"

Lex scoffed. "By *you*, maybe."

"He's actually been nicer to me, too, lately," Bryan went on. "His problem is that he's just so consumed with proving himself to my dad. Ever since Corey came home from Switzerland, he's been on this, like, mission to move up in the company."

"And that's why he's working with this Dr. Wesley guy," Clark said. "Who, you told me, has a super-shady past."

Bryan motioned toward Lex. "I'll let *him* tell you about Wesley. He knew him back in Metropolis."

"He's a really, really smart guy," Lex said. "But he's not in it for the science. He's in it for the money. More power to him. But I know all the people who funded his work back home are now in jail. Which is how he ended up in a town like Smallville."

Clark was just about to ask another question when a balding, middle-aged patron several tables away began railing at their server, Margie. Everyone in the restaurant craned their necks to watch the dramatic scene unfold. Clark recognized the man right away, though he couldn't recall how he knew him.

"You call this rare?" the man shouted, pointing at the hunk of steak on his plate.

"Sir, we're happy to fix it," Margie said in a calm voice.

"Damn right you'll fix it! And when you finish, you can go back to your own goddamn country!"

Clark sprang out of his seat and started toward the commotion. He didn't know what he was going to do, but he couldn't stomach seeing anyone treated so poorly.

Margie pursed her lips and tried to steady herself. "Please, sir, you will have to keep your voice down."

"You don't get to tell *me* what to do!" the man shouted, sweeping a hand across the table. His food went flying everywhere, along with plates and glasses that crashed to the floor and shattered.

The server jumped back, horrified.

The entire restaurant went silent.

You could have heard a pin drop.

"Hey," Clark said, shifting in front of Margie. "What's the problem over here?"

The man looked Clark up and down. "Go sit down," he said. "This is none of your business."

The owner, David Baez, hurried toward the table. "Sheldon, I'm going to have to ask you to leave."

He reached for the man's arm, but Sheldon knocked his hand away, growling, "Don't you touch me!"

Clark couldn't stand witnessing one person mistreat another. But this was even worse. This was clearly racially motivated. The man had now cursed out both the Mexican server and the Mexican owner. And all he'd said to Clark was that it wasn't his business. It gave Clark a rare glimpse into a dark ideological minority here in his hometown. One that rarely bubbled to the surface, at least not in public.

Just as Clark was about to speak up again, the longtime restaurant manager, Mike Caulkins, who was white, came over and said something that seemed to temporarily calm the man. He took his jacket off the back of his chair and began putting it on, and his two friends did the same.

Clark pushed up his glasses and retreated to his booth, trying to slow his mind down. But he was having a hard time. It could have been Gloria taking that barrage of bigotry. He peered over at her now. She was sitting at her table with her brother, staring down at her plate of food. She didn't look up. And it broke Clark's heart.

He sat down at his booth, where the others were talking about the man's outburst.

Bryan looked around the restaurant. "Please tell me someone

got that on their phone," he said. "Post it tonight and I guarantee it'll go viral by morning."

Lana was patting Clark's shoulder. "You know who that was, right? Sheldon Ealing."

Now Clark remembered. Sheldon was a mean old cattle herder who lived in a trailer just outside town. He'd lost his farm a few years back and blamed his predicament on everything from the growing Mexican population to the US government to China. According to Clark's dad, the real reason had been terrible farm management.

Clark took a deep breath and let out a slow exhale, hoping it would relax him, but instead something shocking happened. His breath turned to frost and instantly froze his entire glass of water. He stared in horror at the now-solid block of ice.

Lex, Lana, and Bryan were still rubbernecking the overcooked-steak drama. They watched as Mike led Sheldon and his friends outside, muttering under their breath. A busboy was now cleaning up the overturned steak and potatoes. Another swept up the shards of glass.

Before his friends turned their attention back to their own table, Clark quickly grabbed the frozen glass and put it on the floor, under the table.

So, he was breathing *ice* now? Great. He couldn't even have dinner with friends without some random new power messing everything up.

"Fun fact," Lana said. "Guess who's one of the most vocal advocates of that proposed stop-and-search law?"

"You see how he treated the *owner* of this place," Bryan said.

Lex shook his head.

"Be right back," Clark said as nonchalantly as possible. He pointed to Lana. "Hold off on the Dr. Wesley stuff until I get back."

Lana shot him a confused look. "Okay."

Clark ducked into the small bathroom, locked the door, and looked at himself in the mirror. Without warning, a cacophony of overlapping voices and revving car engines and barking dogs and buzzing insects slammed into his consciousness. The ear-piercing sounds were utterly debilitating. And there seemed to be no way to stop the onslaught. No way to escape the deafening roar that threatened to overtake him.

Clark's knees buckled. He collapsed onto the cold tile, cupping his hands over his ears and rocking back and forth.

When would it end?

What if it *didn't*?

A flash of fear tore through Clark. What if he was actually losing his mind?

Then, just as quickly as the sounds had come on, they were gone, and all he could hear was his own frenetic breathing. And the faucet water he'd left running.

Clark hesitantly climbed back to his feet and gazed at his reflection in the mirror, wondering how long he would be able to go on this way. Hiding from all of Smallville. Hiding from *himself.*

Fire didn't burn him.

Bullets couldn't pierce him.

But standing here, Clark didn't feel powerful at all. If anything, he was at the mercy of his gifts.

And he'd never felt so desperately alone.

The only way forward, he decided, was to go back into the old barn, lift up the tarp, and confront his truth. No matter what it was.

The time had come for him to *know.*

On his way out of the bathroom, he passed the table where Gloria and her brother were eating dinner. "I gotta say," he told them, trying to pull himself together, "that the guy who went off on Margie . . . he was *totally* out of line. He should never be allowed in this place again."

Gloria glanced at her brother. "Things like that seem to be happening more and more," she said. "I don't understand it."

"*I* do," Marco said. "We've let people push us around long enough. It's time to fight back."

Gloria slapped him on his arm. "That's what guys like him want. You're better than that."

"I'm not, Glo." He shook his head. "And I don't want to be."

"You remember what Uncle Rene told us," Gloria said. "We have to fight it peacefully. It's the only way."

Marco seethed.

Clark tried to think of something else to say, but the tension between Gloria and her brother was palpable. And the longer the silence went on, the more uncomfortable it felt. "Anyway," he said, "I just wanted to tell you how angry it made me."

They said their awkward goodbyes, and Clark made his way back to his table. The food had been delivered, and everyone was already eating.

"You okay?" Lana asked discreetly after Clark had sat down.

He nodded and pulled his plate closer.

When Lex began quizzing Bryan about his new workout routine, Lana leaned toward Clark and said, "I didn't know you were talking to Gloria Alvarez."

Clark was caught off guard.

She motioned toward Bryan and Lex. "That's what I hear."

He shook his head. "It's not like that. I mean, she's definitely nice and everything. And smart. But . . ."

Lana was grinning. "Apparently you didn't want to share this with your so-called best friend?"

"There's nothing to share," Clark argued.

Lana shrugged and turned to Bryan. "Before we get to Dr. Wesley, I want to ask a question about your dad's business. Does he ever work with any . . . military groups?"

Bryan shook his head. "Never. He actually thinks we spend way too much on defense in this country." He looked to Lex. "*His* dad's business, on the other hand . . ."

Lex wiped his hands on his napkin. "You name an industry in Metropolis, my dad's got some kind of vested interest. So?"

"Did he ever work with Dr. Wesley?" Lana asked.

Lex shook his head. "We have our *own* team of scientists."

Clark tried to shake off everything that had happened in the past ten minutes and focus on the reason they were here. "We were surprised when we found out it was Wesley's company that had bought the Jones farm. We assumed it was your dad, Bryan."

Bryan set down his burger. "I'm not entirely sure what Wesley's company is up to and how my brother fits in. But I do know this: there are precious minerals in some of the craters around Smallville. And these minerals factor into the way we genetically engineer our seeds—which has always been highly secretive. My theory is that Wesley has uncovered our process and wants a piece of the pie. But I can also tell you that my dad will crush him before he gets very far. Whether my brother is involved or not."

The craters. Now it made sense that Wesley had those photos pinned to his wall.

Bryan glanced at Lana, who was writing all this down in a small notebook. "If you guys really want to know what Wesley's up to," he said, "you'll have to visit the secret lab he runs on the outskirts of town."

"'Secret lab'?" Lana repeated. She looked at Clark.

He nodded. They were on the same page. This was the best lead they'd found so far.

"Wait a minute," Lex said, his usual grin suddenly gone. "What secret lab? I never knew anything about a secret lab."

"I didn't either, until a couple days ago." Bryan tossed his napkin onto his mostly empty plate. "Corey took me. I can show you where it is, if you want."

"Interesting," Clark said.

"Very," Lana agreed.

Lex was just staring at Bryan like a hungry wolf.

After they said their goodbyes outside the restaurant, Clark and Lana broke off and headed in the direction of her car. "A secret lab," Lana said. "Obviously, we have to get inside."

Clark agreed. "This could be big."

They walked together in silence for a few seconds before Lana cleared her throat. "Hey, Clark. Sorry if I weirded you out about Gloria or whatever. I . . . You know you can talk to me about anything, right?"

Clark opened his mouth to answer, but just then his super-hearing picked up on a desperate crying sound in the distance. This time the sound came to him without any interference, as though his ears were hearing only what they were *supposed* to hear.

When Clark didn't respond right away, Lana stopped walking. "Clark?"

He heard voices *around* the cries now. Men laughing and encouraging each other. He heard the muted sound of ribs getting kicked. A fist smashing into a fleshy cheek. It took Clark a few seconds to understand what he was listening to.

A brutal, one-sided fight.

"Clark!" Lana demanded.

He turned to her, distracted. "I know this is kind of sudden, but . . . I gotta go."

"What? *Why?*"

"I just . . . I need to be by myself for a minute. To think." He knew he wasn't making any sense, but his mind was stuck on the scary sounds he was hearing.

"But I'm your ride home," Lana said.

Clark waved. "See you tomorrow, okay?" He didn't wait around for her response. He started jogging away. From the sound of things, someone was in serious trouble. And if he didn't hurry, he might be too late.

As soon as he'd turned the corner and was beyond Lana's line of vision, a flash of energy shot through his entire body, and the world opened itself to him. He had that feeling again, the one he'd had when he saw Bryan's helicopter plummeting toward his farm. He felt like he could fly. He hesitated briefly, remembering what had just happened to him in the diner restroom. But that hardly mattered now. Someone needed his help.

He ran at a dizzying speed and reached out his right arm and leapt into the air. At first it was exhilarating. He was slicing up into the sky. But just as he made it to a safe height above the buildings below, he began tipping forward. Within seconds, he was turning over in the air and falling out of the sky.

He crashed through the roof of an auto-body repair shop and slammed against the concrete floor.

He sat up, still hearing the fight in the distance.

Flying wasn't going to work, but he had to get there. He climbed out a window and took off running instead. And almost immediately, he was at full speed.

His full speed.

The sounds were coming from the south end of town, at least a few miles away. Clark cut down a dark, deserted alleyway. He ran so fast, his jacket began ripping at the seams, the friction of his movements tearing the light fabric, the useless material trailing behind him like some kind of makeshift cape.

When Clark arrived at an alley behind a bar called Bootleggers and saw the brutal scene, his whole body went cold.

CHAPTER 16

Five men were gathered around a bloody heap on the pavement. They took turns kicking the victim in his ribs. His legs. The side of his head. The man on the ground shielded his dark face with his hands, trying to protect himself, but the attempt was futile. He was getting pummeled.

Clark could somehow feel the impact of each fresh blow.

He could smell the man's fear.

At first he just stood there, stunned by the sight of such a beating, the men shouting obscenities as they kicked and stomped and cheered each other on.

Three of the five men did not appear to be locals. They wore black leather jackets. Militant-looking eagles were embroidered all over their clothes. Several distinct tattoos on their arms confirmed their racist beliefs. Clark assumed they owned the massive choppers parked out front.

The other two attackers wore plaid shirts and cowboy hats.

Worn boots covered in spit and blood. Wrangler jeans with pucks of chewing tobacco in the back pockets.

But they weren't the men he'd caught trespassing on his farm.

Clark recognized both of the locals. One was a man named Justin Walker, a long-distance trucker who used to be married to one of the cafeteria workers at school. The other was Sheldon Ealing, the man who'd caused the scene at the All-American Diner only an hour or so before.

"Go back to Mexico!" the tallest of the attackers shouted.

"You and your kind are ruining this town," another added, after smashing a bottle against the ground. "You're ruining the whole country!"

Clearly, they were all drunk. Even the victim's desperate pleas for the men to stop were slurred. The smell of booze hovered above the entire scene like a gas.

Booze mixed with testosterone.

And desperation.

Confusion.

Clark's jacket and shirt were in pieces around his bare, heaving chest. He'd shown up so suddenly that it took the men a few seconds to notice his presence.

"Who are *you*?" the heaviest one finally asked.

"Get lost, kid!" another shouted. "This ain't your business."

"We said, get out of here!" Sheldon barked. "Unless you want some of this yourself." He was squinting from a distance of twenty feet and didn't seem to recognize Clark.

The man on the ground rolled over and groaned. A tooth tumbled from his mouth into a pool of blood.

"Go home," Clark heard himself say in a calm, stern voice. "All of you."

One of the bikers took note of Clark's ripped shirt. The cuffs were still intact, and shreds of cotton hung from his wrists.

"What are you doing back here anyway, kid?" the man asked suspiciously. "And why are you dressed like that?"

"You're just as bad as him in my book," the tallest of them said, motioning toward the Mexican man on the ground. "Making a mockery of this whole proud nation."

Clark's eyes burned with anger. How could these men have so much hate for people they didn't even know?

He moved toward them, pulling in measured breaths now, letting them out slowly. He closed his eyes briefly. He didn't want his fury to shoot out of his pupils in the form of incinerating lasers. These men deserved some kind of punishment for what they were doing, but Clark knew it wasn't his place to do the punishing. He was here for one reason only: to protect someone who could no longer protect himself.

Once he had his anger in check, he opened his eyes and stared the men down. "Go home," he repeated, louder this time. "You're done here."

"What'd you just say to me?" Sheldon shouted.

Clark motioned toward the man on the ground. "You will not touch him again, understand?"

Sheldon grinned and stepped away from the man on the asphalt. "Are you telling me what to do, boy? 'Cause I'll put you down right next to him."

One of the bikers threw an empty beer bottle, which shattered against the wall, and shouted, "We're the only ones out here protecting this town anymore!"

All five began moving away from the beaten man.

They circled Clark instead.

Clark took a few more breaths, trying to think. Trying to prepare himself for what was about to happen. He considered taking off his glasses but didn't. He'd never been in a legitimate fight. The closest was what had happened at the party. He didn't know what to expect next. Or how to carry himself. He had superhuman strength that he knew they weren't prepared for. And superhuman speed. But there were *five* of them.

And his powers were out of control. He'd just tried to fly, and he'd crashed through the roof of a building.

Would he really be able to impose his will against five grown men?

One of the men lunged at Clark from the side.

Clark saw the whole thing as if in slow motion. The man leaning forward, eyes narrowing, fists clenching, then hurling a right hook toward Clark's face.

Yet he wasn't able to stop it.

He stood there paralyzed as the man's fist slammed into his jaw with a sickening crunch, but then a curious thing happened. The spell of uncertainty was broken.

The man retreated, howling in pain and staring at his shattered hand.

Clark moved forward. Unfazed now. Committed.

Sheldon grabbed a broken pool cue out of a nearby dumpster and swung it at Clark's face, but Clark calmly blocked it with his forearm, snapping the thing like a twig.

He continued forward.

Two more of the men charged him, one from behind, the other from his right side. They both threw wild haymakers, which Clark ducked easily. But it was impossible to keep track of them all at once. A third man slammed a brick into the back of Clark's skull.

The brick exploded in a cloud of red dust and pebbles, leaving a loud ringing sound in Clark's ears.

He emerged from the haze of the exploded brick with more determination than ever. Even when they hurt him, he now realized, they couldn't actually *hurt* him.

The guy who'd wielded the brick cursed through his teeth, but when Clark spun around, he took a step back.

"Go home," Clark told him. "I don't want to hurt you."

"I'm done messing around, kid," the man answered. He pulled a small switchblade from his waistband and leveled it at Clark's chest.

Clark sucked in a massive amount of air, then focused on the knife in the guy's hand. This time he blew out a stream of ice-cold breath on purpose, as powerfully as he could.

The blast of frosty air that emerged from Clark's lips shocked everyone. It enveloped the knife-wielding man's hand, and he let out a high-pitched squeal and dropped the weapon. Completely frozen, it hit the pavement, where it broke into several small pieces as they all watched.

The man held up his frostbitten hand in horror. He screamed again, more desperately this time, before passing out. The other men turned to stare at Clark, shock etched onto their drunken faces.

Clark was in shock, too.

"Who *are* you?" one of the men said in awe.

"I'm nobody," Clark told him. And the minute he said it, he knew it was true. He had given himself fully to protecting this man who was in trouble. And in doing so, he had shed himself. He had become someone new. Someone without fear.

Three of the four conscious men turned in a drunken panic and scattered in different directions. The fourth picked up his unconscious friend and dragged him away from the scene.

Clark pulled in several deep breaths, trying to calm himself, before hurrying over to help the victim to his feet. "Come on," he said. "We gotta get you to the hospital."

"No, I can't go," the man said with a thick accent, made thicker by his bloodied mouth. "For me, it's not safe." He shook out of Clark's grasp and tried to reach into his pocket for his phone. But his hands were shaking so badly that he couldn't do it.

"See?" said Clark. "You need help."

The man turned painfully to look at Clark. "They will take me from my family." He began stumbling down the alley, occasionally using the wall as support.

Just before the man rounded the corner, Clark saw a smallish woman emerge from the back door of the bar. She was sobbing. "Moises!" she called out into the night. "Moises, wait!"

"You know the guy who got jumped?" Clark asked her.

She nodded. "He told them not to bother me! That's it!"

Clark pointed in the direction of the man who had fled. "Go to him. Make sure he gets help." He watched her hurry after the man.

Once they were both out of sight, Clark knelt and studied the bloodstained pavement. He didn't feel like he'd just saved a person's life. He felt dark and cold and alone. A cloak of sadness seemed to descend upon him, even though he knew he'd done the right thing.

Maybe true heroism, he thought, didn't actually feel heroic.

Maybe it felt lost.

I'm nobody, he repeated to himself.

Clark touched the back of his head where the brick had hit him, trying to process everything that had just happened. But it was all a blur to him now. And he knew he couldn't talk to anyone about it, either. Not his parents. Or Lana. Or Bryan. Or Gloria. He felt more isolated than ever before. He didn't know where to go or what to do, and as the stars shone on him from above, he stared down at the bloody concrete, and then through it, into the dark earth below.

A loud semi drove past the alley, and Clark was still kneeling there.

A faraway dog began howling into the night, and Clark was still kneeling there.

CHAPTER 17

The next day was a blur for Clark.

As he sat in his classes, his mind kept drifting back to the fight behind the bar. He replayed it, over and over. Every word that was said. The blatant racism. The drunken threats. The bloodied victim staggering away, claiming he couldn't go to the hospital because they'd take him from his family.

Clark didn't understand why, but he felt a connection with the Mexican victim. Maybe because he believed those men would try to do the same to him if they knew his secret.

And then there was Clark's freak discovery of his freezing breath—yet another power he didn't know how to control. He cringed when he thought about the guy's frozen, blackened hand. His bloodcurdling cries of pain. The way his skull had bounced off the concrete after he fainted. Clark had meant only to chill the man's hand enough to make him drop the knife. But he'd gone too far.

He was so stuck in his own head that he avoided all conversation. Even with Lana. When he saw her in the hall after third period, he quickly spun around and went the other way before she could spot him. And he still hadn't answered the two texts she'd sent during lunch. She wanted to discuss everything happening in Smallville, but there was only one question on Clark's mind at the moment: Had he done the right thing in the alley behind the bar?

At the time, he would have answered yes. A man was in serious trouble, and Clark had come to his aid.

But now he wasn't so sure. By the time the skirmish was over, not only was the victim seriously injured, but so was the man with the frozen hand.

Clark had once heard that the first rule of being a doctor is to do no harm. He wasn't a doctor, of course, but by that same logic, his initial rescue missions had been disasters. He'd harmed just about *everyone*.

By the end of the day, Clark was an emotional wreck. He felt like he was teetering at the lip of some invisible mountain peak. One more step in any direction and he'd find himself tumbling down the rocky face of the crag. He stayed in his last class longer than usual, pretending to read his history textbook. When everyone else had cleared out, he slipped the book into his backpack, zipped it up, and hurried out the door—only to slam right into Gloria.

She bounced off him like a Ping-Pong ball, and her books went flying.

Clark instinctively shifted into super-speed and caught both Gloria and her books in a single motion. He then dropped down on one knee, cradling her in his right arm, inches above the hard tile floor. At least he had more control over his powers now.

She looked up at him, startled.

Clark stared into her big brown eyes, transfixed. When her lips parted in surprise, an intense feeling came over him. He'd never wanted to kiss a girl as much as he did in that moment. He *didn't* kiss her, of course. He simply remained frozen with her in his arms.

Gloria cleared her throat. "Clark, do you think you could, uh, help me up?"

"Oh. Yeah." He lifted her upright. "Sorry about that."

"I think it was my fault." She put a hand to her chest. "I wasn't paying attention."

"Hey, Gloria?" Clark ran his fingers through his hair. "Do you think we could maybe talk for a minute?"

"Sure." She looked up and down both halls before turning to him with the beginnings of a grin on her face. "What are your general feelings about licorice?"

Clark frowned. "Licorice?"

"Licorice." She unzipped her backpack and pulled out a fresh pack. "I won this in my psych class this morning, and I've been looking for someone to share it with."

"Actually, I *love* licorice," he told her.

"Cool. Follow me."

Clark's heart pounded as they walked through the hall. He couldn't believe he'd just asked Gloria to talk. Maybe this was a positive side effect of feeling so lost: you might as well say what was on your mind.

Gloria led Clark outside and over to the soccer field. He sat beside her in the grass, and they both pulled off their backpacks and set them by their feet. Gloria tore open her licorice pack. She pulled out two strands and handed one to Clark. The men's soccer team was on the field below them, running through a series of dribbling drills. "Your brother, Marco," he said, pointing down the hill.

She nodded. But Gloria's mind now seemed elsewhere. She

was troubled by something, which was exactly the way he'd felt all day. He could guess what had Gloria so upset. He stared at the side of her face, wondering how it might feel to live on the south side of Smallville these days. The Mexican part of town. Where your loved ones could up and vanish at any moment. "So, who do you think is responsible for what's happening in your community?" Clark asked.

Gloria smiled politely and shook her head. "You don't want my actual opinion."

"No, I really do—"

"People like *you*, Clark!" she barked, her eyes suddenly bright with anger. "Perfectly nice Smallville residents who open doors for you and invite you to their church, then turn around and vote to allow cops to stop you just because you're brown."

"There's no way Smallville will let that become law."

"Yeah. . . . We'll see."

Clark swallowed, nodding, and turned his attention back to the soccer practice. He felt small sitting beside her now. And guilty. But he didn't blame her. If he were in her shoes, he'd be angry, too.

Actually, he *was* angry.

"You're right," he told her. "People like me are sitting around doing nothing while families are being torn apart."

Gloria let her head fall into her hands. "I'm just sort of messed up right now," she admitted. "About everything. Last night my uncle got beat up real bad at a bar." She looked up at Clark. "Some neighbors rushed him into our apartment . . . and it was awful. He'd lost teeth. He was covered in blood. And he swore he didn't *do* anything."

Clark froze.

"His girlfriend told us that if some random guy hadn't come

along to break up the fight, the attackers might've *killed* my uncle Moises."

The assault last night . . .

That had been Gloria's uncle.

Clark couldn't believe it. "That's awful. I hope he's going to be okay. I swear, Gloria, everyone claims we're experiencing some kind of heyday in Smallville right now, but I think it's the opposite. We've never been more divided."

After a long pause, she looked up at him and said, "Do you wanna know the real reason I was so upset that day you found me in the classroom?"

Clark's phone buzzed just then, and he glanced down to see who the message was from. Lana. He looked up at Gloria again. "Because of the people who've disappeared."

"That was part of it," she said. "But there was also a much more selfish reason." She hesitated.

Clark sat up straighter, understanding that what Gloria was about to share was important to her. And he wanted her to know that made it important to him, too.

She reached into her backpack and pulled out a wrinkled letter and unfolded it. "A couple weeks ago, I found out I qualified to be one of the two valedictorian candidates for the senior class."

"Wait, but that's amazing."

"I had to decline."

Clark was confused. "Why?"

She handed him the letter. "All that extra attention might've led the school officials to dig around in my background. And my mom . . . she wasn't born here. We're a mixed-status family. With the way things are going right now, I couldn't risk putting us in any kind of jeopardy." Gloria pulled her legs to her chest and rested her chin on her knees.

Clark's heart sank. Gloria was one of the two smartest and most deserving candidates, and *nothing* should have stripped her of that opportunity. He could feel his blood starting to boil as he read the short letter. He handed it back, shaking his head. "That's not fair, Gloria."

She shrugged, folding the letter up. "But maybe that's what getting older is all about, right, Clark? You start to realize just how much of the world is unfair. And how few people care. It's not about justice, right? It's about power. And the people where I live . . . we don't have any. Not yet."

Clark's heart ached for Gloria. But it ached for himself, too. He was afraid to let anyone know who he really was, for the exact same reason. To protect *his* family. "I wish there was something I could do."

"Me too. But I wish for a lot of things. I wish my parents didn't have to worry about money. I wish I was going to college next year." Gloria smiled wistfully. "I wish someone would take me ice-skating."

"Ice-skating?" This last one surprised Clark. His phone buzzed again, but he ignored it.

She nodded. "I've always wanted to do that. It seems so . . . American. Gliding across the ice with your friends. Maybe doing a little twirl or going backward." She laughed at herself and tucked a long strand of dark hair behind her ear. "Anyway, I didn't mean to unload all that on you."

"I'm glad you did," Clark told her.

She placed her hand on top of his and gently squeezed, then

crumpled the letter and stood up. "Well, I better go. My uncle Rene is organizing a rally this weekend in front of city hall, and I promised to help run the meeting tonight." Gloria handed Clark another strand of licorice before stashing the rest and shouldering her backpack.

Clark could still feel the warmth of her touch on his hand. "What are you doing with that?" he asked, gesturing toward the crumpled letter.

She glanced at the ball of paper in her hand. "Tossing it. I'm not sentimental when it comes to stuff like this."

"No matter what happens," Clark said, pointing at her with his strand of licorice, "you should feel really proud, Gloria. Valedictorian. That's amazing."

When she smiled at him this time, he felt it all the way inside his chest.

"Clark, you may be the kind of guy who runs women over in school halls, but you're also a really good listener. Thank you. And if you ever need me to repay the favor, come find me."

He chuckled a little, beaming.

"Seriously," she said. "Doesn't matter when or where. I'll drop everything."

"Okay. Thanks." And then another bold thought occurred to Clark. "And, hey, maybe one day we'll go ice-skating."

"And do leaps and twirls?"

Clark nodded. "All that."

"Count me in." She waved, and Clark watched her start back toward the school building, stopping only to toss her crumpled letter into a nearby trash can.

Before Clark left, he decided on a whim to pull Gloria's letter out of the trash. Just in case she might want it in the future. He smoothed the paper and slipped it into his backpack, then checked the messages on his phone.

There were four, all from Lana:

Hey, let's talk at lunch.

Clark, where ru???

I'm sorry if I made things weird last night. But stop ignoring me!

Hey, I stopped by your farm because you were IGNORING me. You need to get over here ASAP. Your parents just invited Montgomery Mankins INTO YOUR HOUSE!!!

CHAPTER 18

The first thing Clark noticed after sprinting home from school was the shiny black car parked outside the farmhouse. It was a fancier, more modern version of a Lincoln Town Car, and anyone who lived in Smallville would have recognized it immediately. It was the car Montgomery Mankins was chauffeured around in.

Inside the house, Clark's mom and dad were seated at the dining room table across from Montgomery and a man who wore a business suit and had a briefcase open in front of him. He was shuffling around some papers while Montgomery spoke.

". . . really think you'll find it more than generous," he was saying. He paused when Clark entered. "Clark, good to see you again!" He stood and reached out to shake Clark's hand. "Please join us. I'd like the whole family to be present for this."

"We're talking about the value of the farm," Jonathan said. "You're welcome to sit with us. But just so you know, Lana's upstairs waiting for you."

"She claims you were ignoring her?" Martha said.

"My phone was turned off." Clark looked at his dad. "Everything okay?"

His dad nodded. "We're having a good conversation."

"Okay." Clark eyed Montgomery and his associate as they passed a few papers back and forth. "I'll see what Lana wants."

As Montgomery held a document out toward Jonathan, Clark left the room, but in the hallway outside the kitchen, he stopped short of the stairs to eavesdrop. He could see a portion of the table reflected in the antique mirror hanging on the wall.

"It really is a very generous offer, Mr. Mankins," Jonathan said, looking over the sheet of paper the man had just handed to him.

"Please call me Montgomery."

"But like I said on the phone," Jonathan continued evenly, "this place just isn't for sale."

Montgomery nodded and folded his hands together on the table. He looked at his associate, who pulled another sheet of paper out of the open briefcase and handed it to Montgomery. "Ah, here we go," he said. "Option two. If I can't *buy* the land, then what if I were to lease a percentage from you? We have this alternative offer prepared, which I'm sure you'll find quite satisfactory." He slid the paper to Jonathan and Martha.

Clark watched them look it over with genuine intrigue.

Martha glanced up at Jonathan, who said, "Wow, this is a great deal. But I can't help wondering, Mr. Mankins: Why us? Why *this* farm?"

"I want to be completely transparent. According to our research, your property has the ideal soil for a new hybrid crop we'd like to start growing outside the lab." He took the paper back from Jonathan and read it again. "This way, you keep the land, and we pay you rent for access to just a small percentage of the field near that old barn we saw out there. So the bottom line for you is . . . more money for less work. And the farm stays with the family." He turned to his associate and chuckled a little. "Mark, who the hell drafted this offer? Saying it out loud like that . . . I'm having second thoughts."

Mark added with a straight face, "And we're only asking for a five-year lease. Short term, low risk."

Clark watched his dad nod thoughtfully and read through the document Montgomery had handed back to him. It looked like he was considering the offer, which shocked Clark. Would he actually go for it? Jonathan had high blood pressure, so maybe he saw this as an opportunity to slow down. He passed the paper to Martha, who read through it again, too. She gave him a blank look when she passed it back, which meant she was skeptical.

When Clark saw his dad slide the document across the table, he knew the deal wasn't happening. "I'm sorry," Jonathan said, "but we're just not interested. We like farming our own land. This place goes back three generations in my family. When I went off to college, I swore I'd never return. But I did. And then I took over when my old man passed. Now it's just sort of in my blood."

Montgomery smiled and nodded. "Well, you can't really argue with that, now, can you? Listen, Jonathan, Martha, I respect where you're coming from. And I admire your principles. Shoot, a part of me respects you two even more for turning me down today."

"We appreciate you seeing it that way," Martha said. "We really do."

Now that Clark knew his parents weren't selling, he continued upstairs, where he found Lana sitting on his twin bed, staring out the window. She was wearing jeans and a school sweatshirt, and her red hair was in a messy bun. Lana used to come over a lot when they were younger, but once they got to high school, things changed. Instead of going to each other's houses, they met at more neutral sites. The All-American Diner. The library.

He stood there a second, looking around his small room, trying to see it from Lana's perspective. The faded posters of his favorite sports teams tacked up on all the walls. The blinking alarm clock that was off by over an hour. The bent Nerf hoop that hung over his closet door, and the lumpy old beanbags.

Clark was almost eighteen years old, but his room made him seem like a child.

He cleared his throat. "Hey, Lana."

She spun around. "So? What's happening down there?"

"Montgomery made an offer on the farm, but my folks gunned it down."

"Of course they did," she said. "I bet it was a pretty hefty one, too."

"Sounded like it." Clark looked out the window at Montgomery's fancy black car. "You think he's interested in the crater?"

"Maybe." She looked out the window, too, then turned to Clark. "I can't help but think of the one on the Jones property."

"And the way they were digging it up, I know." Clark shook his head. The police were aware of the men trespassing on his property, and they'd promised to make the Kent farm part of their rounds, but now Montgomery was trying to buy it? "So, what brought you over here, anyway?" he asked Lana.

She pushed off his bed. "I think we need to talk, Clark."

"I'm sorry I didn't text you back. It's just . . . I was studying for finals."

Lana ignored his excuse. "Have things gotten *weird* between us?"

"I don't think so." Clark pulled out his rolling desk chair and sat down. A second earlier, he'd thought his parents might lease Montgomery Mankins part of their farm. Now he was talking to Lana about . . . Actually, what *were* they talking about?

Lana sat back down on his bed. She was looking at him intently now. "Let's just get this out of the way, Clark. So we can focus on more important things."

"Okay."

She opened her mouth to say something, but nothing came out. A few seconds later, she tried again. "I shouldn't have taken that tone with you last night. When I brought up Gloria. It probably sounded like I was mocking you. And that wasn't cool. And it caused you to run away. Literally."

"When we were leaving the diner?" Now Clark understood. "That wasn't it, Lana. Honestly." Clark paused, trying to figure out how to explain his hasty departure. He couldn't exactly tell her the truth. "Watching Sheldon yell at our server like that . . . It messed me up, I think. I kept replaying it in my head the rest of the night, trying to figure out if I could've done more."

Lana nodded. "I get it," she said. "Still, I apologize. I didn't mean it to come out that way. I was just surprised to hear about Gloria from Bryan and Lex. You usually tell me stuff first, and . . . Listen, if you like someone, it's cool. Okay? And you can talk to me about her whenever you want. I won't get upset or anything."

"Thanks," he said, shoving his hands into his pockets. It was awkward talking about how this kind of conversation shouldn't be awkward. "Same goes for you, too."

Lana grinned. "So are you going to ask her out or what?"

"Who, *Gloria*?"

"Yes, Gloria!" Lana play-punched him in the arm. "C'mon,

Clark, don't be so serious all the time. Look, we don't have to talk about her if you're not ready."

He rubbed the back of his neck, feeling self-conscious. "No, we can."

"I'm saying, though—we don't have to."

Clark shifted in his chair. It was true. Growing up, they'd confided in each other about everything from school bullies to cow tipping to dealing with the expectations of their parents. This was the first time they were actually agreeing to *not* talk about something. And he didn't know how he felt about it.

"So, is everything okay, then?" he asked. "Between us, I mean?"

Lana chuckled. "I think things will always be okay between us, Clark. That's what I'm beginning to realize. Until they're not. Know what I mean? And even *then* they'll probably still be okay."

Clark shook his head, smiling. It was such a Lana thing to say.

He stood up and went to the window when he saw Montgomery Mankins and his associate heading back toward the fancy black car. "Check it out," he whispered to Lana. A driver walked around toward the rear passenger door, preparing to open it. But before he got there, Montgomery slammed the hood of the car as hard as he could.

"Whoa, temper tantrum, anyone?" Lana said quietly.

"Weird," Clark whispered. "He seemed okay about my folks not selling when they were all sitting at the dining room table."

They watched Montgomery angrily clenching and unclenching his fist. He pointed at the driver and barked, "Open the goddamn door!"

The driver opened it, but before Montgomery climbed inside, he turned and looked out over the farm one last time. Then he got into the car, and the driver shut the door. His associate got in by himself on the other side. Alone, the driver wiped a hand down his face, then returned to the front.

As the car pulled out of the driveway and moved down the county road toward the highway, Clark turned to Lana. "What was *that* all about?"

She shrugged. "When we interviewed him in his office, he seemed like such a cool customer, like he couldn't even get mad if he tried."

"I guess now we see where Corey gets it from."

"You mean my boyfriend?" Lana said.

Clark grinned. "Exactly."

Lana looked out the window to where the car had pulled down the driveway, leaving a thin layer of dust hovering in the air. She turned to Clark and said, "Now that we got our little talk out of the way, it's on to the next order of business. We just have to figure out what that is."

Clark held up his phone for Lana to see. "I think it's time for me to text Bryan about Dr. Wesley's secret lab," he said. "I'm going to take him up on that little behind-the-scenes tour he offered."

Lana smiled. "I like how you think, Clark."

He unlocked his phone and texted Bryan to see if they could visit the lab that night. It took Bryan less than a minute to hit him back:

Just finishing up a workout. Me and Lex can swing by at 8.

Clark wrote back *Cool*, then held up his phone so Lana could read the exchange.

CHAPTER 19

Just after dark, Clark finally heard the distant honking sound he'd been waiting for. He grabbed his backpack and made for his bedroom door, only to be cut off by his mom. "Your new friends?" she asked.

Clark nodded. "We're gonna hang out, maybe grab something to eat."

"They can use the driveway, you know."

"I think Lex is worried about his car getting dusty. You've seen what he drives, right?"

"Oh, we've *all* seen what he drives," Martha said, unimpressed. "Clark, before you go . . ." She held up the tattered, shredded remains of his jacket from the night before. "I found this in the kitchen trash this morning. You've got to stop doing this, son."

Clark cringed. There was nothing he hated more than disappointing his mom. "I know. I'm really sorry about that."

"I realize you want to practice your powers, Clark. But between you and me . . . we just can't afford to keep buying you new clothes.

Your friends out there may have unlimited resources, but we don't. You understand, right?"

"Absolutely." Clark never wanted to cost his parents extra money. They worked so hard just to make ends meet. He wished he could at least tell her it was for a good cause. That he'd helped someone who was in real trouble. But he couldn't.

He had to own her disappointment.

His mom's face softened, and she reached up to tousle his hair, like she used to when he was a kid. "Now go tell those hotshot friends of yours to use the driveway next time. We don't bite." She went onto her toes to kiss him on the cheek, then left with his ruined jacket.

Clark rumbled down the stairs and jogged along the farm's gravel road to where Lex's fancy red car was idling. Bryan got out of the passenger's seat, and Clark climbed in back, saying, "Thanks again for agreeing to do this."

"The question is," Lex said, "will we even be able to get in?" He hit the gas before anyone could answer, and all three of them were thrown back in their seats. He reached over a hundred miles per hour before he let off the gas and allowed the car to gradually slow down.

"We'll get in," Bryan said.

"Just so you know," Clark said to Bryan, "your dad stopped by the farm today and made an offer to buy the place."

Bryan craned his neck so he could look at Clark. "You're kidding. I'm guessing it was a waste of time?"

"Yeah, my parents turned him down," Clark told him. "But I think they were genuinely flattered by the offer."

Bryan shook his head. "Ever since my dad found out Wesco is

buying up farm properties, too, he's been out of control. He can't *stand* competition."

That would definitely explain Montgomery's outburst, Clark thought.

"You heard about what happened last night, right?" Lex asked, making eye contact with Clark in the mirror. "That guy Sheldon Ealing from the restaurant claims he and his friends were assaulted by an actual alien. Like, from another planet."

"An *alien*," Clark repeated. He'd had a feeling this topic might come up with Bryan and Lex, and he was ready. "Isn't it weird how alien sightings and racism seem to go hand in hand?"

"The thought of aliens alone disgusts me," Lex said.

"Maybe it isn't normal to spend so much time outside," Bryan said. "The quiet, clear nighttime sky must just overwhelm some people."

"Also they were drunk, right?" Clark asked.

"But get this," Lex said. "One of Sheldon's buddies showed up at the emergency room claiming his hand had been frozen solid by the alien's breath. Keep in mind it was almost sixty degrees last night."

Clark shook his head, playing along. He'd scanned the internet while waiting for Bryan and Lex to show up. He was relieved that the only stories he could find said the man was expected to make a full recovery.

When they neared the outskirts of downtown Smallville, Lex slowed to a crawl along a street of nondescript, closed-down warehouses. "Not sure you guys heard about this," Lex went on, "but apparently a couple of undocumented workers have gone missing lately. I wouldn't be surprised if Deputy What's-His-Name makes a statement that they may have been abducted by aliens."

This comment stung Clark a little. Lex was making fun of small towns again. But Lex was an arrogant, rich city kid. He just didn't understand small towns. And that was *his* problem. What Clark chose to focus on instead was the fact Lex had heard rumors about the missing workers. The more attention the story received, the more people would want to *do* something about it.

"There!" Bryan said, pointing toward a huge, mostly empty parking lot tucked between several abandoned warehouses. Clark knew this was a remnant of a different era, back when Smallville was home to a number of leather-treatment companies. Or skin-houses, as some of the old-timers jokingly referred to them. They'd all shut down long before Clark was born.

He pulled out his phone and quickly texted Lana. He pinned his location to where Lex was parked and told her they were going into the lab. He slipped the phone back into his pocket without waiting for a response, saying, "*This* is where Wesco's labs are?" It looked more like a ghost town, especially at night.

"Where else can you find so much square footage?" Lex asked. "I bet it's dirt cheap."

"I wonder if my dad knows how involved my brother is," Bryan said. "He'd be *pissed*."

As they quietly approached a long stretch of dark, dilapidated structures on foot, Clark felt slightly anxious. There were no lights anywhere. No security guards outside. No front entrances. He wasn't worried about his own safety. But the whole setup seemed sketchy, like the company's main objective in being out here was absolute secrecy. And if that was the case, what was Wesley trying to hide?

"Do we know where we're going?" Lex asked Bryan, after they'd walked almost three blocks.

"I think so," he answered uncertainly. "Though it was always light when I came here before. I remember that we have to go in through the back."

Finally Bryan led them up to the structure he'd been looking for. It was a full four blocks away from where Lex had parked. Bryan pulled a key card out of his pocket as they reached a large industrial door around back. He lifted the cover of the small touch pad underneath a filthy window protected by rusted security bars.

"You have a key?" Lex asked in a quiet voice.

"My *brother* has a key. And I know where he keeps it."

"Wait," Clark said, grabbing Bryan's wrist before he could extend the card toward the pad. "Are you sure this is a good idea? I know I'm the reason we're here, but I didn't realize we'd have to sneak around like this."

"He's sure," Lex answered, pushing Clark's hand away.

"Bryan?" Clark said. "I don't want you to get into trouble."

"I'm not gonna lie," Bryan said to Clark. "I could get in deep shit if my brother finds out I borrowed his card. But I also know he's out drinking with his buddies tonight. And that usually means he comes home late and passes out. I'll be able to sneak into his room easily to replace the card."

"And Dr. Wesley?" Clark asked.

"He's at a conference in Metropolis today and tomorrow." Bryan looked at Lex, then at Clark. "Last chance. You guys in?"

"Hell yeah, we're in." Lex motioned toward the touch pad. "Let's go."

"Clark?" Bryan said, staring back at him.

Clark didn't hesitate for long. It was time to be decisive. And he was almost positive that Corey and Dr. Wesley and Wesco were somehow connected to the men who'd tried to rob his farm as well as the men who had shot at him and Lana. He just needed proof.

"I'm in," he told Bryan.

"Cool. And check this out." Bryan pulled a gold badge out of his pocket and hung it around his neck. "With Corey's access badge, we can go almost anywhere in this place. Follow my lead."

"Just act like you belong," Lex added, clapping both Bryan and Clark on their backs.

A quiet beep was followed by the click of the heavy metal door opening.

"I'll do the talking," Bryan told them. He pushed the door open the rest of the way, and the three of them walked inside.

The place might have looked like a dump on the outside, but the inside told a completely different story. They walked down a short white hallway that led to a large lobby area. There was absolutely nothing on the white walls. The place was pristine and smelled like disinfectant. The few people Clark saw milling around in the distance were dressed in lab coats and wearing hospital masks. An armed security guard sat at a small desk that bordered a large X-ray machine. The man nodded at Bryan as they entered, then cocked his head toward Clark and Lex.

"Potential investors," Bryan explained.

"This late?" the man asked.

"My brother, Corey *Mankins*, wanted me to show them around."

The guard eyed them until Lex made a show of checking his Rolex with a huff. Seeing the expensive timepiece, the guard nodded and hit a switch under the desk so that two glass security partitions slid open. The three of them dropped their phones and keys into a plastic bin and passed through a metal detector.

Clark collected his stuff on the other side, making a mental note about how tight security was. It seemed odd they would need metal detectors in a medical and agricultural research facility, especially since it was located on the outskirts of town.

Bryan held up his badge to a second wave of security guards, who made them stop and sign in on a small computer tablet.

Bryan typed in: *Corey Mankins.*

Lex typed: *Kevin Sanderson.*

When the tablet finally got to Clark, he paused. He stared at the blinking cursor, trying to figure out what to write. Lex and Bryan shot him dirty looks. Finally, Clark typed: *Kenny Braverman.*

One of the security guards waved them through.

The hallways of the facility smelled new and clean. And it was quiet aside from the low hum of the bright fluorescent lights.

"This way," Bryan said in a soft voice.

Halfway down a second long hall, Clark asked, "So, what kind of research do they do here?"

"All kinds, I think." Bryan led them through a labyrinth of much narrower hallways. "At least that's what Corey told me. Wesley's got projects going on in here that are far ahead of anyone else in the world."

They finally stopped at a two-way glass partition that looked into a lab. There were several dozen tables and chairs inside, but only one woman was working this late on a weeknight. She wore thick goggles and industrial rubber gloves, and she was carefully measuring chemicals into vials. Large, expensive-looking electronic equipment lined the wall in front of her. Microscopes and various machines sat atop a long stainless-steel table to her left.

"What's she doing in there?" Lex asked.

"Chemical development and testing," Bryan answered.

"Chemicals for what, though?" Clark asked.

Bryan shrugged. "Lots of stuff. This is where we picked up the supplement I'm taking."

Clark didn't know what he was looking for, exactly. The place seemed like an ordinary science lab, and the woman inside looked like a scientist. He wondered if he'd even know it if he stumbled across something out of the ordinary.

"What else has your brother shown you?" Lex asked. Clark had never seen him so eager. He kept looking all around, like he was searching for something specific.

Bryan pointed toward another hallway, and the three of them headed in that direction. Halfway down the hall, just before they reached an antiquated freight elevator that looked out of place, Bryan stopped at another room. "Here's the part I really wanted to show you guys. It's one of their agricultural genetics labs."

There was no one inside, and the room was mostly dark, but once Clark's eyes adjusted, he saw something that blew him away. There, on top of several tables near the window, were four ears of corn the size of small logs. Each one was at least four feet long and twice as thick as the barrel of a major-league baseball bat. There were other enlarged crops on nearby tables as well. Tomatoes as big as pumpkins. Stalks of wheat three times the normal size. A single watermelon so large that it sagged under its own weight and dwarfed the table it rested on.

"Are these real?" Clark asked.

Bryan nodded. "According to Corey, they are."

"But they seem so . . . unnatural."

"Dude, almost all farm corporations are experimenting on crops now. My dad does the same thing. You pretty much have to in order to compete in futures markets."

"It can't be healthy, though. Or ethical." Clark thought of his own farm. Everything was organic and natural. And the appropriate size.

"Why not?" Lex butted in. "Genetic defects are freak occurrences, right? They're not supposed to happen. Genetic alteration is nothing more than science correcting nature's mistakes."

"Yeah, but—"

"We do the same thing with vaccines," Lex added. "Treatments for cancer and other diseases. Are you saying we shouldn't apply the same methodology to the production of food?"

"Look how big that watermelon is. I get fixing genetic mistakes. But this is something else." The freakish crops Clark was seeing didn't sit well with him, but he was having a difficult time expressing why. "So . . . what if this keeps going on and on? Like, how would you feel if they did this to animals? Or *humans*?"

"Ever heard of factory farms?" Lex grinned. "And you're telling me you wouldn't want to be bigger, faster, and stronger?"

Clark shook his head. "Not if it took chemicals to make me that way. Or genetic alterations. I'd feel . . . artificial."

"Not everyone's born like you, though, Clark," Bryan said. "And you didn't do anything to deserve it, right? I mean, I didn't do anything to deserve to be born thin and scrawny. Why *shouldn't* people look for ways to level the playing field?"

Clark turned back to the watermelon, considering his special powers. What if he *was* the product of something like this? What if his powers *were* artificial?

"Think about this," Lex added. "If we can grow bigger and better crops that still taste good, maybe we can help end world hunger. Or at least drive food prices down. That's a good thing, right?"

Clark shrugged, ready to put this whole conversation on hold. This definitely wasn't the best setting for some deep philosophical discussion about the future of agriculture.

"Okay, Lex," Bryan said. "We've seen the inside of the lab. It's probably best if we get out of here now."

"Hang on," Lex said. "Isn't there anything else interesting we can see? I feel like we just got here."

Bryan shrugged. "I've only been in here once. And this is as far as we got. Corey said he wasn't able to take me into the restricted wing."

"The *restricted* wing?" Lex looked down the hall before turning back to Bryan. "We definitely gotta keep going. Just a couple more minutes. You can't tell me you aren't curious."

Bryan looked around nervously. "Two minutes. Then we go, okay?"

But Lex was already continuing on.

Clark tapped Bryan on the arm. "If you think we should go, let's go. I don't want you getting into trouble."

Bryan shrugged. "I guess a couple more minutes isn't gonna make much difference. Come on."

Clark thought about letting the two of them go on without him. But he knew he couldn't do that. Instead, he switched his mind-set from investigating the lab to looking out for his friends.

They turned down a hallway to the left. Most of the rooms they passed now were dark and empty.

Clark froze when he saw the shadows of two stooped figures pass slowly from one hall to another. But when he and Bryan and Lex reached that spot, Clark didn't see anyone. It was as if the figures had disappeared.

As they came upon a large conference room, a voice from behind stopped them in their tracks. "Who are you? And what are you doing here?"

The three of them spun around and found a large man in a suit standing just down the hallway with his arms crossed. He had blond hair and some kind of phone device in his ear.

"We're f-fine," Bryan stammered. "I was sent here to track down—"

"You have no reason to be here. This area is strictly off-limits." The man raised a walkie-talkie toward his mouth, barking, "Security, we have a code red in section C, zone four. Request immediate intervention."

"No, I'm friends with Dr. Wesley," Bryan pleaded. "He knows we're here."

Clark turned discreetly to size up the large conference room. He tried the door, but it was locked. The sign above read RESTRICTED— PROJECT DAWN.

Lex was staring at it, too.

The man marched right up to Bryan and looked at his badge before shoving him against the wall. "You don't have clearance, asshole. If I were you, I'd be looking for a way out. The men who are coming aren't fully trained yet. Mistakes have been known to happen."

Clark's ears tingled as he closed his eyes briefly and focused on the sounds all around him. A glass beaker tapping against a table. Water streaming out of a sink. Classical music. Several people speaking quietly in Spanish. A chorus of clinking chains pulled tight. And then Clark heard what he was listening for.

Footfalls in the distance.

Three people, at least.

"We need to go," Clark barked at Bryan and Lex, taking charge. "Follow me."

The blond man stepped in front of Clark, who went to shove him aside. But the man hardly budged. He was even stronger than he looked.

The man grinned and made a move to grab Clark's arms, but Clark ripped out of his grasp and slugged him in the stomach.

The man doubled over.

"Whoa!" Bryan said, looking on in awe.

"We need to go!" Clark growled. "Now!"

Just then, three men dressed all in brown came racing down the hall toward them. All had shaved heads, and their eyes were abnormally dilated. Two looked Mexican, and one was black. Clark flashed back to the knife-wielding man downtown. The one who'd come after his ex-football teammates. He froze, trying to understand the connection, but there was no time.

The blond man shouted up to Clark, "You're screwed now!" He barked into his radio. "I repeat, code red. Lock down all exits!"

The men in brown were only fifteen yards away now and closing fast. Clark grabbed Bryan and Lex by their arms and all but dragged them down the hall the other way, moving quickly as the trio in brown pursued. Clark's powers came to him easily now. His X-ray vision allowed him to see through walls, into the rooms ahead. He led them along the labyrinth of hallways, and he was able to determine, based on sound alone, that a second group of men was now after them. The men were coming from the opposite direction, trying to pin them down.

Clark spotted a closed door near the end of one hall. He hurried ahead of Bryan and Lex and tried the doorknob, but it was locked. Before they caught up to him, he quickly snapped off the doorknob and chucked it away. "In here!" he shouted, and the three of them ducked inside the dark room and closed the door.

"Shit!" Bryan said under his breath. "Shit, shit, shit!"

"What?" Lex asked.

"I just messed up my foot."

"Jesus, Bry," Lex said. "What'd you *do?*"

"I don't know. I turned it over coming in here."

"Quiet," Clark said when he heard the men coming.

The three of them breathed as quietly as they could, listening to the men run right up to the door, then past it. After a long stretch of silence, Clark used his phone to illuminate the room. They were in some kind of large computer center. Fifteen desktop computers were lined up on a long table, all their screens showing the same screensaver: the Wesco logo. Clark couldn't make sense of it. Wesley had a tiny, run-down office downtown. Yet he seemed to also own this secret facility full of expensive-looking equipment.

And then there was Corey. How did *he* figure in?

"Clark," Bryan said between frantic breaths, "what am I gonna do? I can't put any weight on my foot."

Clark checked his phone. No signal. But Lana had texted back: *On my way!*

"They're just trying to spook us." The normally cocky Lex looked genuinely scared, his typical grin nowhere to be found. "No one's actually going to hurt anyone, right? Clark?"

"No one is going to hurt us," Clark said.

"Either way," Bryan said, pulling out his phone, "I'm calling the cops. I don't even care if Corey finds out I was here." He stared at his phone for a few seconds, then slammed it against the tile floor. "Shit. No service."

"Me either," Lex said.

When they turned to Clark, he shook his head. "No service for me either."

While Bryan and Lex began arguing about whose idea it had been to enter the restricted area, Clark told them he'd be right back.

"Wait!" Bryan called to him. "We should stick together!"

But Clark was already out the door. He crouched in the hall, listening intently for footfalls or voices. He heard only footsteps now, and they weren't close. Straining to make use of his X-ray vision, his eyes buzzing, he felt like he was rising toward the high ceiling. His stomach sank. Then his vision suddenly punched through the wall directly in front of him.

Another dark room.

He went through the far wall in there, too. And now he was seeing the hall they'd been in when the blond man had approached them. He saw two men in brown walking past the restricted area. He paused on the sign above the door again: RESTRICTED—PROJECT DAWN.

What did it mean?

When Clark tried to see through the Project Dawn wall, his sight grew fuzzy, and then he lost his X-ray vision altogether.

It took everything he had to will it back, and this time he focused on finding a way out. Security guards were waiting near the door where they'd entered. And the blond man had a small crew with him at a second entry point. But then Clark spotted an old fire escape with no one nearby. It was clear on the other side of the building, and Bryan was hurt, but the fire escape was their only chance.

Clark burst back into the room and explained the situation. "Bryan, you're coming with me. I'll help you get around."

Bryan stood without arguing and wrapped his arm around Clark's shoulder. The three of them quietly left the room and began making their way across the building, keeping their eyes peeled for the blond man, anyone wearing brown, or security.

Bryan and Lex were looking to Clark for guidance now. He couldn't let them down.

His X-ray vision was less reliable when he was on the move like this—it kept cutting in and out—but he was able to determine a few key pieces of information. The fire escape they were looking for was only accessible from the third floor. And they were on the first. He remembered seeing an antiquated freight elevator behind the genetics lab.

"Here they are! Down this hall!"

Clark spun to find one of the security guards pointing at them. Two men in brown came marching around the corner, gripping police batons. When they spotted Clark, Bryan, and Lex, they started jogging down the hall toward the boys.

"This way!" Clark shouted at Lex. He hefted Bryan over his shoulder, and he and Lex sprinted the other way, out of the restricted area, back in the direction they'd come from and toward the elevator. As they gained a little ground, Clark kept expecting the men to shout at them, order them to stop. But they said nothing. Just hurried after Clark and Lex in silence, wielding their batons. They seemed more like robots than actual men.

When they came to a fork in the hallway, Clark remembered that one way led toward the genetics lab. He had no idea where the other passage went. Before the men in brown could round the corner, Clark said to Bryan, "I need one of your shoes."

"My shoes?" Bryan said, anxiously pulling one off and holding it out for Clark. "Take it."

Clark tossed the shoe down the unknown hall, hoping it would at least give the men pause. He took off down the other hallway with Bryan, Lex following closely behind.

When they made it to the freight elevator, Lex pushed the up button, over and over, but nothing was happening. "Come on," he growled.

Clark set Bryan down and peeked back along the hall. Still no sign of the men in brown. He hurried over and put his ear to the elevator doors but didn't hear a thing. The old elevator didn't work. He had to think of something else.

"What now?" Bryan barked from the floor.

Lex was now straining to pull apart the doors. "I can't even budge them!"

"I need the other one, Bry," Clark said, and Bryan immediately ripped off his remaining shoe and handed it over. Clark hurried to Lex and gave the shoe to him, saying, "Go break something. A window. A lamp. Anything."

Lex looked at the shoe in his hand, and a devious smile spread across his face. "I can do that." He spun around and continued down the hall.

Clark wedged his fingers into the elevator doors and pried them open easily. He looked down. No elevator car. He looked up. There it was, stuck on the third floor. But he also saw a gap between the elevator car and the back of the shaft. Just as he was turning toward Bryan, who'd been watching him the whole time, he heard a loud crash in the distance.

Lex returned, out of breath. "Just took out a whole row of beakers. Hope there wasn't anything important inside." When he noticed the open elevator doors, he turned to Clark. "Jesus, how'd you—"

"Hurry," Clark said tersely. "We have to climb the cable."

As Lex raced to the open elevator shaft, Clark lifted Bryan again and tossed him over his shoulder. He carried him to the shaft, where Lex was already gripping the thick cable. "Up?" he shouted.

Clark nodded. "Go!"

Lex leapt onto the cable, wrapping his legs around it and beginning to climb.

Clark could hear footfalls coming toward them now. "Can you climb?" he asked Bryan.

"I don't know." Bryan looked toward the open shaft. "I can try."

But there was no time for uncertainty. "Wrap your arms around my neck," Clark told him.

"What?"

"Just do it." With Bryan clinging to him, Clark leapt onto the cable and closed the door with his feet. Then he scurried up the cable, quickly catching up with Lex. "There's a gap in back," he said. "See if you can climb up onto the roof of the elevator car."

It took Lex several tries, but he was finally able to shimmy up the small gap between the elevator car and the shaft and climb on top of the elevator. When Clark and Bryan got up there, too, Lex was already climbing down off the elevator, through the open shaft and onto the third floor.

"What now?" Bryan said, after he and Clark got down, too.

"The fire escape," Clark said.

"There," Lex said, pointing out a large window half-covered in tar.

Clark sprinted over and lifted the window, and the three of them climbed out onto the fire escape, one at a time. Clark threw Bryan's arm around his shoulder again, and the trio hurried down the stairs, toward the street level. Lex hopped down onto the crumbling pavement first, then reached up to help Bryan. Clark leapt off last, his phone buzzing the second his feet hit the ground.

It was a series of texts from Lana:

Here. Next to Lex's car. Where are you?

Everything okay????

TALK TO ME, CLARK!

Clark looked at Lex. "Lana's parked by your car. Can you go over there and come back to get us?"

"Yeah, wait here."

"And, Lex, tell Lana to cover her license plate somehow," Clark added. "I'm sure there are cameras everywhere. They'll know who we are, but I don't want them finding out about her."

"I got it," Lex said, and he hurried off to retrieve his car.

"*Of course* this would happen," Bryan said, pointing at his right foot, covered only by a white ankle sock now.

"It's not your fault," Clark said, trying to console his friend. "*I'm* the one who wanted to come here."

Bryan shook his head. "No, I don't want to do that anymore." He looked right at Clark, glassy-eyed.

"Do what?"

"Pretend."

"Bryan, it's okay, though," Clark said. "We got out. We're good." Clark looked up the fire escape. No one coming. He scanned the street. All clear.

Bryan gazed at the night sky. "You know why I like flying, Clark?"

"Why?" Clark asked, surprised by the non sequitur.

"The world actually makes sense at ten thousand feet."

Clark glanced at the sky, trying to think of something supportive to say.

"When you're flying," Bryan went on, "you look down at your city or your town, and you see how small everything looks. And you realize maybe your problems are small, too. And all the important people, like my dad—they're small, too, you know? And it sort of puts everything into perspective." Bryan looked at Clark with a pained smile. "Because the world is a really, really big place. And it existed for billions of years before we came along. And it may exist a billion more after we're gone. And up there . . . you *get* that."

Clark nodded as he listened, but the truth was, he found Bryan's words a little unsettling.

"The problem is," Bryan added, "a plane can only hold so much fuel. Eventually you have to land."

Just then Clark heard the familiar sound of Lana's car coming down the road. "See?" Clark said.

Bryan didn't say anything.

Lana's front license plate was covered with a sweatshirt. She pulled right up to them and reached across the car to throw open the passenger-side door, shouting, "Get in!"

Clark helped Bryan into the back seat, then jumped into the front. "Where's Lex?"

Lana shrugged. "He made me promise we'd keep him in the loop from now on. Then he peeled out." Lana pulled away from the weed-covered sidewalk a little less dramatically. Glancing back at Bryan, she added, "I think I'm your ride home now."

Bryan nodded, staring out the window.

Clark looked back as they continued down the street. No one was following them. "We're not going to the police this time," he said to Lana.

"Nope. No police." She glanced at Clark as she drove. "You guys okay?"

He nodded. "I think so." He motioned toward Bryan in the back, but Lana didn't notice.

"Good," she said. "Now tell me what happened in there. I'm assuming we've zeroed in on our guy. But I want to know *everything*."

CHAPTER 20

Bryan wasn't at school the next day. And when Clark texted him during his lunch period, to check in, Bryan's side of the conversation was clipped and dismissive. So after school Clark set off toward the downtown Body Reserve gym, where he knew Bryan had been working out.

"Thought I might find you here," Clark said as he walked into the mostly empty gym. His friend was stacking forty-five-pound plates onto the ends of a barbell, and it looked like he had a black eye. "Whoa, what happened to *you*?"

Bryan brushed the question aside. "It's nothing."

Now that Clark was closer, he saw how nasty the bruising was around Bryan's half-closed left eye. "What are you talking about, Bryan? Who did that to you?"

Bryan paused to look at Clark. "It's no big deal. I fell when me and Corey were wrestling around. What are you doing here, anyway?"

Clark watched Bryan lie on the bench and line his hands up on the bar. In addition to the black eye, he had a brace on his ankle. As Bryan did his set, Clark thought back to his cryptic comments right before Lana had picked them up outside the Wesco research lab. He'd sensed it at the time, that something had broken inside his friend's psyche, but seeing Bryan now . . . It was even worse than he'd thought.

Complicating things even more, Bryan was tossing around a tremendous amount of weight like it was nothing. He had only been on his workout kick for a short time. How was this possible?

"Listen," Clark said, after Bryan had set the bar back on the rack, "maybe you don't want to talk about your eye right now, but we *have to* talk about what happened at the lab. This is important for all of Smallville."

Bryan sat up and stared at the plaque-covered wall in front of him. "Going out there was a mistake," he said, wiping his brow with his gym towel. He sighed. "Listen, I don't mean to sound rude, but . . . I'm kind of busy. Can we do this another time?"

"I'm worried about you," Clark said. "You weren't at school. And you've barely answered my texts. And now I see your eye . . ." Clark trailed off, trying to figure out the best way to reach his friend. He didn't want to push Bryan so far that he closed himself off completely. But at the same time, Clark wasn't going to just turn around and leave.

Bryan stood up and motioned for Clark to take his spot at the bench. "If you're gonna be here, you might as well work in."

Clark saw his chance. "Sure, I'll lift with you." He walked closer to the bench, stretching out his arms. He didn't need to stretch, of course, but he'd seen so many others do it inside weight rooms, he assumed it made him appear more normal.

"Want me to take some of this weight off?" Bryan asked.

Clark shook his head. "Let me give it a try."

After Bryan stepped away, Clark lay down on the bench. He pushed the bar off the rack and began a slow, laborious-looking set. Ever since freshman football, he'd felt silly inside a gym. Truth was, Bryan could put a half dozen more plates on either side and Clark *still* wouldn't break a sweat. Which turned his whole gym experience into nothing more than a performance. He strained whenever it seemed like an appropriate time to strain. He let out little grunts whenever it was an appropriate time to grunt. When he was done with his ten reps, he reracked the bar and sat up.

"Ten," Bryan said. "Not bad."

Clark stood up, stretching some more. "I guess I sort of remember how to do this."

As they each hefted a third forty-five-pound plate onto either end of the bar, Bryan cleared his throat. "I know that what happened last night sucked. But it's all under control, okay? We're not going to let some small-time company like Wesco take *any* of our market share. You'll see."

"*We?*" Clark said, moving out of Bryan's way. "When did *that* happen?"

Bryan sat down and lined up his hands. "You know what I mean."

Clark wished Lana were here, too. She'd know what to make of this sudden shift in Bryan's demeanor. But she was spending the afternoon on the south side of Smallville, trying to get a better sense of how big the upcoming protest might be and how the organizers planned to publicize the fact that people had gone missing from their community.

Bryan hoisted the bar off the rack and did a quick set of ten, then reracked the bar and sat up. "Anyway, things are getting a little better at home," he said. "I feel like my dad's treating me different now."

"Really? How?"

Bryan shrugged. "He said we're at an important crossroads as a company. And he needs me."

"He 'needs' you," Clark repeated. "And what does that mean?"

Bryan only gave a shrug, though, and started in on his next set.

Over the next fifteen minutes or so, they continued adding weight to the bar, and Bryan met every challenge. Clark was genuinely impressed. But there was something gnawing at him about this display of strength. Something that didn't add up.

When Bryan put a fifth plate on, Clark knew he had to fight his competitive instincts and bow out gracefully. "That's it for me, man. I've hit my limit."

"Yeah?" Bryan asked.

"Yeah, you got me." Clark moved into a spotting position. He looked at all the weight on the bar, thinking there was no way Bryan would be able to lift it. Clark would have to be ready to help.

Bryan lay on the bench, stretched his pectoral muscles, and took a series of yoga-style breaths while working out the position of his hands. He then let out a deep growl as he hoisted the bowing bar and slowly brought it down to his chest. Both arms trembled as he inched the tremendous weight back up, iron plates rattling, his face pinched in concentration. When he got the bar to its high point, he locked his elbows and guided it back onto the rack, where it clattered into place.

A few serious-looking weight lifters who had stopped to watch nodded their approval. One guy hooted. A proud-looking Bryan saluted them as he sat up, sucking air. He turned to Clark. "New personal high."

"Impressive." Clark gave Bryan a minute to towel off before addressing the elephant in the room. "But you and I both know people don't improve that quickly on their own." He left off there, without saying the word *steroids*, hoping Bryan would address it himself. But he didn't. He just walked over to the drinking fountain and took a long sip.

"Bryan?" Clark tried again.

This time Bryan turned to look at Clark. "I don't want to play it safe anymore. That's gotten me nowhere." He paused for a few seconds, shaking his head. "Do you want to know why I finished the year at Smallville High?"

"Yeah," Clark answered. "Of course."

"It's not because I got kicked out, like everyone here seems to think. It's because a few close friends at my boarding school started gambling in the city. Like, a lot. At these super-shady places. I went with them a few times. I've always been good with numbers, and it was no different when I sat down at the poker table. Soon as I learned the rules, I started making money. And it freaked me out. Not because I was scared of getting in trouble. I was scared by how much I liked beating people. I couldn't stop, so I transferred here. Because it was safe."

Clark nodded along as he listened. He understood what Bryan was saying, but his mind went somewhere else. Hearing the guy be honest like this, and vulnerable, gave Clark the feeling he was actually seeing the real Bryan for the first time. "Thanks for telling me that."

Bryan scoffed. "I didn't tell you so you'd thank me. My point is,

I've decided to try and be someone with more of a backbone. No matter the consequences." He paused for an uncomfortably long time, like he was still trying to process all this himself. "Maybe it's better to have a short, brave life than a long, gutless one."

"But, Bryan—"

"Anyway, I should probably do legs now," Bryan said, cutting Clark off. "And I usually do this part alone. So . . ."

"Okay," Clark said, backing up. "We can catch up later, I guess. Text me?"

Bryan nodded.

"Cool." Clark turned to leave, but he didn't go all the way out the door. He sort of loitered near the locker room, watching Bryan. The guy squatted two sets of heavy weight, despite the bad ankle, then went over to his duffel bag in the corner of the weight room. He looked around, making sure no one was watching, and then took out a small green kit. He pulled a light green liquid into a syringe, tapped the needle, and then yanked down one side of his sweatpants and discreetly stuck himself in the right butt cheek. The sight made Clark feel physically sick.

Bryan tossed the syringe into the trash and went back to the squat bar, where he attacked the next set with an astonishing level of intensity. Not even the football players Clark knew went that hard.

Stinging with disappointment, he watched Bryan for a few more seconds. Then Clark turned and left the gym. He knew Bryan wasn't open to talking yet, and he needed to figure out a way to help his friend.

It was time to answer some questions about himself, too.

CHAPTER 21

After all the chores were finished for the night, Clark wandered into the small living room, where his parents were reading. Clark picked up the comics section and sat on the couch. But he didn't read. He watched his folks instead. From his earliest memory, he'd always felt close to them. But he'd also sensed that there was some kind of family secret being kept from him. It was the way they'd sometimes look at each other when they thought he wasn't paying attention. Or after he'd demonstrated one of his powers for the first time.

Tonight was the night, he told himself. No turning back this time.

"Dad?"

Jonathan looked up from his paper. "Yes, son?"

Clark pulled off his glasses and looked at his mom, then at his dad again. "Honestly . . . what *am* I?" As soon as the words left his mouth, butterflies ravaged his insides.

Jonathan took a deep breath and looked across the table at Clark's mom.

She studied Clark, then gave Jonathan a firm nod.

Jonathan turned back to Clark and met his stare. "From the very beginning, we've always known this day was coming." He looked down at the table for several seconds, shaking his head. "But now that it's here . . ."

Clark's heart began pounding inside his chest.

His dad stood up. "Martha?"

She shook her head. "You go on. I want to talk to him after."

After what? Clark thought, slipping his glasses back on.

Jonathan motioned for Clark to follow him.

Out of habit, Clark scooped up his backpack on the way outside and put it on.

"It happened seventeen years ago," his dad said, leading Clark toward the old barn.

"What did?" Clark asked.

Jonathan pulled a set of keys out of his pocket as he walked. "Well, that's when we . . ." He turned to Clark. "It's when we found you."

"When you *found* me?" Clark didn't understand. Did he even *want* to?

Jonathan stopped at the barn and sifted through his keys. When he located the right one, he forced it into a new lock and turned. The old wooden doors groaned loudly as he pulled them open.

The barn was as dark and musty as it had been the night Clark snuck in here alone. The ground was still littered with dusty old tractor parts. Ancient tires. Tools that Clark had accidentally snapped in half in his youth. Cobwebs draped from every corner, and this time Clark heard the faint sound of flapping wings up near the ceiling.

They moved toward the back corner. Jonathan began dismantling the much smaller pile of rubble that now covered the object. He tossed a couple of tires out of the way, then strained to lift a large chunk of rusted sheet metal and leaned it against the wall.

Clark took off his backpack and anxiously stepped forward to help.

After several minutes of working in the dim light, they found themselves staring at a tarp lying across a large oblong object. It was a little smaller than an SUV, and Clark could now see that there was a metallic point poking out of one end of the tarp.

A wave of nerves hit him hard as his dad grabbed the edge of the tarp and slowly pulled it off the object. Dust billowed across the old barn, and for a few seconds, Clark could hardly see a thing. When his eyes adjusted, though, his mouth fell open.

What he saw seemed impossible.

"Seventeen years, four months, and eleven days ago." His dad put a hand on Clark's shoulder, then removed it. "That's when you arrived in this."

Clark's heart dropped, and he had to sit down.

It was a spaceship.

Nearly fifteen feet long and shaped like a teardrop. A geometric hexagon made up the larger end. It came to a sharp point at the other end. A spherical metallic bubble bulged up from the middle. The whole thing sat on low tripod legs. It was almost six feet high at the thickest portion.

Clark rubbed his hands down his face, trying to comprehend what he was seeing.

Why would he have been inside a *spaceship*?

Who had put him there?

There were so many questions flooding his brain that he could hardly think straight.

His dad let out a long sigh and went on. "It all started when we saw a streak of light in the night sky. At first we didn't think much of it. Just another meteor. You've seen many of them yourself over the years."

It was true. Working outside at night, Clark had seen a lot of strange things. Lights that danced in random patterns. Meteors. Satellites. Unexplainable shapes on the horizon. But what could any of those things have to do with *him*?

"Then it grew larger," Jonathan said. "And brighter. And it was heading directly toward the field just south of the house. I'll never forget the sound of the impact that night. The way it lit up the sky."

"The crater outside," Clark said, making the connection. He knew that part of the farm like the back of his hand. It had always been his safe space. But now . . .

"We headed over right away," his dad continued. "Based on the size of the explosion, I figured there'd be a huge boulder in the crater. That happens around these parts sometimes. Never in my wildest dreams did I expect to find . . . *this*."

Clark's dad reached down and hit a switch on the spaceship. Then he cranked open the top half of the metal bubble in the center.

Clark leaned over to peer inside, feeling a strange combination of fear and fascination. There was a soft pad covered in blue-and-red blankets. Despite having sat in a dusty barn for nearly two decades, the blankets were still bright and clean, the colors as vibrant as if the material had been dyed yesterday. A strange-looking control panel ran all along the rim of the opened cockpit.

"You were safely tucked inside here, wrapped in blankets," Jonathan said. "And you looked like a perfectly normal human baby boy."

"Except I *wasn't*," Clark said under his breath.

"Well, there's more to it than that." His dad pointed at a glass square in the middle of the control panel. "Put your hand in there."

Clark hesitated.

The square had strange green symbols etched all over the dark surface. Most were entirely foreign, but one of them resembled the letter *S*.

"Go on, Clark."

He slowly pressed his hand against the surface of the glass. The panel lit up instantly, and the symbols began to glow—especially the *S*. A beam of blue light suddenly emerged from the center console, displaying a hologram in the middle of the barn. Clark started to remove his hand, but his dad held it firmly in place, saying, "It's time."

The image of a man's face flickered into being. He appeared to be in his late thirties. He had a chiseled face and dark eyes, and there were silver streaks running through his coarse black hair.

Something about the man felt oddly familiar.

"*My name is Jor-El,*" he said in a deep voice. "*And I am from the planet Krypton.*"

The color drained from Clark's face.

Another . . . *planet?*

Jonathan stared at the ground, unmoved. This obviously wasn't the first time he'd seen the message. And since it required Clark's hand to activate, he wondered if he'd seen it, too, when he was too young to comprehend it all.

As the hologram continued, it shifted from the face of Jor-El to an image of a bright blue-and-green planet orbiting a distant red star.

"*Some time ago,*" Jor-El's voice went on, "*we became aware that our planet was doomed to inevitable destruction. My wife, Lara, was pregnant with our first child. You, Kal-El.*"

"Who?" Clark swallowed uncomfortably.

"You, Clark," Jonathan answered. "Your given name was Kal-El."

"But . . . that's impossible."

"*We knew we did not have time to save ourselves,*" Jor-El continued, his face reappearing in the hologram. "*But we had enough time to construct a spacecraft equipped to carry you to the nearest planet that, we hope, will sustain life from Krypton.*"

The man's mouth moved slightly out of sync with his words, like a poorly dubbed foreign movie. Even in his shock, it occurred to Clark that some strange technology might be translating the words from an alien language into English.

"*Because of your genetic and cosmic makeup, Kal-El, we believe you will react to the natural environment differently than the planet's indigenous beings. What this means for you is hard to say. It is our hope, of course, that it will not render you weak and vulnerable. Regardless, it is a risk we must take. There is no other choice.*"

The hologram cut out for several maddening seconds, then reappeared.

"*By the time you see this, our home planet of Krypton will long have been destroyed. Gone for hundreds, perhaps even thousands, of solar revolutions. Your mother and I, I'm sorry to say, will also be gone. But you, Kal-El, must carry on in the name of Krypton. Be well, my son. And do your family and planet proud. We love you very much and always will.*"

The hologram cut out again, only this time the spaceship also went dark.

Clark sat down in the dirt, physically and emotionally wrecked. He wanted to go back to his room and sleep for days. And when he awoke, maybe this whole thing would turn out to be a dream.

Only he knew it *wasn't* a dream.

It was real life.

His life.

He pictured an eight-year-old version of himself lifting a thousand-pound four-wheeler off his neighbor's legs. Pictured sparks flying when he'd touched the electrified wire in the steer pen. Pictured himself taking a handoff for the very first time on a football field, defenders bouncing off him like rag dolls.

"Clark," Jonathan pleaded. "Clark, listen to me."

All these things he could do. His powers. But it wasn't because he was special.

It was because he was an alien.

A freak.

"Clark, please." His dad reached for his trembling shoulder. But Jonathan wasn't his dad at all. He was some random human who had just happened to find a spaceship in his field.

It could have been anyone that day.

In any field.

In any world.

"We thought about reporting the crash," Jonathan was saying in his ear. "Or bringing you to the authorities. But I have to believe things happen for a reason. And once we held you . . ."

Clark heard the words, but he couldn't make sense of them. He couldn't make sense of *anything*. Not the spaceship or the folded blankets or the hologram with the man's shocking message. That *he* was Clark's real dad. This strange alien from Krypton.

"You see, we'd recently discovered we could never have children of our own. So when you showed up like that, out of nowhere . . . well, we decided to raise you as our own, Clark. We became your family—at least here on Earth. And I promise you, we've always done our very best."

Clark shrugged out of Jonathan's grasp and stood up. "I gotta go."

"But, Clark—"

"I gotta go!" He put his backpack on.

His entire life had been a lie.

Jonathan slowly moved toward Clark with a profound hurt in his eyes. He reached an open palm out, but Clark ignored it and took off out of the barn.

He heard Jonathan's voice calling after him, but Clark didn't turn back.

He could never turn back.

Not now that he knew the truth.

CHAPTER 22

Clark ran faster than he'd ever run before. These powers were all he had to hold on to now. They were his protective shield. His salvation.

Soon he reached speeds that blurred everything around him. Winds battered his face and tore a hole through his jacket. His shirt. He ripped the torn clothing off his back and flung it away as he bounded over neighbors' fences, trespassing through farms and cattle ranches and cornfields. This town, Smallville, was all he'd ever known. Yet now he understood it was no longer his to claim. Home was millions of miles away. Home was out beyond the solar system somewhere. Among the distant stars.

No, that wasn't right. According to the man on the hologram, his birthplace, Krypton, had exploded. So his *real* home no longer existed.

Clark Kent no longer existed either.

That was a made-up name. A made-up persona.

He was Kal-El.

His mind drifted to the missing undocumented workers. If the people of Smallville only knew there was a *real* alien living among them . . .

He stopped at a large barn on the Pullman farm. He knew the Mankins Corporation had recently purchased it but had yet to take over, so it was all but vacant. Clark climbed atop a massive tractor and stared blankly at the wall in front of him—then *through* the wall. He scanned the fields and the farmhouse, confirming he was the only one around.

If his whole life was a lie, then what mattered?

Nothing.

Clark shifted the tractor into neutral, hopped off the springy seat, and gave the hulking machine a powerful shove. The tractor lurched forward, crashing through the barn doors and caroming down the hill, toward a large pond.

He sprinted in front of the runaway tractor and spun, closing his eyes and holding out his arms and waiting for the massive machine to knock him senseless.

For once in his life, he wanted to *feel* something.

That wasn't what happened.

The tractor slammed into Clark's bare chest, but he hardly budged. The front loader crumpled in the collision and fell off, and the grille folded in on itself. The remainder of the machine stopped cold and settled in front of him with a kind of sigh.

Clark had hardly felt a thing.

No marks on him anywhere.

He grew so angry, he grabbed the cab of the machine in his bare hands and spun around and heaved it toward the pond. He fell onto the ground, watching the tractor land with a great splash in the far end of the water, where it slowly began to sink.

Clark climbed to his feet and bounded down to the pond and let out a long, deep exhale—an exhale that froze the entire body of water in an instant.

Freak!

You're an alien freak!

He stared at the frozen pond, trying to figure out how he could possibly go on with his life. No matter what he did, no matter who he befriended, he would never be one of them.

He was destined to be alone.

Forever.

And what kind of an existence was that?

He glanced back up the hill, where the broken loader still lay. Then he looked at the frozen pond again. A silly idea occurred to him, and he marched back into the barn and began sifting through the junk drawers for a ball of twine. He found the twine inside the bottom drawer and ripped off four large pieces and shoved them into his pocket, then turned and left the barn.

Seconds later, he was kneeling in the grass in front of the loader. He tore off eight small strips of the steel from the side, each one about a foot long. He then pressed each strip in his bare hands to flatten it. Next, he concentrated on the middle of each piece until a thin laser shot out from his eyes and he was able to weld two perpendicular pieces together, and then he burned a small hole through the center of the bottom one. He did this three more times and let them cool for a few minutes before slipping them into his backpack.

He then pulled out the crumpled letter Gloria had tried to throw away.

He took out a Smallville High T-shirt from a recent pep rally and put it on while studying her address.

A few minutes later, Clark found himself moving through downtown Smallville.

It was almost nine, and the moon had overtaken the sun in the sky, but many of the businesses were still open. The restaurants and cafés. The two-screen movie house. And there were dozens of people out and about. Young couples on dates. Families. Old people with canes moving slowly down the wide sidewalk. He recognized almost all of them. This was his community. But it also wasn't.

What would happen if he told them the truth?

What if he stood atop the library steps right now and announced that he was really an alien named Kal-El? That he'd landed here in a spaceship when he was only a baby.

Would they run away screaming?

Would they call Deputy Rogers?

And what would the police do once they had him in custody? Stare? Prod him with a stick? Draw a sample of his blood?

He walked south through the downtown and out the other end. Smallville was too tiny and rural to have an actual "bad" area. But the neighborhoods in the south end were more downtrodden. The streets grew narrower and were full of potholes. Some store signs were in both Spanish and English, and there were bars over many of the windows. A few dilapidated fences surrounding abandoned lots were covered in graffiti, and he remembered Mrs. Sovak's lecture about Smallville's hidden history of redlining. It hit him even harder in the context of what he'd just learned about himself.

When Clark arrived at Gloria's building, he glanced at the letter again, this time looking for her apartment number. It was 3B. He glanced up at the faded facade of the structure, assuming the number three meant the third floor. There were only three windows on that level, and one was high and very small, which made Clark think it was a bathroom window. That left two possibilities. He picked up a tiny pebble and lobbed it at the closest one.

The pebble tapped the glass and fell away.

The window remained dark.

He waited a minute before tossing a second pebble, this time at the other window. A light turned on. The blinds were slowly swept aside, and a silhouette of what looked like Gloria appeared in the window.

Clark waved, heart racing.

In a few seconds, she disappeared from the window.

His shoulders slumped and he cursed himself. Why did he just show up at her apartment building uninvited, after dark, and think she'd be happy to see him?

But hadn't she said they could talk anytime? That she'd drop everything?

Just as he was turning to leave, he heard the lobby door creak open behind him. He saw Gloria standing there, dressed in jeans and a Smallville High sweatshirt, her hair pulled up.

"You okay?" she asked.

The kindness in her voice made his chest ache.

He shook his head.

She motioned for him to follow her to a short stairwell on the side of the graffiti-tagged building. She sat down and patted the spot next to her. "What is it, Clark?"

He broke eye contact when he felt like he might get emotional. He knew he wasn't actually going to cry, of course. He'd never shed a tear in his entire life. Not even as a kid. And now he understood why. That was the whole point.

"Clark?"

He shook his head again. "My dad told me some stuff tonight, and it . . . I don't even know."

Gloria hesitated, then slowly reached out her hand to him, palm up. He took it, and the second their skin touched, an electricity surged through his entire body. "It's okay if we just sit here awhile," she said. "We don't have to say anything."

She gazed up at the dark sky. If only he could explain to her what was up there. And where he'd come from. He gently squeezed her hand and said, "Can you go somewhere with me?"

"When?" she asked. "Now?"

He nodded. "I sort of planned a surprise for you. But I understand if it's kind of late."

"No, I wanna do your surprise." She looked up at her building. "Wait here a sec. I have to get my mom's permission. With everything happening around Smallville right now, I don't want her to worry."

Clark watched Gloria hurry back into her building.

She came out less than a minute later, saying, "I could really use some kind of distraction, Clark. Lana was here earlier, talking to people. Did she tell you it's not just Smallville? People are missing from neighboring counties and cities, too. Like Metropolis. And some of them aren't undocumented."

Clark stood, crushed by this news. "What's happening, Gloria? Who's responsible?"

She shook her head. "I can't even talk about it right now. Can we just do your surprise? Please?"

He nodded and looked out over her neighborhood. "Come on."

As they walked, they talked about Smallville and the protests outside city hall, and they wondered what it would be like to go somewhere else. Gloria had been to Metropolis for a summer camp once. She told him it was dirty and loud, but at the same time she'd felt at home because there were so many other people like her. Clark talked about the one time his family had driven to Iowa for a hog show. But the town they'd stayed in, he told her, felt even more like Smallville than Smallville. So he really didn't know anything else.

"The weirdest part," Gloria said, "is sometimes I feel alone when I'm surrounded by my family. Like, when I bring up college, for example. Everyone gets quiet. Like they don't even wanna *go* there. And it gets super awkward. I used to take it personally, but now I just sort of . . . I don't know. I guess I've accepted that I'm different from them in some ways. And maybe that's okay."

She had just put words to the way he'd felt his entire life.

Maybe Gloria was right. Maybe it was okay to be different from your family.

He turned to her, relieved, and said, "Even though they get weird when you bring up college, I'm sure they still love you." He realized he was talking about more than just Gloria's situation now. "And support you."

She nodded. "They do."

"And you still love them."

Gloria smiled. "More than anything."

As they walked side by side toward the Pullman farm, Clark glanced at Gloria's profile. He wanted so badly to confide in her the way she was confiding in him. To reveal what he really was. Where he really came from. But he kept his mouth shut. Because that was what his real life would always be now: a secret trapped inside.

Gloria stopped when they came upon the fence. "What now?"

"We're going over."

She frowned. "Really? You always struck me as a rule follower."

"I am," he said, grinning. "The people who owned the place have already moved out. And the new people aren't here yet." He boosted her over the fence, then followed.

Soon they came upon the frozen pond.

It sparkled under the moonlight, and Clark watched Gloria's face light up.

"Whoa," she said under her breath. "How's this possible?"

Clark smiled. "I don't know, but I had to show you."

She turned to him then, a genuine look of curiosity in her eyes. "But . . . why *me*, Clark?"

"Because," he told her, "you're the kind of girl whose wishes should come true." Clark opened his backpack and removed the four strips of metal and the twine. "Can I see your shoes?" he asked.

"My shoes." There was confusion mixed into her smile as she pulled off her shoes and handed them over.

Clark used his strength to make sure her soles hugged the beds of his crude skates. The blade sat firmly underneath in a straight line. He then secured everything tightly into place with a good bit of twine.

"Wait a second," she said, catching on. She glanced at the pond, then back at Clark. "Are you serious?"

He was grinning from ear to ear now. "You told me you wanted to try ice-skating," he said, securing makeshift blades to the bottoms of his own shoes. Clark stood up and took her hand and led her toward the pond.

"I'm going *ice*-skating," she mumbled to herself. "In spring. What is this life?"

They stepped onto the ice together tentatively, Clark pulling her toward him. "We should probably hang on to each other," he told her.

"So we don't fall," she said.

"Exactly."

A few steps in, though, Gloria slipped and dragged Clark down to the ice with her. They both laughed as they climbed back to their feet. The blades weren't perfectly even, so it was difficult to move with any real fluidity. Holding on tightly to each other and taking little choppy steps, they were soon clumsily gliding across the ice on their jagged strips of metal. Gloria's warm hand in Clark's. Her eyes piercing his chest whenever she turned to look up at him. They skated like this for a long stretch, until Gloria let go of him and drifted a few feet away.

"Ready?" she said.

"For what?" he answered.

"My twirl."

"Oh, man, I don't know if that's such a good—"

Before he could even get the sentence out, she was swinging her arms around and attempting to leap into the air like some kind of Olympic figure skater. One of her skates caught and the other flew out from underneath her, and she went tumbling toward the ice. Clark lunged forward to try to catch her, but he slipped, too, and she landed in an awkward sitting position on his back.

He craned his neck to look at her. "Saved you!"

They both laughed as she slid off his back and he picked himself up so that the two of them were sitting on the cold ice, face to face. Their eyes locked, and slowly their smiles began to fade.

"Thank you," she said in a soft voice, placing a hand on his knee.

He brushed a stray lock of hair behind her ear, then traced a finger lightly down her cheek. She reached up, stopped his hand, and held it there as she looked into his eyes.

He leaned toward her slightly.

"Clark," she whispered.

And then he kissed her. Softly at first, molding his lips to hers. When she began kissing him back, the kiss grew more urgent. He buried his hands in her hair, pressing her against him. They fit together perfectly. Like this was exactly where he belonged.

Clark reluctantly drew back, knowing he needed to slow himself down, though he could have kissed her full lips all night.

Gloria smiled against his neck and then rolled onto her back on the ice so that they were both staring up at the stars, still holding hands.

His head was spinning like a top.

His heart swelled in his chest.

Tonight he had learned that he was from another planet. That he was an alien who didn't belong on Earth. So why did he feel so . . . human?

CHAPTER 23

After walking Gloria back to her building, Clark wandered the quiet streets of downtown Smallville, trying to process everything that had happened. He pictured Gloria and him ice-skating across the pond, fingers linked, their eyes finding each other's, the feel of her lips against his. He pictured Jonathan's wounded expression as they stood across from each other in the old barn, staring at the half-buried spaceship. "You were safely tucked inside here," he'd said to Clark, "wrapped in blankets."

And now another face came to mind.

Jor-El.

His biological father.

What if he could've seen Clark with Gloria tonight? Not only safe on a planet called Earth but ice-skating. Holding hands with a girl he really liked.

Clark was beginning to understand what his biological parents had sacrificed for him. Yes, they'd strapped him into a cold space-ship when he was just a baby, all alone and left to fend for himself.

But they hadn't abandoned him. No, they'd given him a chance to live. And wasn't that what every person migrating from one place to another was really seeking?

It was well after three in the morning when Clark finally checked his phone.

He had three messages from Lana, two from Lex, and one from his mom. Lana's and Lex's messages all said a version of the same two things: In the past several days, the number of people who had officially disappeared had multiplied significantly. And tomorrow night they were going to meet outside the library, minus Bryan, to go on a top-secret mission. Clark needed to be there by eight o'clock at the latest.

The message from his mom was different. She was worried about him. She asked him to please come home so they could talk. Her text was as straightforward as it got, but that didn't stop him from reading it over and over, a lump rising in his throat every time.

He put away his phone, forcing the image of his mom out of his head.

He wasn't ready.

Instead, he shifted his focus back to Lana and Lex. When had they started working together? It was way too late to call either of them back, so he spent the rest of the night wandering all over Smallville in a kind of emotional haze. He was able to see his hometown from a totally new perspective now. Through the lens of an outsider. But also as someone who had just gone ice-skating with Gloria Alvarez.

Life, he realized, was a profoundly complicated thing. It was filled with awe and wonder and beauty, but it was also filled with heartbreak and loneliness. Maybe that was what made it so precious. You could never know what to expect next, or who might step into or out of your world. And the truth was that we were all navigating the mystery together.

That was why it was so important for Clark to help people.

Because all life, he was beginning to understand, was really *one* life.

And what if everyone could see it this way?

He didn't start heading for home until he saw the first few rays of sunlight climbing into the sky.

He made a pit stop at Alvarez Fruits and Vegetables, his heart dropping when he saw it boarded up. Carlos and Cruz were always at the stand before dawn on Saturday mornings—setting things up, stocking fruit, listening to their Spanish radio station. Clark peeked through the wooden slats. Only a few pieces of fly-infested fruit were still there. How could anyone think it was a good idea to put an end to their business? Who were they harming?

The Kent farm was quiet when Clark returned. He looked up at the old farmhouse and felt a strange sense of nostalgia. As if the childhood he'd experienced here was gone now, and something else had taken its place. He walked down the gentle slope toward the old barn, studying the crater in the field.

Clark pulled open the door and was relieved to see the spaceship still in the corner of the barn, covered only by the tarp. He was surprised Jonathan hadn't piled all the junk back on top of it. But maybe once something so important was uncovered, it didn't seem right to cover it right back up.

Clark removed the tarp and stared down at the capsule. It

wasn't quite as shocking to him now. It felt strange yet familiar at the same time. He undid the latch, and the top opened with a hiss.

He watched the hologram of his biological father again, this time concentrating on the man's face as much as his message. He *saw* himself now. It was the man's eyebrows. And his mouth and strong chin. Clark studied the details in the background, too. A strange picture of a robot. A rounded doorframe. Just beside his father was some kind of large control pad.

When it was over, Clark watched it again.

And then a third time.

This was as close as he would ever come to his home planet. To his own flesh and blood. And he wanted to soak it all in. After the third time through, he lowered the lid and stared at the spaceship, trying to imagine the state of his planet when his biological parents were forced to place him inside and send him off on his own.

Just as Clark finished replacing the tarp, he spotted Jonathan standing in the barn doorway. He was wearing the same clothes from the night before. "You came back," he said, entering the barn and coming to stand alongside Clark.

Clark nodded. He could tell there was something wrong by the blank look on Jonathan's face, and he knew it was their difficult conversation the night before. Clark softened, studying the new lines of worry on the man's face. And he realized something: all the traits he most valued about himself—his work ethic and principles, the way he treated others—were the direct result of being raised by Jonathan and Martha. Talking to Gloria had made him understand this. If he'd had to crash-land on Earth from another planet, he couldn't have done any better than the Kent farm.

Clark stood up to face Jonathan. "Dad," he said, "I owe you an apology."

Jonathan held up his hand. "The things we kept from you all these years . . . I'd understand if you *never*—"

Clark moved forward and hugged his dad.

When they separated, Jonathan was teary-eyed. "Your mother and I . . . we love you very much."

"I love you guys, too." Clark looked at the spaceship again, an anger suddenly rising in his throat. Someone had tried to break into the barn to steal a piece of his story. "You don't think anyone knows about this, do you?"

Jonathan shook his head. "Even if those men had made their way in here before you could run them off, they wouldn't know what they were seeing. No one can activate the holographic message without your hand—that much we do know. It's more likely they would think we'd built this ourselves or stolen some kind of government tech and hidden it away in here." Jonathan put a hand on Clark's shoulder, adding, "We do need to find out what they wanted, though."

Clark nodded as he and his dad looked at each other.

It almost seemed as if his dad was giving him permission to use his powers, without actually saying as much.

"Come with me," Jonathan said. "Your mom has something to show you."

The two of them walked up the hill together in silence. And when they went through the front door, Clark found his mom sitting at the kitchen table with a medium-sized wrapped box in her lap. He was surprised to see a fire going in the adjacent living room. He hadn't spoken to his mom since he learned about his true origins, and just seeing her made the world feel a little more sensible. He dropped his backpack and went over and hugged her.

She hugged him back, whispering in his ear, "I wish I could take away all the confusion, Clark, but just remember: your greatest strength is inside here." She tapped the side of his head with her finger.

Clark nodded as they separated. Before he could say anything, she handed him the box. "It's a little early for a birthday present," she said, "but now feels like the right time."

"What is it?" Clark asked.

She motioned toward the package. "See for yourself."

His dad cleared his throat. "We meant to give it to you sooner. But it never quite seemed appropriate. Until now."

"I also had a little trouble with the material," Martha added.

Clark turned over the box, trying to imagine what could be inside. He tore through the comics-section wrapping paper and lifted the top of the repurposed box. Inside was a bright, spandex-like material. Only denser. Stronger. Colored a familiar blue and red.

He unfolded it, assuming it was a coat, and held it up.

It wasn't a coat.

"I made it from the blankets inside your ship," his mom said. "It's for you to wear whenever you need to use your powers."

Now his mom was saying it was okay to use his powers, too?

"Hopefully, this will cut down on the amount of clothing you ruin," she added with a grin.

It was some kind of bodysuit. All in one piece. The entire body and legs were a deep navy blue that shimmered unnaturally. There was a red-and-yellow symbol on the chest that looked like an S inside a diamond. And a deep red cape draped from the back.

Clark tried to hide his confusion. They didn't expect him to actually *wear* this, did they? He looked up at his mom and dad. "Uh, thanks, guys."

His dad was beaming. "It's an amazing suit, isn't it?"

"It's, uh . . ." Clark didn't know how to phrase it without hurting any feelings. "I'll definitely wear it when I'm practicing my powers around the farm."

He made sure his mom was still smiling. The last thing he wanted to do was offend her.

Martha came over and took the suit out of Clark's hands. "Watch this," she said, throwing it directly into the fire in the living room. Flames quickly engulfed the bright fabric.

"Mom!" Clark shouted.

Martha pulled the tongs off the tool rack and reached them into the fire. She pulled out the suit and tossed it to Clark. Not only was it entirely unharmed, but it was still cool to the touch.

"It's some kind of strange space material," his mother explained. "Unlike anything we have here on Earth." She lifted the bottom of the cape and pulled as hard as she could. The material stretched, then snapped back into form. "Doesn't rip. Doesn't burn. Doesn't stain. It's really something."

"Your mother had to make sewing needles out of wire from the ship's control panel," his dad said. "That was the only thing that would penetrate the material."

"It took me some time, all right," his mom said.

Clark looked down at the suit again. He appreciated all the work that had gone into the gift, and it *was* pretty cool that it couldn't be burned or ripped. But what was he supposed to *do* with it? He looked up at his mom. "So, what's with the cape?"

This seemed to excite her even more. "There was a good bit of leftover material. And I thought . . . Well, you kids have your own styles these days. And I felt like the suit could use a little extra . . . *flair.* I remembered one of the jackets you ruined. I kind of liked the way it looked flapping around in the wind behind you."

Clark laughed nervously. The last thing a shiny blue jumpsuit needed was extra flair. He pointed to the chest of the suit. "What about this *S*?"

"That's my favorite part," Jonathan said, turning to his wife. "Your mother was very adamant about this, actually."

Martha met eyes with Clark. "Listen, you will always be our son. You know that. But there were two important people back on your home planet who loved you very much. We thought it was important to honor them."

"The *S*," his dad added, "is so you'll never forget who you are."

Clark fingered the letter on his suit.

"It's not actually an *S*, of course," Martha said. "It's some kind of symbol."

Jonathan nodded. "We believe it's your family crest. It's on the front of the spaceship, too. And I don't know if you remember from the hologram message, but it was also etched into the collar of your father's shirt."

"Wow." Clark now understood the weight of their gesture. "This really is an amazing gift. Thank you." He gave his mom and dad a hug. When he saw that they were still staring at him, he said, "What?"

"Why don't you go try it on," his dad said.

"Now?"

"Oh, leave him alone." Martha took Jonathan's hand and held it. "We don't need to force Clark to play dress-up."

Jonathan nodded. "I guess you're right."

Clark was relieved. He'd feel too ridiculous, even in front of his parents. He took the suit up to his room and hung it in his closet.

It looked so out of place next to his jeans and T-shirts and flannels. He sat at the end of his bed and stared at it. The suit seemed to almost glow. He imagined his ex-teammates all giving him grief if they ever caught him wearing a tight suit with a cape. Looking like some kind of space freak.

Clark slumped down on his bed. He lay back on his pillow and stared at the ceiling, thinking of the hologram again. And the spaceship. And someone trespassing on his family's farm. Then he turned onto his side and looked at the strange suit in his closet again.

The cape was the most ridiculous part. Other than a magician, who in the world would intentionally wear a cape? He stood up, pulled the suit off the hanger, and spread it out across his bed. He stared at it. The *S* on the chest was cool, though. He loved that his mom and dad were so respectful of where he'd come from.

It was still so strange to think that he was actually from *another planet.*

Out of pure curiosity, Clark stripped out of his clothes and stepped into the suit, one leg at a time. He pulled it up over his torso and slipped his arms into the armholes, and the suit automatically nestled into each contour of his body. It was the strangest feeling Clark had ever experienced, like being cocooned inside some familiar echo of who he was supposed to be.

When he looked in the mirror, an odd feeling came over him. He was no longer awkward Clark Kent from Smallville, Kansas. He was someone new. Someone greater. He reached a hand up to touch his family crest, the framed *S*-like symbol resting directly over his heart.

Now you understand who you are, son.

Yes.

You are Kal-El. Lone remaining survivor from the planet Krypton.

Clark's chest heaved. I'm Kal-El.

You have found refuge on Earth, where you will love and protect. But you must never forget where you come from. And who you were meant to be.

I will never forget, he promised the mirror.

Not ever.

CHAPTER 24

When Clark awoke from his nap, he found himself lying across the foot of his bed, still dressed in the suit. He stretched and reached for his phone to check the time.

7:34 p.m.

He bolted upright, looking out his window. The sun hung low in the sky, which meant he'd been sleeping for hours. Now he was supposed to meet Lana and Lex in front of the library in less than thirty minutes.

He had two texts from Lana and one from Gloria.

All three of them asking where he was.

Clark slid off the bed, put on his glasses, and went to his closet, trying to take off the suit. But the material had sucked to his skin so tightly that it now felt like a part of him. He wrestled with the thing for a few minutes before giving up and throwing his regular clothes on *over* the suit.

He'd figure out how to take it off later.

Once Clark was fully dressed, an odd sense of calm came over him as he stood there in his room, studying his reflection. What if his whole life had been a journey to this very moment, when he was finally able to reconcile his two separate identities?

On the outside, his everyday, ordinary self. Clark Kent.

But beneath this earthly, constructed persona lived something more primal, something closer to the truth. And the suit seemed to free that side of his nature.

Maybe the trick was learning how and when to pass from one to the other.

Maybe this was his way forward.

The sun was just beginning to set by the time Clark made it to downtown Smallville. In front of the new Mankins facility, workers were constructing a large temporary stage with two big screens, one on either side. He assumed the screens would broadcast the feed so everyone would be able to see. He couldn't remember the last time a Smallville event had required such a grand setup.

The streets were littered with flyers advertising the next day's festival. Clark picked one up and read about the elaborately planned celebration. There would be dozens of food trucks in the morning and live entertainment in the evening, all of it entirely free to the public. The mayor was going to kick the whole thing off with a big public address.

Clark folded up the flyer, shoved it into his pocket, and continued toward the library. He didn't even have to climb the steps, though. Lex's car was idling near the far sidewalk. Lana hopped out and folded the passenger's seat up for him. "Hey, look, it's my long-lost friend. Where have you been, Clark?"

He averted his eyes. "I had to deal with something sort of . . . personal. Long story."

"Well, get in," she said. "I have a little surprise for you."

As Clark went to climb in, he saw Gloria sitting in one of the two back seats and froze. "Gloria?"

She waved. "Hey, Clark."

Lana and Lex laughed.

"Hey." Clark climbed in, checking to make sure his suit wasn't visible underneath his clothes. "Not a bad surprise," he said, touching her hand.

"Told you," Lana said, getting in after Clark. "So, you guys ready to break this thing wide open?"

Before anyone could respond, Lex peeled out onto the road.

As they merged onto the highway, Clark leaned over to Gloria. "How'd you—?"

"Lana called me this morning," Gloria said. "She filled me in on the plan and asked if I was free. I dropped everything. This is all that matters to me now."

"I assumed you'd be good with it, Clark," Lana said.

"Of course. Yeah." Clark shot Gloria a look, thinking of their night ice-skating. She smiled a bit and shook her head discreetly, and Clark could tell they were on the same page. She hadn't mentioned anything to Lana. The magical experience would stay between them.

Clark looked toward the front of the car, ready to switch mindsets. He'd taken up enough time worrying about himself. Now it was time to focus on Smallville. "No Bryan?" he asked.

"I tried calling him, like, ten times," Lana said, "but he never answered. And he never called me back."

The only thing that surprised Clark about this was that Lex didn't say anything. "Lex?" Clark pressed. "Any word on Bryan?"

"He's a big boy," Lex said. "If he doesn't want to help, that's his problem."

Clark decided to worry about Bryan later. "Okay, somebody catch me up."

"This is a recon mission," Lex said from the driver's seat. "Lana told me about the last time you guys went out to the Joneses' farm. And I happen to know things have progressed."

Clark nodded.

"Lex brought hidden cameras," Lana said. "And all sorts of other high-end surveillance equipment." She held up an overstuffed backpack to prove it.

"Really?" Clark tried to figure out why Lex was being so helpful all of a sudden. Was it because of their experience at the Wesco research lab? It definitely wasn't out of the goodness of his heart. Clark had known Lex only a short time, but he was certain the guy would never be motivated by pure altruism. "So, what's in it for you, Lex?"

Lex didn't answer right away.

Clark and Gloria shared a look. He realized he'd have to fill her in about Lex later on.

"I have my reasons," Lex finally said as his fancy sports car blasted down a narrow road, headed in the general direction of the Jones farm.

Clark noted that they weren't taking the usual route to get there, instead angling toward the back of the farm this time.

"Check these out." Lana held up a pair of black-framed glasses. "Apparently, there's a small camera inside the lens."

Clark took the glasses and looked them over. At first glance they seemed pretty ordinary, aside from the thick frame. But when he looked more closely, he saw a little camera lens in the upper right corner. "So, we're going to record what we see."

Lex made eye contact with him in the rearview mirror. "There's a switch on the side. Once it's turned on, the signal goes directly to my cloud database."

"The trick is to get close enough so that the footage is clear," Lana said. "I've been messing with them, and you can't really zoom in or out."

"What are you guys planning to do with the footage?" Gloria asked.

"If they're doing what I think they're doing," Lex said, "I'll have proof on my computer."

Clark flipped the switch on and off and held the glasses out to Gloria.

She grinned. "*You* try them."

Clark turned away from her and pulled off his normal glasses. Then he slipped on these thicker-framed glasses. He shifted slightly so he could see his vague reflection in the window. He looked more bookish. A thought occurred to him as he discreetly lifted his shirt to peek at the blue suit beneath his clothes. Maybe looking bookish was a good means of fitting in. There was no way someone with superpowers would need glasses with such thick lenses.

He turned to Gloria. "What do you think?"

She nodded. "Ooh, I like the cute, brainy look."

Lana spun around. "Whoa, Clark, I agree. You might want to rock those full-time."

"You think I can keep these?" Clark asked Lex.

"Let's do the mission first," Lex said humorlessly. "We can divvy up the tech later."

"So that's it?" Clark said, still wearing the glasses. "We're just trying to figure out what they're up to? And recording them if we can, so we have evidence."

"I also lined up an interview with Corey tomorrow," Lana said. "During the festival. I want to see if he knows who cosigned for the Joneses' farm. I'm thinking Dr. Wesley might still be connected to those mob leaders who used to bankroll his work back in Metropolis."

"There was a cosigner?" Clark asked. Maybe Dr. Wesley wasn't doing all this alone.

"I did some digging around in public records," Lana said. "As usual, the devil's in the details."

They pulled off the gravel road near a large human-made pond. The sun had fallen below the horizon, but there was still a bit of light in the sky. Lex maneuvered behind a broken-down Caterpillar tractor, put the car in park, and cut the engine. When he got out, Lana, Gloria, and Clark followed. Lex grabbed a second backpack from the car and locked the doors.

"We're still pretty far away," Lana said.

"Look," Lex said, "I can't have anyone tracing this shit back to me. But don't worry—if we need to get out of there quickly, I've got us covered with vehicles for extraction." He lifted a pair of binoculars to his eyes and scanned their surroundings. "Now, let's get our stuff on."

They geared up with body cameras, miniature flare guns, and their special glasses. Each of them wore a backpack filled with various other equipment. Clark felt like it might be overkill, but he went along with it anyway. Obviously, Lex had put a lot of thought—and money—into all this stuff. Which told Clark that Lex believed the payoff would exceed his investment. Clark was almost as interested in Lex's motivation for being out here tonight as he was about what was happening on the Jones farm.

Clark turned to Gloria, watching her adjust her glasses. He was hit with a sudden bout of nerves as he remembered what had happened the last time he was here. If there was more gunfire, it would be impossible to position himself in front of both Lana and Gloria.

"What?" Gloria said.

Clark shook his head. "Just . . . we have to be careful."

Gloria nodded.

"We walk due east for about a half mile," Lex instructed them. "There we should encounter one guard, who we'll have to take out. At that point we will have a clear path to these new structures I was telling Lana about. They have rotating lookouts every twenty minutes, so we'll have to be quick. In and out. And then to our getaway location. Got it?"

"How do you know so much about what's going on out here?" Clark asked.

"Satellites."

"*Satellites?*" Lana repeated.

"Look," Lex said smugly, "LuthorCorp is light-years ahead of everyone else when it comes to defense and weaponry, okay?" Lex gazed off into the distance, a grim look washing over his face. "And we plan to keep it that way."

Here it was, Clark thought. Lex's real motivation.

"Now, they've built two temporary structures at the back of the Jones farm," Lex continued. "A large one and a much smaller one." He looked from Clark to Lana to Gloria, adding, "I should warn you: my most recent satellite images have revealed what might be minor military hardware. And a bunch of trucks and jeeps. Suggesting there may be a dozen or more people out here now."

They walked a long way down the road, then cut through the rear of the farm. As they began picking their way through the field of knee-high corn, Clark marveled at the scale of this operation. When they'd been here for the party, he had no idea the space would soon have two mysterious structures.

What exactly was Wesco up to?

When they finally neared the edge of the field, they crouched among the short cornstalks. Then, seeing that they were in the clear, they hurried across a small opening, into a thick grove of trees. It was the same grove where Clark and Lana had hidden the last time they were here. But this time, Clark reasoned, they were approaching from the opposite side.

From behind the base of a thick tree, Lex motioned to the right, but Clark had already seen it: maybe fifty yards away, on the edge of the grove, was an armed guard in familiar black military fatigues. He was guarding some kind of perimeter.

"We gotta take that guy out," Lex said. "Quietly."

"And how are we supposed to do that?" Lana asked.

Lex took off his backpack, unzipped the main pocket, and pulled out a small gun.

"No way," Clark said, reaching out and pushing the muzzle of the gun toward the ground. "We're not going to *shoot* anyone."

"It's a dart gun," Lex said, irritated. "It's not going to kill him."

Clark backed off and watched Lex take aim. A small green dot from the laser sight appeared on the guard's arm. Just as the light caught the guard's eye and he began to raise his machine gun, there was a burst of compressed air near Clark's ear. A small dart lodged in the guard's right shoulder, and he immediately collapsed to the ground.

"Jesus," Lana said. "I'm officially a believer in LuthorCorp."

"Is he okay?" Gloria asked.

"When he wakes up in a couple hours," Lex said, "he'll be a little groggy. But that's about it."

Clark was impressed. *Why hurt someone if you can simply put him to sleep?*

The moon was rising above them as they raced through the thick trees to the far edge of the dark grove, then stopped. In the clearing—the same one that had been an empty patch of weedy grass just a few days ago—Clark saw two single-story metal structures, just like Lex had said there would be. One was large, boxy, and windowless. A single door in front. The other was a smaller structure on wheels, with three jeeps parked outside.

The crater was just beyond, two tractors parked near its lip.

The rest of the massive clearing had been closely mowed and was marked with an array of spray-painted white lines. It looked almost like the setting for some odd sporting event, but Clark knew this wasn't a game. Whatever was going on here was far more serious than he'd ever imagined. Clark scanned the area for potential dangers as they crept toward the side of the larger structure, to the left.

"Shit," Lex whispered. "I assumed there'd be a window somewhere. These camera glasses are useless if we can't see inside. Especially now that it's dark."

Clark stared at the exterior of the building in front of him until his X-ray vision punched through. The wall was made of a thick metallic substance, however, so his view was blurry. He believed he was looking at two dozen or so men sitting in folding chairs, watching a theater-sized movie screen. What was on the screen, he couldn't tell. But all the men were dressed in brown and had shaved heads—like the guy who'd rammed the SUV into the retaining wall downtown.

The men sat completely still. Coming up out of the floor, Clark saw, were chains that connected to a leather belt around each man's torso.

Clark's vision soon cut out, but the image was seared into his brain. The men inside the structure were being kept against their will. They were prisoners. His thoughts flashed back to the night at the Wesco lab. He'd heard the sound of chains there, too. Inside the large conference room labeled Project Dawn. Whatever was happening here had begun at the lab.

"What's in there?" Gloria whispered. *"People?"*

Clark almost blurted out what he'd just seen with his X-ray vision. But he stopped himself in time. Instead, he said, "There's gotta be a window somewhere. At least some kind of ventilation shaft on the roof."

"Hang on." Lex pulled a small handheld device out of his backpack. He punched in a series of numbers and waited, saying, "Come on. Come on."

But Clark was no longer willing to wait. He was sure the guards would walk the perimeter again soon. He peered around the building when he heard the sound of men speaking quietly. There were two, guns in hand. They stood beside one of the jeeps. It seemed to Clark that they were the only guards who stood between him and getting a look inside the structure now.

Lex tapped Clark on the shoulder and said in a quiet voice, "You were right." He held out his device so Clark could see. And there, on the tiny screen, was a detailed satellite image of the compound where they were standing. Lex zoomed in so that

Clark could see the single skylight on the roof of the structure before them.

"But how do we get up there?" Lana whispered.

Gloria was shaking her head now. "I don't understand. Why not just call the police?"

"We already tried that," Lana whispered. "This time we want to go to them with proof."

Lex knelt and dug into his backpack. He pulled out three pairs of black gloves and fabric booties. They were made from a strange metallic material. "Put these on."

The three of them slipped the gloves on and then slid the thick socks over their shoes. Buckles snapped them into place around their wrists and ankles. The material was soft but heavy, as if some kind of metal was mixed into the fabric.

"To make it cling," Lex said, "just take a step. Or reach your hand out for the metallic surface. To release, slide right." He switched them all on and, to Clark's surprise, began scaling the side of the building, reaching up a hand or foot and sticking, then sliding right to release and climb higher.

Lana, Gloria, and Clark shared a look before following.

Clark was amazed at how the gloves and grip socks clung to the wall through some kind of magnetism when he secured a foothold, then released when he stepped to the right. It was awkward at first, especially remembering to slide right, but by the time he neared the top of the structure, he'd figured out the technique. He also noticed that there was a second button on the side that held the magnetic connection firm even when he tried to step or push right.

At the top of the structure, the four of them removed their grip socks and crept over to the lone skylight to peer inside.

Gloria gasped.

She could now see what Clark had seen earlier.

Lana and Lex looked, too.

Dozens of men sat motionless, chained to the floor of the structure, watching some kind of instructional video. It showed an older man in a business suit who was speaking directly into the camera while every few seconds a seemingly random image flashed onto the screen, never long enough for Clark to make out what it was. The only source of light inside the room was the screen, but Clark could clearly make out that all the men had IVs coming out of their arms, which were strapped to their sides. A scientist Clark didn't recognize was going down the line of chairs, reading the machines connected to the men and recording information on a small tablet.

But what made Clark's entire body go numb was something he was just now beginning to recognize. A single characteristic linked all the men chained to the chairs.

The color of their skin.

Brown.

Fury boiled inside Clark's chest. He turned and saw the horrified look on Gloria's face. "I'm going down there," he snarled.

"No," Lana said. "Lex is recording. We'll take the footage to the cops, and they can come out here with the proper reinforcements."

Clark shook his head, repeating, "I'm going down there. Now." When he stood up, Lana and Lex both grabbed hold of his arms. He easily brushed them away.

But then Gloria stepped in front of him, saying, "Don't, Clark! It's suicide."

The desperate emotion in Gloria's voice stopped Clark in his tracks.

He took a deep breath and tried to think. The men inside this building had been taken against their will. They were chained to the floor, IVs forced into their veins and propaganda forced into their brains. They needed help. And Gloria probably knew some of them. Yet she was still telling him to wait. Maybe she was right. If he barged into the building now, people could get hurt. Maybe even killed.

Lana or Gloria could get killed.

Clark balled his hands into tight fists and growled soundlessly. Then he knelt beside the skylight and stared down at the men again. When his eyes had adjusted to the dim light, he picked up on more troubling details. Some of the men were older, some in their thirties and forties. Others hardly even looked eighteen. And the IVs were feeding a light green liquid into each man's veins. It looked similar to the substance he'd seen Bryan inject at the gym.

He spun around to Lex. "You're getting all this?"

Lex nodded. "Every bit of it."

There was a commotion near the small building. Men shouting.

"Let's get out of here," Lana whispered.

Clark scurried to the edge of the roof, where he saw three Mexican men being led from the smaller structure to the bigger one.

Lex was suddenly beside him, aiming a tiny digital camera down at this new cluster of men. Lana was there, too, pointing at Lex's watch. "Seriously, we gotta go. Now."

One of the guards looked up. Clark quickly backed away from the edge, pulling Lex and Lana with him. Gloria remained behind them, looking all around. Clark listened for movement. He heard the guards mumbling to each other below. Using his super-hearing, he could just make out some of what they were saying:

"They're not ready," one said.

"They have to be. We don't have any more time."

"Should I increase the dose, then? Or wait on the improved formula?"

Clark saw the beam of a flashlight pass over their heads. He was pretty sure they hadn't been spotted.

But had the men *heard* them?

They quickly put their grip socks back on and readied themselves to climb down the side of the building. But just as Lana was turning around to descend the wall feetfirst, the top of a ladder swung into view and came to a rest against the edge of the roof right next to them. Clark's stomach dropped as he heard someone beginning to climb the aluminum rungs.

He pulled Lana away from the wall.

Gloria was beside him now. "We have to go down the other side," she whispered.

Clark put a finger up to his lips. He quickly moved around the perimeter of the roof, peering down at every other option before coming back to Lex and Lana. The man climbing the ladder was closer now.

"I got him," Lex said, pulling out his dart gun.

Clark watched Lex raise the narrow barrel and wait for the man to come up over the side of the roof. His hand was shaking.

When the man finally emerged, Lex fired, missing badly.

Before Lex could reload, the man had swung himself onto the roof. He bounded to Lex, grabbed the dart gun, and chucked it away.

Clark lunged for the man, quickly taking him down. Within a fraction of a second, Clark had him in a tight sleeper hold. When the man's body went limp, Clark gently set him on his back.

Gloria stared at Clark, wide-eyed.

"Come on," he said to her. He motioned for Lana and Lex, too, and the four of them made a move for the opposite side of the roof. But in the chaos, none of them were able to use the grip socks correctly. They kept forgetting to slide right and tripping. "Take the socks off," Clark said. "I'll help you down."

Clark descended the wall using only his hands. When the others made it to the edge of the roof, he held out his arms, motioning for them to jump. "Gloria, you go first," he said in a loud whisper. She hesitated, then dropped into his arms. He caught her, making sure he went to the ground once she was secure, so that it appeared to take a great effort.

Then Clark and Gloria together caught Lana.

And all three of them caught Lex.

As they scurried off into the night, Clark heard a great commotion behind him. One of the guards had climbed into a jeep, started the engine, and peeled out after them.

Clark led the group into a thick patch of trees near the other end of the cornfield. They hid there as the jeep sped back and forth a few times, shining a flashlight into the brush. But the man never got out, and eventually he headed back to the buildings.

"They were all chained in place," Gloria said angrily. "Did you see it?"

"Disgusting," Lana said.

Clark slapped the ground, saying, "I know how we can nail these guys."

Lana turned to him. "How?"

Clark felt a surge of energy just imagining it. "Tomorrow at the festival. In front of everyone."

Lex looked up from studying his glasses. "What are you *talking* about?"

"I'll explain as soon as we get out of here." Clark watched the jeep pull up to the smaller structure, where another guard climbed in. They started spinning around for another pass. "In the meantime, you're up, Lex. Where to?"

"This way," Lex said, and the three of them sprinted into the cornfield, crashing through stalks until they arrived at a small clearing, where four brand-new four-wheelers sat.

"Our escape," Lex called to the others as he climbed onto one of the machines and started the engine. Clark, Gloria, and Lana followed his lead, and soon they were racing from the back of the Jones farm, Clark's mind still stuck on the image of all those men strapped to chairs, their brown faces angled toward the screen, IVs pumping a light green liquid into their bodies.

Clark was horrified that something like this could be happening right here in Smallville.

And he vowed to stop it.

He turned toward Gloria as he rode. He wouldn't give up until every one of those men was free.

CHAPTER 25

They dropped off the four-wheelers near the rusted tractor and got back into Lex's car. As Lex drove them home, Clark reviewed his plan. The following morning at the festival, they would take Lex's footage and broadcast it for all of Smallville to see. Then the local police force would have no choice but to believe them.

"And how are we supposed to do that?" Lana asked.

"When I was walking over to meet you guys at the library," Clark explained, "I saw the workers building the stage. They were putting up two big screens, which I'm assuming will broadcast whatever is taking place onstage. We're going to hack the feed."

Lana shot him a skeptical look. "And I suppose you have secret hacking skills I don't know about."

"Not me," Clark said, turning to Gloria. "But I know someone who does."

Her eyes grew big. "Me?"

Lana pounded the dash. "I love it. Can you really do this, Gloria?"

"If it's a standard HDMI connection," she answered, "then, yeah, I guess I could probably figure it out."

"Interesting idea," Lex said, touching his glasses. "I got over six minutes' worth of footage. We'd just have to figure out where to start it from. Or . . . I guess I could edit it down tonight."

"I'd leave it exactly the way it is," Clark said. "I don't want anyone thinking we tampered with evidence." He turned to Lana. "But what if we splice in pieces of your interview with Corey? Then we could prove that he's complicit, too."

"If I can get him to say anything worthwhile," Lana said.

Clark scoffed. "If Corey has anything to say, you'll get it out of him."

Lana nodded, staring out the front windshield. Then she met eyes with Clark in the rearview mirror. "I can't believe we're actually going to use the celebration to expose these assholes. It's brilliant."

They all agreed, and Clark turned to Gloria. "You okay?"

She shrugged. "What we just saw out there . . . it made me physically ill."

The look in Gloria's eyes devastated Clark. His plan had to work. There was too much at stake.

Gloria took a deep breath and let it out slowly. "I take it back," she said. "No matter *what* kind of AV they're using tomorrow, I'll find a way to hack the feed."

Clark squeezed her hand. "I know you will." Then he touched his suit under his regular clothes. *We're going to pull this off,* he told himself. Because they had to. There was no other option.

"I still don't completely understand what Wesco is doing with those men," Lana said. "But they had them chained to their chairs."

"They tore them away from their families and friends," Gloria added.

"It's obviously about race," Lana said. "We know that much, right?"

Lex shook his head. "That's naive," he told Lana. "It's about money. And power. It's *always* about money and power. Remember that."

"Maybe it's both," Clark said. "Think about it. They're *using* people who are different from them. People they view as vulnerable, expendable."

"They know some of us can't just go to the police," Gloria added. "Which makes us easier to prey upon."

Clark could feel Gloria's words in the pit of his stomach. Because it could just as easily be *him* chained up like that. If they knew what he really was.

"We won't let them get away with it," Lana said.

Clark and Gloria nodded, and Lex said, "We get this right, it'll be a public takedown of epic proportions."

"And since Mankins is a nationally known corporation," Lana added, "I'd be shocked if there weren't at least a few media outlets from outside of Smallville at the event." She glanced back at Clark. "It'll be a national story. Plus, we'll be doing it peacefully, right, Clark? No violence."

Clark nodded. But his mind had drifted back to what he'd seen on the Jones farm.

"Clark?" Lana said as Lex pulled up to the foot of his driveway. "You okay?"

He looked at her. "I just want this to work."

Lana glanced back at Gloria. "We'll *make* it work." She opened the passenger-side door, got out, and flipped the seat forward for Clark.

Before getting out, he turned to Gloria. "I'll see you tomorrow, okay?"

"Let's go," Lex said.

Gloria ignored him and reached across the seat to touch Clark's cheek. "Bye, Clark."

He climbed out of the car, then watched as Lana got back in and Lex's car pulled away.

Instead of going straight into the house, Clark went down to the crater near the old barn and sat with his head against the lip, his usual spot. He pulled out his phone and checked to see if Bryan had texted him. Nothing. Clark slipped his phone back into his pocket and thought about Gloria and what they'd all just seen together, and then he looked out over the crater before him, trying to imagine that long-ago version of himself crash-landing here. Jonathan and Martha opening the top of the spaceship and carrying him into their home. Treating him like their own.

None of it seemed real.

Or even possible.

Yet it was the truth. *His* truth.

Instead of feeling sorry for himself or trying to make sense of something so incredible, he vowed to deal with it another way. He would do everything in his power to make his adopted planet a better, safer place.

CHAPTER 26

Clark woke up to a text from Gloria.

Freaking out. Nobody can find Cruz.

Clark froze, picturing the Jones farm, the men chained to the floor. He called Gloria, but she didn't answer. He left a message and texted, too, telling her to call him back as soon as possible.

He put away his phone and sat up in bed, an awful feeling moving through his entire body. Cruz was just a kid. And he was a citizen. Maybe there was some other explanation.

While waiting to hear back from Gloria, Clark went over to his closet and looked at the suit. He'd managed to remove it the night before. But now he had a strange desire to put it back on. Like it was some kind of armor on such an important day. He took it off the hanger and slipped it on, then put his regular clothes on over the suit. He also wore the thicker-framed glasses Lex had given him instead of his regular glasses. The new ones seemed more Clark Kent to him now, and it felt important to make sure that the two different sides of him contrasted greatly.

He tried calling Gloria one more time but got her voice mail, so he started for downtown.

Two hours later, he still hadn't heard anything from Gloria. He looked for her outside city hall, but she wasn't among the crowd of protesters. And she wasn't anywhere around the square. He eventually left to meet Lana and Lex on the steps outside the library.

And there was Gloria.

But no Lex.

"Hey," he said to Gloria. "I've been trying to reach you."

She nodded, clearly upset. "I left my phone in the car while we looked around the neighborhood for Cruz."

Clark hesitated before asking, "Did you find him?"

She shook her head. "You don't think he could be on the Jones farm, do you? He's just a kid."

"I didn't see him last night." Clark glanced at Lana, who looked at the ground, shaking her head. "We have to get this right," he told Gloria. But he was saying it for his own benefit, too. "If we get this right, everything will be okay."

"Lex texted," Lana said. "He's going to be late. We don't have access to any of the footage without him."

Clark looked around, trying to figure out what to do. He'd never felt so anxious. "Maybe we should go talk through the plan. We can catch Lex up whenever he gets here."

The three of them ducked into a quiet room in the library and sat at a round table. Clark motioned to Lana. "So, you'll start your interview with Corey a few minutes before the first speaker, right? That way you can cover the charity angle and get him comfortable."

Lana didn't look very confident.

Clark's whole body tensed. "What's wrong?"

"I've been texting Corey all morning," Lana said. "He told me he didn't have time for an interview. When I pressed him, he went silent. So I sort of had to try a Hail Mary."

Clark waited for her to explain. It felt like everything was unraveling.

"I told him I'd heard a rumor that there was something strange happening on the Jones farm. And I was hoping he could clarify for me personally."

"And?"

"He agreed to meet me," Lana said. "But he's definitely not happy about it. I think the whole charity angle is out the window. We'll just get right to it." She held up a small black duffel bag. "I brought the digital camera and tripod from school. So at least I have that part covered."

Clark wanted to believe this part of the plan could still work, but he had his doubts. "Where are you guys meeting?" he asked.

Lana tried to seem more upbeat. "Corey said he talked to the courthouse manager. She's letting us use one of the meeting rooms for the interview."

"Okay. So you'll be at the courthouse." He turned to Gloria. "And were you able to get a look at the AV they're using?"

Gloria nodded.

"It only took her, like, two minutes to figure out how to do it," Lana said.

Gloria shrugged. "For outside events like this, people don't usually do anything too sophisticated." She held up a thin laptop. "I enabled split-screen capability in case we want to have the interview running alongside the footage. Up to you."

"That would be great." Clark still had doubts about the Corey piece, but if anyone could pull it off, Lana could. And he loved the split-screen idea. "I'll be right next to the police stand the whole time. Soon as we cut the footage, I'll lead them directly to Wesco."

"We just need Lex to show up," Lana said.

Gloria's phone buzzed just then. She stood to answer it, saying, "Marco? Did you get in touch with Carlos yet?" She stepped out of the room to continue the call.

Lana looked at Clark. "You don't think Cruz could be on the farm, do you?"

"I sure hope not," he said. "But I'm not putting anything past these people."

"When this is over," Lana said, "I want to see them all rot in jail."

They both went quiet for a stretch, and then Clark said, "Can you text Lex again?"

"I've been texting and calling all morning," Lana said. "What are we gonna do if we don't have the footage? Then everything's ruined."

Clark stared at the floor, replaying everything that had happened the night before, searching for any sign that Lex might have been putting them on. Clark definitely didn't trust the guy to do anything out of the kindness of his heart, but in this case it seemed like their interests were aligned. Clark, Lana, and Gloria wanted to expose Wesco and save the people held prisoner on the Jones farm. Lex wanted to take down the competition.

A few seconds later, Gloria came back into the quiet room. She was followed by a thin, middle-aged black man with a bushy mustache. He was wearing a Hawaiian shirt, jeans, and a leather backpack.

Clark and Lana looked to Gloria, who said, "This is Leonard. He was looking for us outside the library."

Leonard nodded, removing his backpack and unzipping the front pocket. "Unfortunately, something came up, and Lex is unable to make it. But he sent me to give you this." He held out a thumb drive.

Clark took it.

"It's the footage you guys need for the hack," Leonard said.

Clark looked up at the guy as he was putting his backpack on again. "And how are you connected to Lex?"

"I work for LutherCorp."

Clark and Lana and Gloria all looked at one another.

"Anyway," Leonard said, backing up toward the glass door, "I was told to deliver that. Good luck with everything." And then he turned and left.

After sitting there stunned for several seconds, Clark shook his head. "I knew Lex wasn't in it for the same reasons we are, but . . . can you believe he didn't even show up?" Clark softened when he looked at Gloria. "Everything go okay on your call?"

She shook her head. "It's like you said earlier. We have to get this right."

They all nodded, and then Lana said what was on everyone's mind. "I wish we could speed up time. Those men shouldn't have to spend another second chained up like that."

By eleven the public square outside the new Mankins headquarters was packed. It was easily the largest crowd Clark had ever seen in Smallville. People were sitting in lawn chairs all over the closed-off street, heaping plates of food in their laps. Dozens of food trucks were parked outside the library, and long lines snaked from each window. The beer tents were already overflowing. Giggling kids chased after one another in the grassy area in front of the library steps. Or they waited in line for the ball pit or the bounce house. Smoke from industrial-sized barbecues curled into the sky as crowds of people waited for food-service workers to dish up pulled pork and brisket and baked beans and coleslaw.

The two large video screens were mounted well above the stage, one on either side of the podium. They were blank, since the speeches had yet to start, but Clark hoped they'd soon be filled with Corey's face as Lana interviewed him live. And then the footage they'd recorded on the Jones farm.

Clark kept glancing down at Gloria, who was sitting at the tech table to the right of the stage. He knew how devastated she was about Cruz. And it had to be hard on her to be sitting down by the stage when so many people from her community were protesting up the hill, in front of city hall. He glanced up there now, watched men, women, and children march in a large circle, shouting about equal rights and brandishing signs in both Spanish and English. When the protests had begun a few weeks earlier, it was only Latinos marching. Now it was everyone. Blacks, whites, Latinos, Asians. Anyone who wanted to fight for equality.

Clark texted Gloria and Lana to make sure everything was progressing. Lana responded right away, saying she was on her way to meet with Corey. Gloria replied a minute later—she had already gained access to the feed. And no one seemed to question her claim that she was an intern working for the city. *Just say the word, and I'll make the switch.*

Clark paced back and forth. He kept glancing at the officers stationed beside him, hoping they'd take immediate action after the footage aired. Hoping they'd rush out to the Jones farm, sirens blaring, to return the innocent men to their families and friends.

A wave of nerves hit Clark twenty minutes later, when he saw a man climb up onstage and approach the microphone. The huge video screens behind him flickered to life and displayed the man's face. The plan was for Gloria to stick with the regularly scheduled programming until she got a signal from Clark. And Clark wouldn't signal Gloria until he got the signal from Lana.

He checked his phone again.

Nothing.

Where *was* Lana?

The man in the blue suit onstage welcomed everyone. Then he began listing all the special programs Mankins Corporation was initiating. The company was sponsoring youth sports leagues and tutoring centers and a brand-new children's wing at the Smallville Medical Facility. "And this is just the beginning," he bellowed into the microphone. "I'm proud to announce here today that Mankins founder and president Montgomery Wallace Mankins has just made a three-million-dollar commitment to Smallville schools. Three million, folks."

The crowd erupted in applause.

Clark imagined that if he weren't so stressed, he might be cheering, too. He thought of Bryan again. Clark hadn't seen him anywhere at the celebration yet, and he still hadn't texted Clark back.

"Yes. Yes. That's right." The man paused, smiling. "And Mr. Mankins will be here later today, just before the fireworks. Don't miss his speech about his desire for our small town to be a leader in education. He's vowed to help our community hire the best teachers. Build the best facilities. Provide the widest range of extra-curricular activities. Our schools will be among the greatest not only in Kansas but in the entire nation."

More wild applause.

Clark looked around at all the people cheering. He checked his phone, but there was still nothing from Lana, though he *did* have a text from Gloria now: *Everything okay?*

Clark started to text her back, then decided to call instead. "I still haven't heard from Lana," he said when Gloria picked up.

"Could something have happened to her?"

Clark scanned the square, thinking about Corey's reluctance to do the interview. "You know what—I'm gonna see if I can find her. Call you back in a minute."

He left his spot next to the police officers and began fighting his way through the crowd, toward the courthouse. He'd made it only a few yards, though, when he heard someone calling his name. He stopped near a food truck serving pizza slices. Paul, Tommy, and Kyle were waving at him from the line.

"Hey," Clark said, peeking at his phone again.

"Wanna go play home run derby?" Kyle said. "We need a fourth."

Tommy held up a bat with the Mankins Corporation logo branded on the side. "Me and Paul won these already, but Kyle still needs to win one."

"I wish I could," Clark said, distracted, "but I'm sort of busy. Anyway, good to see you guys."

"Hold up," Tommy said. "Where you rushing off to?"

"I'm looking for Lana."

"We just saw her," Paul said. "Over by the courthouse building. She was with three chumps. One of them was that rich dude from the party."

She *had* met up with Corey.

So why hadn't she texted, like she was supposed to?

"Speaking of the party," Paul said, "I just wanted to say, Clark . . . I was pretty tanked that night, and you stepped up—"

Paul was interrupted by the sounds of shouting in front of city hall.

Clark spun around, spotting two college-aged protesters who had broken away from the others and were pushing through the crowd, toward the speaker. They hopped the rope near the back of the crowd gathered in front of the stage and held up signs that read VOTE NO ON ISSUE 3! SMALLVILLE IS OUR HOME, TOO!

Mankins security corralled them just before they could reach the stairs to the stage, and a minor scuffle ensued. A buzz spread through the crowd as the police officers Clark had been standing beside earlier loped over to help subdue the college students.

"I had a feeling shit was gonna get out of hand," Kyle said. "You got the protesters up here and the celebration down there. We all know that's not a good mix."

Seconds later the officers were leading the students away.

"You look stressed, Clark," Tommy said. "Want us to help you find Lana?"

Clark studied the crowd again. Kyle was right—this wasn't going to end well. And it was going to mess up his plan.

"Clark?" Tommy said again.

"I'm sure I'll find her. Good running into you guys." They all bumped fists and said their goodbyes.

Clark maneuvered through the crowd again, moving toward the courthouse, until he heard feedback coming from the stage mic. He stopped to see what was happening.

The Mankins representative straightened his tie and stepped to the microphone to resume his speech. "We're okay, folks! Someone, bring those two some food! Seriously! We love everyone who's come out to celebrate with us today. . . ."

As the man went on, Clark pulled out his phone and tried reaching Lana yet again. This time his call went straight to her voice mail.

He could feel it in his gut: something was seriously wrong.

Clark put away his phone and hurried through the crowd. He cut across the wide lawn in front of city hall and the courthouse, which were separated by a narrow alley. City hall was loud and crowded with marching protesters. And police. The courthouse looked relatively quiet. There were several families on the lawn outside, but the building seemed empty.

Clark entered through the open front door and went from room to room, looking for Lana and Corey, but he found no one. A security guard approached him. "May I help you, young man?"

"I'm looking for a girl named Lana. She was coming here to interview Corey Mankins."

"An interview?" The guard shook her head. "I wasn't told anything about any interviews. You must be mistaken."

"Corey Mankins set it up. Montgomery's son."

"I'm sorry," she said. "There's nothing on the books. Unfortunately, I'm going to have to ask you to leave."

Clark was stunned. Had Corey lied to Lana? And if he'd lied to her about the interview location . . . Fear rose in Clark's throat as he turned to leave the small courthouse. On his way out, he peeked into all five rooms. None were occupied. No sign of Lana anywhere.

Outside the courthouse, he stood watching the crowd and thought, *If Lana isn't here, then where can she be?*

He peered across the square, toward the stage area, trying

to figure out what to do next. He scanned the entire area, then checked his phone again.

Nothing.

As Clark was putting away his phone, though, he spotted a small black duffel bag lying on top of an industrial trash bin. His entire body went cold.

Clark hurried over and unzipped the bag. Sure enough, the digital camera and the tripod were inside. Lana had been here—and someone had trashed her equipment. His heart pounded within his chest. He turned away from the bag and looked toward the alley. About halfway along the passageway, on the city hall side, a small staircase led down into the bowels of the building. He made a beeline for it and saw a door held open by a wooden block.

Had someone taken Lana in there?

Clark bounded down the stairs, quietly pulled open the door, and entered a long, dark corridor. He passed a large boiler room, then several empty concrete rooms. He heard the faint sound of water dripping and light footfalls in the distance. But no voices.

A few seconds later, a door creaked on its hinges in the distance. Clark moved at super-speed through the dark hall, catching the door just before it clicked closed. He held it there for several seconds, until the sound of the footsteps ahead of him had faded. Then he went through the doorway and down a short hall, where he encountered a closed red door. This was the end of the line. There were no other doors or hallways.

Clark hesitated. If he barged in and Lana got hurt, he'd never forgive himself.

But if he *didn't* barge in and Lana got hurt, it'd be just as bad.

He slid a hand under his shirt to feel the slick blue material beneath. For whatever reason, it gave him strength. And confidence.

He had to go in and save Lana.

But he also had to be smart about it.

Clark turned to the solid concrete wall beside the door. He focused all his energy on his eyes until his vision pierced through and he could see inside. Two male figures were hovering over an object strapped to some pipework near the floor. They were moving nervously, with a kind of frenetic energy.

The object they were tinkering with beeped.

Clark's heart sped up as he considered what the sound might mean.

It beeped again.

He strained to get a better look. Three long metal cylinders were strapped together with a small electrical device and a digital clock affixed to the front.

A bomb!

Clark's mind went white with panic. His X-ray vision began cutting in and out, but he was able to determine two final details. Flashing red numbers were steadily ticking down.

9:39

9:38

9:37

And a small figure was tied to the pipework with a thick chain.

Lana!

She'd be the first to die.

Clark charged forward, blasting the red door so forcefully that it split into two twisted shards of metal as it exploded away from its hinges.

The men spun around in a panic.

One of them was Corey Mankins, whose face twisted in shock.

The other was a big, muscular man with a shaved head. He was dressed in black military fatigues.

Corey quickly regained his composure. He pulled a gun from his waistband and pointed it at the back of Lana's head. "Stay where you are," he demanded, "or your little girlfriend's a goner."

Lana was slumped forward, the chain tying her to the bomb the only thing keeping her upright. Blood trickled onto the floor from a bad gash near the top of her forehead.

Corey had hit her.

He'd actually *hit* her.

Clark saw red. He wanted to kill Corey. Wanted to bash his face in and rip his limbs off his body. Clark took a steadying breath, noticing Lana's interview pad on the floor beside her. No, Lana wouldn't want him to destroy Corey. She'd want him to get the truth.

"What are you *doing*?" Clark demanded. "There are hundreds of people out there. Little *kids*!" Clark motioned toward the device strapped to Lana. "And you wanna set off a *bomb*?"

Corey shoved the barrel of the gun against Lana's head. "I told you not to move!"

"Okay, okay." Clark held up his hands. "But I don't think you want to shoot that thing in this small space. Not with an explosive nearby."

The man in fatigues lunged toward Clark, pinning his arms behind his back and looking to Corey. "What do you want to do with him?"

"Might as well tie me to the bomb, too, right?" Clark said.

Corey looked down at Lana, then back at Clark. "There *would* be a bit of symmetry to that." He nodded to the guy in fatigues while turning his weapon toward Clark.

But Clark had no intention of resisting.

8:58

8:57

8:56

"Here's what I don't understand, though," Clark said, looking at Corey. "Why sabotage your dad's grand opening like this? Are you trying to undermine him? Put Wesco on top?"

Corey grinned and placed a hand on Clark's shoulder. "We're not pointlessly harming anyone. There's something much, much larger at stake."

Clark shrugged Corey's hand away. "And how's that?"

"Sir, we need to go *now*," the man in fatigues said, motioning toward the ticking bomb.

Corey nodded before turning back to Clark. "You know, I actually sort of admire you, farm boy. Always trying to do the right thing. But you're missing the bigger picture."

"There's no bigger picture than the hundreds of innocent people out there."

"Wake up, Clark. Your beloved Smallville has *never* been anything more than a diversion to us." He patted Clark on the head, and then he and the man in fatigues moved quickly toward the exit. Corey paused on his way out to study the mangled door.

He looked back at Clark once more, with less certainty this time.

An electric current shot through Clark's body.

He'd restrained himself long enough.

He gritted his teeth and tore through the chains wrapped around his torso. Then he snapped the cuffs off his wrists and flung them against the wall.

Corey was so caught off guard that he didn't even have time to raise his weapon.

Clark lunged forward and punched the gun out of Corey's hand, then pivoted, disarming the second man with a quick swipe to the hand and wrist. He heard the crunch of bone as the gun went flying. Clark spun and slammed an open palm into Corey's chest, sending him flying backward into the cement wall, where he slumped to the ground in a motionless heap.

The man in fatigues cradled his fractured hand to his chest and spoke swiftly into his radio, calling for backup.

Clark glanced at the big gash on Lana's forehead before advancing on the man in fatigues. The guy had blood on the cuff of his shirt—maybe *he* was the one who'd hurt Lana. Clark wanted to obliterate the man. And it would be so easy. But if he acted on this impulse . . . he'd be no better than they were.

The man dropped his radio and swung wildly, just grazing the left side of Clark's face, but Clark felt more at home in a fight now. He read the man's eyes, knowing exactly what he'd do before he did it. It was in the way he leaned. Clark waited for the guy to throw a second punch, which he ducked easily. Then, using the man's momentum, Clark shoved him headfirst into a series of metal pipes running from floor to ceiling. The man's head clanged against two pipes before he dropped to the ground, unconscious.

Clark spun back toward the bomb and Lana.

7:33

7:32

7:31

He had to get her out of here. *Now.* She wouldn't be safe alone with Corey and the man in fatigues. And he knew reinforcements were already on their way.

But could he really save Lana and have enough time to save the town, too?

He'd have to move fast.

Clark pulled Lana out of the chains and tore off her handcuffs. He slung her over his shoulder and hurried out the door and into the hall. When he rounded the first corner, though, he heard the sound of boots rapidly coming down the corridor. In his direction. Maybe four or five people, by the sound of it.

Then he heard the click of ammo being loaded.

Four more men in black fatigues suddenly appeared, blocking Clark's path. One of them was carrying a handgun. But it was the fifth man, dressed in an oversized blue suit and wearing glasses, who caught Clark's attention.

Dr. Wesley.

But why would he be anywhere *near* the bomb if he'd planned this whole thing?

CHAPTER 27

Clark gently sat Lana down, preparing himself for another fight. But this was the one he'd been waiting for. Here was the man ultimately responsible for the disappearing workers. For Gloria's terror. For the blood dripping from Lana's forehead.

"You stole people from their families," Clark snarled. "That was a mistake."

Dr. Wesley shook his head in disgust. "You stupid, stupid people. Meteorites land in several of your backyards, made up of the most valuable substance this world has ever known, and what do you do? *Nothing.*"

The men behind Dr. Wesley began to spread out around Clark. The one with the gun aimed it at his left temple.

"You sent your men to *my* farm," Clark growled.

"Waste of time," Dr. Wesley scoffed. "However, many of the other craters we've mined have produced a precious radioactive ore that seemed useless at first—but after years of experimentation, I've found that it works as the perfect binding agent to better activate the other elements of my Project Dawn compound." Grinning, he held up a small vial of liquid. It was a brighter green than the substance Clark had seen in the lab. Or in the syringe Bryan had injected. "The formula I hold in my hand will change the face of mankind." Looking around, he said, "Now, where's Corey? He said he had a loose end to tie up, but we need to get out of here. *Now*."

It was the grin that made Clark snap. He lunged and shoved Dr. Wesley against the wall. The man's head cracked against the concrete, and he dropped the vial to the ground, where it shattered, the bright green liquid pooling around his shoes.

Clark was suddenly overcome by an intense wave of nausea.

He went to his knees, struggling to breathe.

The guards were moving toward Clark, and he was utterly helpless. He could feel his strength draining from his body. There was only one thing that could be causing him to feel so sick.

The mysterious green substance.

Dr. Wesley righted himself, rubbing the back of his head. "Luckily, there is more where that came from. But what's fascinating is your reaction to the increase in binding agent. Why is that?"

Clark couldn't stand as the dark shapes moved toward him. One man kicked him onto his stomach. Another brandished his gun at Clark.

Dr. Wesley pushed the barrel down with his hand, saying, "Don't be stupid. They've just armed a bomb down here."

The man put away his gun and kicked Clark instead.

And then came a barrage of kicks and punches from the others.

Clark felt each blow on his back, his neck, his shoulders and legs. The shocking pain seared through his entire body, and he let out a bloodcurdling scream. He felt like he was going to die.

By the time the beating had let up, Clark lay facedown against the cold concrete floor, hands over the back of his head. He was able to work up enough strength to turn slightly, and he saw two blurry figures approaching Lana.

"Don't touch her!" he managed to shout, but they paid him no mind.

Clark had never felt so weak or defenseless as he watched Dr. Wesley turn to the soldiers and say, "Finish him quickly." The doctor didn't spare him another look as he hurried toward the exit.

With a sinking feeling, Clark watched two of the men carry Lana back down the hallway, toward the room with the bomb. The pair who remained began to beat him with renewed energy. Blow after blow rained down on his skull as he curled into a protective ball. He took fists and boots to his ribs, his back, the side of his face.

They were going to kill him.

The punishment was relentless, and soon his mind slipped to another place. He saw the people of Smallville out in the streets, eating and drinking and laughing, oblivious to the bomb beneath their feet. One that was steadily ticking down. He saw Gloria's warm smile as he led her toward the frozen pond. His parents walking across the farm, holding hands.

And now an impossible memory . . .

His biological mother holding him in a black rocking chair. Their bodies swaying back and forth, back and forth. Tears streaming down her face. Falling onto his tiny cheeks as she bends down to kiss him over and over. And now his father lifting him out of his mother's arms, carrying Clark toward the open spaceship, strapping him into the blanketed seat.

Both of his parents' faces etched with the pain of letting him go.

They sacrificed everything so you could live.

I understand that now.

So how can you let it end here? Like this?

I can't. I won't.

Just as Clark was steeling himself for one last battle, three new figures crashed into view. They attacked Clark's assailants with bats as his mental haze finally began to dissipate.

Clark summoned enough strength to turn over, then to sit up.

It was Tommy Jones.

And Paul Molina.

And Kyle Turner.

They'd followed him into the basement.

Paul had one of the men in black fatigues in a headlock, and he was shouting, "Don't you ever touch him again! Understand me?" He slammed the man's head against the wall.

Clark rose to his feet.

The farther he got from the green substance, the better he felt.

Paul took the second man to the ground, delivering two speedy rights to the side of his head. Clark met Paul's eyes, and Paul gave a subtle nod before shifting his focus back to the fight.

Clark was still weak and vulnerable, but he had to go after Lana. He moved swiftly past his former teammates, who appeared to have the upper hand.

When he caught up to the guards, they dropped Lana and turned to face Clark. They circled each other for a few seconds, Clark trying to size up his slowly returning strength. He crouched slightly, the way he once had on the football field, then exploded toward the center of the first man, slamming his shoulder into the guy's sternum. For the first time in his life, Clark felt the impact of his blow. The force of the collision reverberated all the way into his spine and knocked the wind out of him.

But it was the man in black fatigues who got the worst of it. He crumpled to the ground, holding his chest and fighting to catch his breath. The other man abandoned Lana and sprinted past Clark, toward the exit.

Tommy was there now, rushing past Clark. He was about to go after the guard on the ground before seeing how much the man was already suffering. Tommy backed off and turned to Clark. Paul was there now, too. And Kyle.

Clark hurried to Lana and crouched over her.

"What the hell's going on?" Paul shouted. "She okay?"

Clark held Lana's face in his hands. "I don't know."

Tommy was beside him, holding two fingers against the inside of Lana's wrist. "Her pulse is strong," he said.

Clark stood with Lana draped in his arms. His best friend in the world. All his strength was back now, and he wanted to stay with her, protect her. But he needed to handle the bomb before it was too late. "Take her to get help!" he shouted at his teammates. "And tell the police to go to your farm, Tommy!"

"My farm?"

"Trust me!"

His former teammates all nodded.

They were looking to him for direction again, like freshman year.

"Who are these guys?" Tommy asked.

Clark shook his head. "Just take care of Lana. And hurry. I'll be right behind you."

Tommy and Kyle dropped their bats, took Lana from Clark, and moved quickly toward the exit.

But Paul just stood there. "I'm coming with you."

"No," Clark shouted, anxious about how quickly time was slipping away. "Your job is to convince the cops to go to Tommy's farm. There's something dangerous going on there. Please go!"

They shared a brief look, and then Paul nodded and took off after Tommy and Kyle.

Clark rushed back into the room with the bomb.

His breath caught when he saw the clock.

1:01

1:00

0:59

He looked frantically around the room. Corey and the other man were gone. All that mattered was the bomb anyway.

Clark knelt in front of the device. He had no idea how to defuse it. Melting a bomb with heat vision seemed like a bad idea. So did freezing it with his breath.

00:48

00:47

00:46

There was no solution. And no one to turn to.

All the physical strength in the world made little difference in this moment. He ripped the bomb away from the pipe and held it in his bare hands, the numbers steadily ticking down in front of him.

00:42

00:41

Clark carried the bomb out of the room.

He raced through the halls, looking for a safe place to let it detonate. He ran so fast that his collared shirt ripped, exposing a large swatch of his blue-and-red suit.

There *was* no safe room to detonate a bomb. When it went off, it would blow up the entire square. And everyone in it.

He burst out of the building and paused to scan his surroundings.

The crowd had only grown in size. Everyone was milling about and enjoying the celebration, completely unaware of the bomb ticking down.

00:31

00:30

Clark looked around wildly. There were wide-open farm pastures outside town. He could throw it in that direction. But what if a farmer was working in the barnyard? Or what if there were day laborers in the fields? He couldn't risk harming innocent people.

00:27

Panic rose in Clark's throat.

He peered up at the sky. Scattered clouds framing a sea of blue. The yellow sun glowing in the distance.

00:23

00:22

He'd tried once before and crashed through the roof of a building. It was impossible. Beyond him.

Clark glanced down at himself. The blue of his suit. The *S* emblazoned onto his heaving chest.

There was no other option.

He tucked the bomb under his arm like a football. Then he raced toward the square. When he'd gotten up enough speed, he took a leap of faith, extending one fist in front of him and rising up into the air, slowly at first, his cape flapping wildly behind him, his heart in his throat.

Clark clutched the bomb to his body as he ascended. Higher and higher. Keeping his weight back this time. His ears popping. Heart pounding. All these years he'd dreamed of flight. And here he was, soaring like a bird.

Because he had to.

Because there was no other choice.

00:11

00:10

Below he saw hundreds of people in the town square. Several looked up. Some pointed. Unaware that their lives were in his hands. But wasn't his own life in his hands as well? Because all he had thought through was getting the bomb away from the masses. Saving his community.

But now it would go off in mere seconds.

And he would go off *with* it.

00:04

00:03

Yet a strange feeling of calm had come over him. There were no more expectations or desires or confusion. He was doing what was right. Because he was no longer lost. He had been found. This was his true self.

He was free.

00:01

And he was flying.

CHAPTER 28

The blast echoed through all of Smallville.

It shook the ground below with the force of an earthquake. The brand-new Mankins facility trembled, and the large windows at the front entrance of the library shattered. People flung themselves onto the ground and covered their heads as the strange object flying overhead suddenly flashed brighter than the sun.

The boom that followed seconds later pressed stomachs to the earth and rattled teeth. The crowd peered up at a massive bloom of fire. They watched it roll across the blue sky, sending waves of intense heat in every direction.

Martha fell to her knees, shrieking.

Jonathan held her tight as they both scanned the horizon for any sign of what they had known was their son.

Others began to speculate about what they were seeing. . . .

Had a plane just exploded in midair?

A man in a strange blue-and-red suit came tumbling out of the fireball in the sky. He spun aimlessly, cape fluttering in the wind.

The crowd gasped as he fell. After several horrifying seconds, he crash-landed on a grassy field just beyond the library.

The crowd held its collective breath and moved as one toward the field. But there was no way a human could have survived such a fall.

Many looked away.

Parents held back their children.

When the dust finally cleared, the figure in the blue suit and red cape rose up out of the crater and staggered several paces before collapsing to his knees. He stared at the stunned crowd, his face hidden behind layers of scorched black soot.

Seemingly unsure of what to say or do.

Or even who he was.

Jonathan and Martha ran to the edge of the circle of onlookers that had formed around the field. Martha sagged in relief and held out her hand, stopping only when Jonathan squeezed her shoulder.

A helicopter buzzed just overhead. Few in the crowd even noticed it.

But the man in the red-and-blue suit did.

He followed the chopper's arcing flight with his gaze until it passed over the square. Then he took off running at a tremendous speed and leapt back into the sky, eliciting a chorus of gasps from the small crowd.

He thrust a fist out in front of him and flew after the forward-leaning chopper.

Kyle, Tommy, and Paul, just arriving at the scene, craned their necks and watched his impossible flight in awe.

CHAPTER 29

Clark knew exactly where the helicopter was headed.

He was thinking bigger than Smallville now. If the bomb had only been a diversion, it meant that Corey and Dr. Wesley wanted the entire community—most importantly, the police and rescue crews—to be focused on the downtown. This would free up the pair to do something on a grand scale back at the Jones farm. Clark still didn't know what they were up to, but if they were willing to blow up a mass of innocent people, it had to be something truly horrific.

As he ripped through the air toward the farm, keeping his distance from the chopper, he couldn't get the exploding bomb out of his mind. His whole body still trembled from the massive blast. His head rang like a bell.

He couldn't remember being on fire or falling out of the sky. But what mattered was that he was still alive. And when he'd stepped out of the crater and found everyone in his Smallville community staring at him in silent amazement, he understood himself on a deeper level. These special powers he possessed—they weren't for his own amusement or vanity. They were for the service of others. Even people who might shun him if they knew what he actually was.

He recalled the quote his father had once told him: "To whom much is given, of him will much be required."

But he'd also realized something else. His regular clothes had completely burned up in the sky, and his glasses had fallen off, leaving him dressed only in the indestructible suit his mom had made. Yet nobody had recognized him. It was as if all they could see was the S symbol, keeping his secret secure.

As Clark drew closer to the helicopter, he craned to see who was inside. Other than the pilot sitting up front, there were two men in black fatigues in back. Next to them, he now saw, were Corey and Dr. Wesley. When they spotted him, they moved closer to the window and stared in shock, mouths agape. Not because they recognized him as Clark. No, they were merely stunned to see someone flying alongside their helicopter, aiming to take them down.

Dr. Wesley summoned one of the guards, who opened the hatch in the side door and began firing with an assault rifle. Most of the bullets missed wildly, but a few pinged off Clark's shoulders and back, each leaving a brief, deep burning sensation. But Clark wasn't as worried about that now. He knew if he avoided the mysterious green substance that Dr. Wesley had been carrying, nothing would slow him down.

Then something else grabbed his attention.

Below he saw people in some kind of organized formation in the clearing with the strange white markings. Men with weapons stood on each spray-painted line. They all had shaved heads and wore matching brown uniforms as they marched in straight lines, like they were doing some kind of military training exercise. Several men in business suits watched from the sidelines.

Clark thought of the man in brown who'd attacked his teammates with a knife, and he thought of the guards who'd chased him and Bryan and Lex through the lab—the men who weren't "fully trained yet." Wesco was attempting to turn the men Clark had seen shackled to their chairs into some kind of enslaved army.

But why?

Who were they going to fight?

Clark put his head down and flew faster. When he drew near the descending helicopter, he finally saw who the pilot was.

Bryan.

His heart dropped.

Had Bryan been a part of the Wesco team from the beginning? Had their entire friendship been a con?

Clark zipped underneath the helicopter's broad belly and grabbed on to the landing skids. He remembered the last time he'd been in such a position, that day on his farm when he'd been trying to save Bryan and Corey and Dr. Wesley.

Now he was trying to save all of Smallville.

Clark grabbed hold of the hulking vehicle. He gritted his teeth as he strained to guide it away from the field of men and over a small hill some fifty yards away. The blades whirred loudly above him, fighting him for leverage. One of the men in black fatigues hung out the window. He fired shots directly into Clark's face, but now that all Clark's strength had returned, he instinctually dodged each bullet, contorting his body in unimaginable ways. He released his grip on the skids, repositioning himself farther back, making it impossible for the gunfire to reach him.

The shots ricocheted off the skids, spraying in all directions.

Bryan soon gave up trying to wrest away control of the chopper. Clark was too strong. Too determined. When they were only twenty or so feet above land, Clark heaved the vessel toward an empty pasture. He and the helicopter crashed to the earth at the exact same moment, Clark tumbling across the field before finally coming to rest face-first in a patch of dirt.

He leapt to his feet and bounded over to the smoking helicopter and tore off the door, flinging it aside.

First, he zeroed in on the guard with the rifle, yanking the weapon from the man's hands and bending the barrel into a U. He tossed aside the weapon, ripped a seat belt out of the floor, and quickly tied the two guards together at the wrists, back-to-back.

Bryan sat there, stunned. But Clark could tell by the look on his face that Bryan didn't recognize him, so he turned his attention to Dr. Wesley first. The man was holding several vials of the green compound that had made Clark so sick. One slipped out of the man's hands and fell to the ground. Luckily, it didn't break. Dr. Wesley didn't recognize him, of course, but Clark wasn't taking any chances this time. He pulled in a massive breath and exhaled a blast of frost that froze both the vials and Dr. Wesley's hands solid.

The man shouted in pain, cradling his body around his frozen hands.

Corey made a move for one of the rifles on a rack against the rear wall, but Clark quickly grabbed him by the shirt and pulled him back into his seat. He then tore another seat from its foundation and bent it around both Corey's torso and the first seat, pinning his arms and trapping him there.

"Lemme go, you freak!" Corey struggled desperately to free himself, but his efforts were futile.

Bryan was out of the chopper now, racing toward the crest of the hill. Clark sprinted after him, slamming into his back and taking him to the ground about twenty yards from the chopper. He sprang to his feet and stood over Bryan, who looked up at Clark with a mix of fear and astonishment.

"Bryan!" Clark barked. "Tell me you weren't in on this the whole time! Tell me you didn't help Wesco separate innocent people from their families."

Bryan climbed to his feet and stumbled backward a few steps before falling. "How do you . . . ? Is that . . . ? *Clark?*" Bryan scrambled to his feet again and slowly backed up. "You can . . . *fly?*"

Clark cursed himself for having given away his identity. He peered back at Corey and Dr. Wesley, making sure he hadn't revealed himself to the others, too. They were just out of earshot. Clark moved toward Bryan, feeling a deep sense of betrayal. He was still trying to process what he'd seen down on the field. And how it related to what he'd seen the night before. The chains. The propaganda video. The IVs.

"Clark . . . you really shouldn't be here. Trust me." Bryan's face was stuck in a kind of pained expression.

"How could you be *working* with your brother and Dr. Wesco?" Clark demanded. "You're not like them."

Corey began shouting a string of obscenities at Clark as he thrashed against the seat bent around his body. He managed to tip himself over and roll out of the helicopter, but all he succeeded in doing was falling to the ground with a loud thump. Now he lay on his side, face pinned against the dirt as he spewed dusty insults at Clark.

Dr. Wesley was fifteen feet away from him, his entire body still folded around his frozen hands, eyes wide with shock and pain.

Bryan was sucking in deep breaths as he stared at Clark. "My dad said he needed me," he said with mock conviction. "He finally believes in me, Clark. He placed me in a position of power."

"Your *dad?*" Clark was furiously trying to put all the pieces together in his head. How could Bryan be working for his dad *and* flying out to the Jones farm with Corey and Dr. Wesco?

Unless . . .

Lana had said Wesco needed a cosigner to purchase the farm.

And Clark recalled Montgomery's strange reaction when he'd asked about Project Dawn. Suddenly it all made sense. . . .

Those men out on the field in formation.

The green substance.

The propaganda film.

This was Project Dawn.

Bryan stood there, staring back at Clark, his face frozen in terror.

"What are you telling that freak?" Corey shouted from near the helicopter. "Bryan, you'd better shut up! I'm warning you!"

The Mankins Corporation had been behind this thing all along.

Bryan pointed toward the other side of the hill. "Potential clients from around the world are over there right now, Clark. They're waiting for our demonstration."

"Demonstration of *what?*" Clark shouted. "You're having them *fight* each other? After pumping them full of that green steroid?"

"Keep your mouth shut!" Corey yelled to his brother.

"What happened, Bryan?" Clark could see the vulnerability in his friend's glassy eyes. Bryan was clearly teetering. Clark had to tread lightly. "You said you wanted to be your own person."

"My dad . . ." Bryan glanced over at Corey and Dr. Wesley. "He told me we've created a tool for *peace*. He said this can . . . help end all wars."

Clark narrowed his eyes and began moving toward his friend. "Those men didn't volunteer for any of this. Whatever they're doing down there, Bryan, I'm going to stop it."

Shifty-eyed, Bryan started moving toward Corey and Dr. Wesley. "No, Clark. It's too late." From his back pocket, he pulled out a syringe. Then he sprinted over to Dr. Wesley, scooping up the vial that had tumbled to the ground. Kneeling, Bryan filled the syringe with the bright green substance and injected it with a practiced ease.

Clark was stunned by Bryan's speed.

Bryan's face contorted wildly. He chucked aside the empty vial, his muscles already beginning to twitch, and moved away from the chopper.

"Kill that thing!" Corey shouted at his brother.

"Why are you *doing* this to yourself?" Clark asked his friend. He could already feel his own body beginning to weaken. He didn't understand how or why this new substance had such a dramatic effect on him, but he felt it all the way in the marrow of his bones.

Thankfully, it wasn't quite as debilitating this time, because the substance hadn't spilled out in the open. He was able to resume moving forward.

Bryan's eyes were now inflamed. He looked like he wanted to tear out of his own skin. He gritted his teeth, let out a low, guttural growl, and charged.

Clark managed to sidestep him, but Bryan spun around more quickly than Clark had expected, and he delivered a wild right hook that slammed into Clark's ear with the force of a sledgehammer. Clark stumbled back, grabbing the side of his face. Being this close to Bryan, who had the green liquid coursing through his veins, weakened Clark even more.

But there was no alternative.

He had to fight his way through it.

Clark could see in Bryan's eyes that he was losing himself. The drug made him physically stronger, but it also changed his psychology somehow.

"I won't let you harm even one more innocent person," Clark said, moving toward Bryan again, this time with more determination.

Bryan turned to Clark, let out a savage yell, and attacked.

He led with another wild right haymaker that tagged Clark near his left temple, putting him on his back. Clark blinked hard as he saw Bryan standing over him. He was stunned by his friend's raw power. In a manner of weeks, Bryan had become a legitimate physical threat. When the men behind Bootleggers had struck Clark, their fists had broken against his skull as if he were a brick wall.

This was different.

This was going to be a real fight.

Clark leapt to his feet and stared at Bryan, who was crouching and leering with angry red eyes. Bryan charged again. They exchanged a series of frenzied, powerful blows to the body and face, then wrestled each other to the ground. Bryan ripped at Clark's hair and gnashed his teeth at Clark's ear.

"Kill him!" Corey shouted.

Clark elbowed Bryan in the gut before pulling back and headbutting him in the face.

Bryan scrambled backward, wiping a hand down his face. Chest heaving, he looked at the gobs of blood in his palm.

Clark thought this might stop him, but Bryan only grinned through bloody teeth and charged again.

This time Clark landed two quick body shots, then lunged at Bryan like a linebacker, taking him down hard. They grappled on the grass for several frantic seconds, until Clark slowly gained leverage and unleashed a flurry of body blows that left Bryan howling and begging Clark to stop.

When Clark finally backed off, gasping for breath, Bryan was curled up in the fetal position, whimpering.

Clark cursed himself and shouted, "I don't want to hurt you!" He crouched there in the grass, slowly getting back his full strength now that there was a gap between him and Bryan. His lungs opened up, and he was able to breathe again. "We have to fix this thing. Before anything else happens."

Bryan sat up, knocking himself in the side of the head with the heel of his hand, like he was trying to expel something from his brain. After a long pause, he wiped a hand down his face, smearing blood everywhere. "Those fighters will take you out in seconds. There are two dozen of them, and they're just as strong as you."

"I don't care *how* strong they are," Clark said.

Bryan leaned over and vomited. He retched and retched and then wiped his bloody face on his shirt. When he looked up at Clark, tears were welling in his bloodshot eyes. "My dad needed me," he pleaded. "He said I was the only one he could trust."

"He manipulated you," Clark said. "Just like he manipulated the rest of Smallville." Clark approached Bryan, putting his hand on his friend's trembling shoulder. It made him feel instantly weaker, but he didn't care. "Imagine all of this from above. Which side do you think is right? Which side do you want to be on? You can help me fix this."

Bryan looked up at Clark. "Why do you even *care*?" He slunk away from Clark and scrambled to his feet, motioning toward Clark's suit. "If the people in this town knew what you really are, they'd lock you away in a cage. They'd run experiments on you for the rest of your life."

"Doesn't matter," Clark said.

"You'll *never* be one of them."

"You're probably right," Clark said. He recalled the signs the protesters had carried. "But . . . Smallville's my home, too."

Bryan shook his head, looking mentally broken. Torn between two drastically different ways of seeing the world: his dad's power-hungry, Machiavellian approach, and the one closer to Bryan's own nature.

"Remember that first time we ate at All-American together?" Clark asked, sensing it was time to stop talking and start acting. "When you said you wanted to make your own path? Find your own success?"

Bryan tilted his head, wary, but listening.

Clark knew that this time he couldn't be the hero. Not with the green substance flowing in the veins of every man down on the field. But maybe Bryan could.

"This is your chance," Clark told him. "You could go talk to your dad. Stall the demonstration until the police get here."

Bryan wheezed. "He'd *never* listen to me." He coughed up blood and spit, staring at the ground for a few long seconds. Then he glanced over at his brother and Dr. Wesley before turning back to Clark. "Wesley developed a substance that reverses the effect of the Project Dawn compound. They prepared it for today in case anything went wrong. But it's in Structure A, which is heavily guarded."

Clark looked toward the field. "How would the fighters have to take it?" he asked. "From a syringe?"

Bryan shook his head. "It can be inhaled. They made the antidote even stronger than the compound itself. For safety reasons."

Clark considered this. He turned to study the helicopter. "Where's Structure A?" he asked, turning back to Bryan.

"It's the smaller of the two buildings down . . ." Bryan's eyes widened when he realized why Clark was asking. "You'd never make it out alive. Even if you did, there's no way you could actually get it to each of those men before they killed you."

"Not alone, I can't," Clark said. "If I'm going to pull this off, Bryan, I'll need your piloting skills."

"Those fighters will be on you the second you walk down the hill. My dad would probably welcome the chance to show off how much control he has over his army."

"There's no choice—"

"*I'll* go," Bryan interrupted.

Confused, Clark looked at his injured friend. "You said your dad would never listen to you."

But Bryan didn't seem to hear Clark. He was looking toward the crest of the hill now. "The fighters will assume I'm still on their side."

Clark studied Bryan and could tell the substance still had a hold on him. "*Are* you on their side?" he asked.

Now it was Bryan who was studying Clark.

There was a long silence between them, and finally Bryan lowered his eyes. "I think I've always been searching for his approval. Secretly. And this time . . . I thought I actually had it." Bryan stood up. "I'll go."

Clark wasn't sure if he could trust Bryan. But at this point he didn't really have a choice.

He moved toward his friend, but Bryan waved him back.

Bryan began to say something else to Clark, but then he closed his mouth and started toward the edge of the hill instead.

CHAPTER 30

After Bryan disappeared from view, Clark walked over to the helicopter, where Corey was still pinned to the ground, cursing him. "My father's going to destroy you, freak!" Clark ignored him and climbed on top of the helicopter, making sure the blades were in working order. He checked the windshield and the cockpit, too, then climbed back down and went to where Dr. Wesley sat on the ground, rubbing his hands against his legs, trying to thaw them out.

"You're going to spend the rest of your life behind bars," Clark told the man.

Dr. Wesley looked up at him, emotionless. "You don't know what you're talking about. Montgomery and I are going to change the world."

Clark was desperately trying to keep his rage in check. "Those are actual human beings down there. They're not pawns for your experiments."

"Sentimentality is a weakness," the man said in an even voice. "The leaders of great empires don't waste their time worrying about perception. They do what is necessary to win. To increase their power. The highest bidder down there will be able to turn his immigrants, his refugees and homeless and indigent populations, into a powerful army that will heed every command. Their physical abilities will be a dozen times greater than that of a normal soldier. And they will fight to the death."

Clark started to respond, but Dr. Wesley immediately cut him off. "I already know your counter. 'But it's wrong. It's immoral.' Well, what do you think we've been doing since the founding of this nation? Answer me that. Remember, it's the winner who gets to frame history."

Clark stood there, fuming.

"Try to see it rationally," Dr. Wesley went on. "These men . . . they've come here to make a better life, right? Well, we're giving them purpose. Meaning."

Clark realized he didn't *need* to put his thoughts into words.

He went over and helped the man to his feet. And the second Wesley opened his mouth to say something else, Clark cracked him right in the jaw.

The man crumpled to the ground and went quiet.

Clark then turned to Corey, who'd been watching the whole exchange.

But he was quiet now, too. So Clark left him alone and went to the other side of the chopper to sit by himself and wait.

When Bryan had been gone for nearly ten minutes, Clark started to get nervous. He wondered if his friend had betrayed him after all.

A few minutes later he heard the sound of synchronized footsteps over the hill. The troops were on the move.

Clark rushed over to the crest and watched dozens of soldiers moving in his direction. They were dressed entirely in brown, machine guns by their sides. They all stared straight ahead as they marched in perfect unison.

He froze.

How was he supposed to fight people he couldn't bear to harm?

Clark crouched, locating Structure A.

It was positioned directly between him and the troops, but there was no sign of Bryan anywhere. His stomach sank. He really had been betrayed.

Instead of waiting there like a sitting duck, Clark decided to plunge right into the fray and try to retrieve the antidote himself. Maybe it was a suicide mission, but he had to do something. He had to act.

He took a deep breath, then sprinted down the hill several yards before taking flight. As he soared into the air, he heard Montgomery shout orders through a megaphone, and he watched the first row of soldiers raise their guns at him and begin firing. To his horror, Clark realized that one of them was Cruz. He was as tall as the soldiers around him, but far scrawnier, his uniform draping off his skinny frame. Clark's whole body went numb as he watched Cruz discharge his weapon without remorse.

Heartbroken, Clark retreated higher into the sky to rethink his strategy.

And from this new perspective, he realized something.

He had assumed that Montgomery had ordered the soldiers to shoot at him, but now he saw that he was mistaken. Because here was Bryan, speeding up the hill in a jeep under a barrage of gunfire.

Montgomery had ordered them to shoot at *Bryan*.

His own son.

Clark swooped back down just as Bryan's jeep skidded to a stop beyond the crest of the hill. There was shouting below, and more shooting, as the line of fighters in their brown uniforms continued to advance.

Bryan threw open his door and called to Clark, "What now?"

"The helicopter!" Clark grabbed a large plastic jug out of the back of the jeep and hurried toward the chopper. He set the jug inside the cab. "What *happened?*"

"My dad saw me going for Structure A!" Bryan shouted. "And he knew!" He hopped into the cockpit, trying to catch his breath, and turned the key. The engine roared back to life, and the blades above them began to turn.

Clark spotted blood trickling down Bryan's forearm. "You're hit!"

Bryan shook his head. "It barely grazed me. Come on!"

Clark hoisted the jug onto his lap. It had to contain at least three gallons of the liquid antidote. He peered through the back window and saw that the soldiers were now coming up over the crest, weapons drawn. "Can you fly over the top of them?"

Bryan quickly lifted the helicopter into the air, spun it around, and started moving forward, directly toward the soldiers in brown, who all raised their weapons at once and began to fire.

An onslaught of bullets peppered the bottom of the helicopter as Bryan made a pass over their heads. Shots pinged against the metal floor and the siding and punched into the belly. Several holes appeared beneath Clark's feet as he unscrewed the plastic lid and attempted to pour a small portion of the sloshing antidote onto the men below. But he stopped immediately when the wind caught the liquid, carrying it into the side of the helicopter.

This wasn't going to work.

Bryan adjusted the controls, and the helicopter lurched higher.

"Bring it down again!" Clark yelled over the hum of the whipping blades. "I'm going to try going underneath!"

As Bryan looped around, preparing for a second pass, Clark watched his friend's fingers move gracefully over the control panel. A look of calmness had settled on his face. This was where Bryan belonged. This was where he was at home.

Clark climbed beneath the helicopter with the antidote. He clung to the lone remaining landing skid, preparing himself to splash it over the soldiers' heads.

As they approached the men again, this time at a lower altitude, Clark saw several police cars pulling into the field in the distance. And he saw some of the men in business suits fleeing in large black SUVs. At the very least, he'd led the cops to the scene of the crime. But what if Montgomery turned his soldiers on the cops? They'd fire back. They wouldn't know any better. And how many innocent people would get hurt?

This had to work.

The soldiers were now kneeling on the crest of the hill, leveling their weapons at the quickly approaching chopper, eyes trained on their target.

Bryan flew right over their heads this time.

Directly into the line of fire.

Bullets seared into Clark's back as he attempted to dump more of the antidote onto the brainwashed men. He saw the spray rain down on one of the men, who dropped his weapon immediately and sat on the grass. Then another man let go of his weapon. But the yellow liquid came out haphazardly. It touched only four of the men, and one continued to discharge his weapon. The other three soldiers had gone to the ground, clearly confused, while the soldiers around them fired at Clark and the battered helicopter.

This wasn't going to work either.

The chopper was already badly damaged, and Clark worried about Bryan. He still had about 90 percent of the liquid left. Their only hope was to somehow create a mist that would rain down on all the men at once.

But how?

As Bryan lifted the helicopter into the sky, Clark climbed up the side and looked around for some kind of tool he might be able to use. But there was nothing.

He studied Bryan. "You okay?"

Bryan didn't take his eyes off the battered windshield in front of him. "We have to go again, Clark!" he called over the roar of the helicopter.

"You're hurt!" Clark pointed at Bryan's jeans, the right side streaked with blood.

"Please, Clark!" Bryan spun to face him. "I have to do this. I can see that now."

Clark crouched there, frozen. Bryan had obviously been hit. More than once, by the look of it. He needed medical help. Now. But Clark also saw the conviction in his friend's eyes.

"One more pass!" Clark shouted. "If this one doesn't work, I'll try something else!"

Bryan quickly spun the machine around. "Clark!" he called, without making eye contact. "I'm sorry!"

Clark could feel Bryan's words land deep inside his chest. "Me too," he whispered. He wanted to say something more, but there was no time. Instead, he hauled himself and the antidote up onto the side of the helicopter, his head only inches from the violently whipping blades. The soldiers knelt on the crest of the hill, readying themselves for another barrage of gunfire.

Clark didn't know how much more damage the chopper could withstand. There were bullet holes in the bottom of the fuselage, as well as in both sides. The driveshaft was smoking, and the tail boom was slightly askew. The front windshield was so badly spider-webbed that he wondered if Bryan could even see where he was flying.

"Ready?" Bryan shouted up to him.

"Ready!" Clark responded. He took a deep breath, and glanced up at the whipping blades.

He knew he only had one shot at this. If it failed, it was over. And he didn't know what would come next.

He couldn't think that far ahead.

As soon as the chopper neared, the men in brown began to fire, and this time the barrage was relentless. Clark waited until the last possible second before heaving the entire plastic container up toward the spinning blades.

Time slowed to a crawl as soon as the antidote left Clark's hands, his brain registering several small details. . . .

The men beneath them, angling their weapons up toward the struggling chopper. The subtle kickback of their weapons after every shot fired.

Bullets punching into his legs and side like firebrands.

The plastic jug colliding with the whipping blades, exploding into a million little pieces, creating a great yellow mist that rained down on everyone and everything below.

Bryan lifted the battered helicopter up into the air, and Clark leaned over the side, watching in awe. Dozens of men stopped firing at once. They dropped their weapons in bewilderment and stood around looking at one another.

The air was thick with the antidote, but in seconds the cloud dissipated, revealing the ground below, coated in yellow, as if the soldiers were kneeling in a field of bright yellow marigolds.

Clark was about to climb back into the cockpit of the helicopter to check on Bryan, when he spotted Montgomery jumping into one of the large trucks, trying to escape the cops who had him surrounded. They aimed their weapons at the vehicle as Montgomery sped directly at two police cruisers parked sideways. Bullets pierced the truck's windshield, but Montgomery managed to crash through the small gap between the cruisers and sped down the old country road.

Clark dropped off the top of the helicopter and extended his right arm outward, zipping through the air as everyone below looked up, audibly gasping. He crashed through tree limbs on his descent and flew to the driver's-side window of the truck. When Montgomery spotted him, he panicked, cranking the steering wheel to the right, and crashed right into a tree. The front of the vehicle folded in on itself and the airbags deployed, trapping a bloody-faced Montgomery in his seat as the car alarm blared.

Two police cruisers screeched to a stop beside the truck. Officers flung open their doors and yanked Montgomery out of the cab and onto the ground, where they cuffed him on the spot.

Clark looked up and saw Bryan's helicopter now hurtling out of the sky.

He sprinted a short stretch before taking flight again. With a desperate lunge, he made it to the battered helicopter just before it crashed. This time Clark didn't even bother with the chopper itself. He yanked Bryan out the side door seconds before the machine hit the ground at a tremendous speed. It exploded on impact.

The plume of fire that rose from the crash site caused Clark to tumble in the air while he clutched Bryan's limp body in his arms. When Clark finally regained control, he saw several slick swatches of blood oozing through his friend's shirt.

He'd taken two bullets in the chest.

One in the stomach.

Clark hurried to the ground, laying Bryan down gently on a pale yellow patch of dirt. He immediately started CPR, pumping Bryan's chest desperately. He pinched his friend's nose and breathed into his mouth. Clark repeated this process again and again and again, his own heart racing, bile rising up into his throat.

But there was no pulse in Bryan's limp body.

No breath in his lungs.

After several minutes Clark set down Bryan's limp head and covered his own face with his hands and rocked back and forth, back and forth, trying to make sense of what was happening.

How could Bryan be gone?

He was just flying the helicopter.

He was just asking Clark to make one more pass.

Clark's chest closed in on itself, and a kind of paralysis spread through his veins.

All his life he'd longed to feel the way everyone else around him seemed to feel. But now it came crashing down on him at once, and it was utterly debilitating. He peered down at his friend's slack face, his eyes open but devoid of life, and suddenly Clark was struck by the precariousness of this world. How quickly a life could end. Even Clark's speed had not been enough to stop Death. Sadness filled his chest with a weight so heavy that it felt like he was sinking into the earth below him.

A swarm of police cars and black SUVs were now pulling up in front of Clark. Men and women in blue FBI jackets were stepping out of open doors and starting toward him.

Clark gently lowered Bryan's eyelids and looked toward the hill, where the men in brown were now standing in the yellow field.

They were going back to their families because of Bryan.

Cruz was going home to Carlos because of Bryan.

Across the field, Clark saw Lex get out of one of the back seats, gripping his handheld satellite device and pointing up the hill to where Corey and Dr. Wesley were. Several federal agents set off in that direction on foot.

The two nearest federal agents raised their weapons at Clark.

He reluctantly pulled away from Bryan's side and stood, holding up his hands. "Leave the men in brown alone," he said. "They've all been drugged and brainwashed by the Mankins Corporation."

A woman in an FBI jacket stepped forward, motioning for her agents to lower their weapons. "Just stay where you are," she said, cautiously approaching. "We need to ask you a few questions."

A group of paramedics hurried toward Bryan with a stretcher. Clark watched them drop next to his friend's motionless body and begin testing for vital signs.

Down by the road Montgomery was being pushed into the back of a police cruiser.

One of the agents came closer to Clark, an uncertain look on his face. "Who . . . *are* you?" he asked.

Clark looked up at the man and shook his head. "I'm nobody," he said.

Then he rocketed back up into the sky.

Everyone on the field stopped what they were doing to look up.

They craned their necks to watch him shoot straight into the atmosphere. Even after he was nothing more than a tiny black dot among the distant clouds, they were still watching.

CHAPTER 31

"Can you believe this?" Lana shouted as they walked through the crowded school hall. She held up the newspaper again, shoving it right in Clark's face this time. "Front-page story in the *Daily Planet*. By some junior reporter who just happened to be in Smallville covering the Mankins launch event. This was supposed to be *my* story, Clark!"

He pushed up his glasses. "I'm sorry," he told her, glancing at the headline now circulating in newspapers and online articles all across the country:

A SUPERMAN SAVES THOUSANDS AMID MANKINS SCANDAL

By Lois Lane

Under the headline was a huge color photo of Clark in his suit. His face was turned away from the camera, but his family crest was clearly visible on his chest, his cape billowing behind him.

It turned out that no cameras had been able to capture his

face that day. In nearly every photo that surfaced in the aftermath, Clark's face either was turned away or was nothing but a grainy, blurry smudge. Even in the one image taken straight on, no one seemed to see Clark.

It was Monday, and everyone, including the teachers, was buzzing about Superman.

"You're still in high school," Clark told his best friend as they stopped at the top of the steps outside. "Your time will come."

"Of course they made it all about Superman," she said. "That's the sensational angle, right?" She reached for his arm. "But Paul told me what you did for me, Clark. Thank you. I would have included that part in the story, too."

"It's okay," Clark said, stifling a grin.

"There's actually a lot of stuff I would have put in the article," Lana said, lowering her voice as a group of freshmen walked past them.

"Like what?" Clark asked.

"Well, for one thing, *officially* the strange chemicals that the Mankins Corporation had been developing were recovered from the company's various facilities," Lana said. "And are now in the possession of *proper* authorities."

"But unofficially?" Clark asked.

She shook her head and looked around to make sure no one else was listening. "From what I heard, LuthorCorp bought out what was left of the Mankins Corporation immediately. Rumor has it they obtained some files that had yet to be recovered by authorities. Protected by some obscure trade law."

Clark nodded. "Why am I not surprised?"

"But I think it goes beyond Lex having ulterior motives," Lana said. "Apparently, his father sent him out here to investigate Project

Dawn. He knew Mankins was behind it all along. And now that LutherCorp has the Project Dawn files, who knows what they'll do with them. I wouldn't put it past them to make a deal with a dictator."

Clark shook his head. "I definitely don't think we've seen the last of Project Dawn. Lex and his dad are smarter, too. Which makes it even more dangerous."

They both went quiet for a few seconds, Clark realizing there would always be another evil to contend with.

"But I don't want to dwell on that right now," Lana said. "What matters is that the soldiers all lived. Thanks to Bryan and Superman." Lana shook her head. "Not that the *Planet* disclosed exactly how. They kept that part weirdly vague."

"So that's what everyone's calling him, then?" Clark asked. "Superman?"

"I guess so," Lana said, clearly irritated. "I would have come up with something much better."

"I just wish they'd highlighted Bryan more," Clark said. "He was the real hero that day."

Lana squeezed his wrist. "Losing Bryan was hard."

Clark nodded, looking at the floor. It killed him that he couldn't scream from a mountaintop about the tremendous sacrifice Bryan had made for Smallville. But, of course, Clark wasn't supposed to have been there, witnessing Bryan's death. Unable to save his friend. "I keep expecting him to text me," Clark said, meeting eyes with Lana. "You know, to go get food at All-American or something."

Lana nodded and squeezed Clark's hand again as a bunch of other Smallville High students moved past them, toward the parking lot.

"We'd better go, Clark." Lana pointed to her watch. "We don't want to miss the march of the scumbags."

They continued to her car and drove downtown, where they were just in time for the march. From the back seat Clark grabbed the poster he and Lana had made the night before in the library. When they arrived at the courthouse steps, there was a swarm of people out front. A handful of reporters fought their way to the front of the anti-Mankins protesters. This time there were as many white people protesting as Mexicans. Everyone in Smallville had seemingly come together to denounce the Mankins Corporation.

Cameras flashed as Montgomery Mankins was led out of the building in handcuffs. Reporters shouted questions, but he ignored them all. He held his head high, trying to hold on to his air of authority and dignity even in the face of defeat. But it was impossible. The man would never see another day outside jail. And that, Clark reasoned, was justice.

As Montgomery neared, Clark and Lana unfolded the poster and held it up over their heads. The man slowed to read the message as he walked past Clark and Lana. FOR BRYAN. Montgomery paled as he made eye contact with them before being pushed along by Deputy Rogers.

Lana turned to Clark as he folded their poster. "It's pretty satisfying to see the once-mighty fall."

Clark stared up into the clouds. "If only it could bring Bryan back somehow."

Lana nodded. The two of them turned to watch Montgomery be loaded into a police van, then started back to Lana's car.

* * *

They made it back to school just in time for their final class with Mrs. Sovak. Clark shifted uncomfortably in his creaky wooden seat, trying to focus on her lecture. Instead of a final this semester, she simply wanted to talk about current events. But unlike all Clark's other teachers, who wanted to talk about Superman and the Mankins Corporation, Mrs. Sovak wanted to discuss immigration. "As you know, several community members and I have been pounding the pavement, collecting signatures to try and kill the stop-and-search issue before it even goes to a vote. Well, I'm thrilled to announce we ended up with more than twice as many signatures as we needed. It has officially been dismissed as of two o'clock this afternoon."

Clark cheered wildly with the rest of his classmates. He knew racism was a much deeper problem than this one battle. But it made him happy that Smallville had landed on the right side of history in this case.

As the clapping slowed, Clark's focus drifted to the sounds all around school. Now it was easier for him to direct his attention. Ever since Clark had begun wearing the suit under his clothes, he could control his powers better than ever. He'd decided to put it on every morning, beneath his regular clothes.

Just in case.

A girl near the back of class was whispering to a friend: "I just wish I knew who it was. I mean, how can he *fly* like that?"

Out in the hallway, a student walked by, retelling the story of what he'd seen that weekend to a buddy on the phone. He made swooshing and swooping noises to mimic Superman's flying.

All the way across campus, Clark heard Moira DeMeyer, Lana's ex-friend, claiming that Lana was actually *dating* Superman. There was one particular sound that he kept coming back to, though. In a distant room on campus, a girl was laughing.

He'd recognize the sound of Gloria Alvarez's laugh anywhere.

As soon as class was over, he hurried out of the room and found her sitting next to Counselor Julius on the steps of the school's back entrance. Gloria was looking up at him, her face filled with joy.

When she spotted Clark, she called him over.

"What is it?" he asked. "What's so funny?"

She handed him a letter.

It was a college scholarship offer. Metropolis University had offered her a Dreamer spot beginning next fall. One of the top schools in the Midwest, if not the whole country.

Gloria stood and gave Clark a kiss on the cheek. "I'm actually going to college," she told him. "Can you believe it?"

"I can," he said. Then he gave her a big hug, whispering in her ear, "I'm so incredibly happy for you, Gloria."

"Thank you," she told him. "Maybe you can help me move in September?"

"I'd love to."

"Come on," she said. "Let's go celebrate. I'm meeting Marco and some friends at All-American. They'd love to see you."

"Sounds great," Clark said.

They began walking the few blocks to the All-American Diner. Gloria was beaming, unable to let go of the letter. She kept reading it to Clark over and over again. Like she needed to make sure it was real. They talked about what she might study, and how excited she was to go back to Metropolis.

But as they neared All-American, Clark heard something else.

It was the steady whine of a failing airplane engine. He heard it approach the area at thirty thousand feet. Pass overhead and then start to fade in the distance.

Then the sounds of the engines were suddenly gone.

Clark strained to hear them, but there was nothing.

Instead, he heard a man's faint voice. "Mayday! We are declaring an emergency. NationAir Five-Zero-Two. Repeat, full engine loss at thirty thousand feet."

A strained robotic voice in the background repeated an emergency cockpit message over and over: "*Pull up. Pull up. Pull up. Pull up. Pull up.*"

Other cockpit sirens and alarms wailed. The noise became so clear, Clark felt like he was with them inside the cockpit.

Clark turned to Gloria. "Listen, I have to . . ." Clark couldn't figure out what to say. "I'll catch up with you guys in a sec, okay? I promise. But first there's something I have to take care of."

Gloria looked confused but eventually smiled. "Of course, Clark," she said. "Do what you gotta do. We'll see you when we see you."

He nodded and jogged away behind a building.

Ducking behind a dumpster in an alley, he tore open his button-down shirt and quickly shed his regular Clark Kent clothes and glasses. Leaping into the air in a blue-and-red blur, he soared toward the falling airplane. Now nearly two hundred miles away. And descending rapidly.

His blue-and-red suit seemed to sparkle and shimmer so close to the sun. The bright red cape billowed behind him. The family emblem on his chest practically glowed, reminding him of who he was and why he needed to drop everything to save this crashing airplane.

And why he always would.

After all, he was more than just Clark Kent.

More than Kal-El, son of Jor-El, from the planet Krypton.

He was Superman.

ACKNOWLEDGMENTS

I'd like to thank the following people who helped make this book possible. First off, a huge debt of gratitude goes out to the entire DC/Warner Bros. team for letting me dip a toe into the incredible Superman legacy. This was truly an honor! Thank you to the talented and tireless editorial team at Random House, especially Chelsea Eberly (you were incredible!), Michelle Nagler, and Jenna Lettice. Thanks to Chris Rylander, who was instrumental in the early part of this process. I'd like to thank so many other folks at Random House who played vital roles in this process: designers Regina Flath and Stephanie Moss; copyeditor Barbara Bakowski; the marketing team, including Lauren Adams, Tara Grieco, Kerri Benvenuto, Elizabeth Ward, Hanna Lee, Kate Keating, Kristin Schulz, and Mallory Matney; publicist Aisha Cloud; Tim Terhune in production; and the entire Random House sales team. I'd also like to thank Afua Richardson for creating such a beautiful Superman poster and Steven Malk for being the best agent a writer could ask for. And most importantly, I want to thank my wife, Caroline, and our two little people, Luna and Miguel. You all are *my* superheroes.

MATT DE LA PEÑA is a #1 *New York Times* bestselling and Newbery Medal–winning author. He has penned six critically acclaimed YA novels, including *Mexican WhiteBoy* and *The Living*, a Pura Belpré Author Honor Book. Matt's picture book *Love* was a #1 *New York Times* bestseller, and *Last Stop on Market Street* was awarded a Newbery Medal. Matt received an MFA in creative writing from San Diego State University and a BA from the University of the Pacific, which he attended on a full basketball scholarship. Matt lives in Brooklyn, New York.

mattdelapena.com
🐦 @mattdelapena

THE NIGHTWALKERS
ARE HUNTING GOTHAM CITY'S ELITE.
BRUCE WAYNE IS NEXT ON THEIR LIST.

#1 *New York Times* Bestselling Author of *Legend* and *The Young Elites*

MARIE LU

DC ICONS
BATMAN
NIGHTWALKER

TURN THE PAGE TO SEE HOW
BRUCE'S ADVENTURE BEGINS
IN THE BESTELLING DC ICONS SERIES!

As Bruce rounded another bend, the wails suddenly turned deafening, and a mass of flashing red and blue lights blinked against the buildings near the end of the street. White barricades and yellow police tape completely blocked the intersection. Even from here, Bruce could see fire engines and black SWAT trucks clustered together, the silhouettes of police running back and forth in front of the headlights.

Inside his car, the electronic voice came on again, followed by a transparent map overlaid against his windshield. *"Heavy police activity ahead. Alternate route suggested."*

A sense of dread filled his chest.

Bruce flicked away the map and pulled to an abrupt halt in front of the barricade—right as the unmistakable *pop-pop-pop* of gunfire rang out in the night air.

He remembered the sound all too well. The memory of his parents' deaths sent a wave of dizziness through him. *Another robbery. A murder. That's what all this is.*

Then he shook his head. *No, that can't be right.* There were far too many cops here for a simple robbery.

"Step *out* of your vehicle, and put your hands in the air!" a police officer shouted through a megaphone, her voice echoing along the block. Bruce's head jerked toward her. For an instant, he thought her command was directed at him, but then he saw that her back was turned, her attention fixed on the corner of the building bearing the name BELLINGHAM INDUSTRIES & CO. "We have you surrounded, Nightwalker! This is your final warning!"

Another officer came running over to Bruce's car. He whirled an arm exaggeratedly for Bruce to turn his car around. His voice harsh with panic, he warned, "Turn back *now*. It's not safe!"

Before Bruce could reply, a blinding fireball exploded behind the officer. The street rocked.

Even from inside his car, Bruce felt the heat of the blast. Every window in the building burst simultaneously, a million shards of glass raining down on the pavement below. The police ducked in unison, their arms shielding their heads. Fragments of glass dinged like hail against Bruce's windshield.

From inside the blockade, a white car veered around the corner at top speed. Bruce saw immediately what the car was aiming for—a slim gap between the police barricades where a SWAT team truck had just pulled through.

The car raced right toward the gap.

"I said, *get out of here*!" the officer shouted at Bruce. A thin ribbon of blood trickled down the man's face. "That is an *order*!"

Bruce heard the scream of the getaway car's tires against the asphalt. He'd been in his father's garage a thousand times, helping him tinker with an endless number of engines from the best cars in the world. At WayneTech, Bruce had watched in fascination as tests were conducted on custom engines, conceptual jets, stealth tech, new vehicles of every kind.

And so he knew: whatever was installed under that hood was faster than anything the GCPD could hope to have.

They'll never catch him.

But I can.

His Aston Martin was probably the only vehicle here that

could overtake the criminal's, the only one powerful enough to chase it down. Bruce's eyes followed the path the car would likely take, his gaze settling on a sign at the end of the street that pointed toward the freeway.

I can get him.

The white getaway vehicle shot straight through the gap in the barricade, clipping two police cars as it went.

No, not this time. Bruce slammed his gas pedal.

The Aston Martin's engine let out a deafening roar, and the car sped forward. The officer who'd shouted at him stumbled back. In the rearview mirror, Bruce saw him scramble to his feet and wave the other officers' cars forward, both his arms held high.

"Hold your fire!" Bruce could hear him yelling. "Civilian in proximity—*hold your fire!*"

The getaway car made a sharp turn at the first intersection, and Bruce sped behind it a few seconds later. The street zigzagged, then turned in a wide arc as it led toward the freeway—and the Nightwalker took the on-ramp, leaving a trail of exhaust and two black skid marks on the road.

Bruce raced forward in close pursuit; his car mapped the ground instantly, swerving in a perfect curve to follow the ramp onto the freeway. He tapped twice on the windshield right over where the Nightwalker's white vehicle was.

"Follow him," Bruce commanded.

SELINA KYLE IS CATWOMAN.

TIME TO SEE HOW MANY LIVES

THIS CAT REALLY HAS.

DON'T MISS THIS NEW DC ICONS STORY FROM

#1 *NEW YORK TIMES* BESTSELLING AUTHOR

SARAH J. MAAS!

CHAPTER 1

The roaring crowd in the makeshift arena didn't set her blood on fire.

It did not shake her, or rile her, or set her hopping from foot to foot. No, Selina Kyle only rolled her shoulders—once, twice.

And waited.

The wild cheering that barreled down the grimy hallway to the prep room was little more than a distant rumble of thunder. A storm, just like the one that had rolled over the East End on her walk from the apartment complex. She'd been soaked before she reached the covert subway entrance that led into the underground gaming warren owned by Carmine Falcone, the latest of Gotham City's endless parade of mob bosses.

But like any other storm, this fight, too, would be weathered.

Rain still drying in her long, dark hair, Selina checked that it was indeed tucked into its tight bun atop her head. She'd made the mistake once of wearing a ponytail—in her second street fight. The other girl had managed to grab it, and those few seconds when Selina's neck had been exposed had lasted longer than any in her life.

But she'd won—barely. And she'd learned. Had learned at every fight since, whether on the streets above or in the arena carved into the sewers beneath Gotham City.

It didn't matter who her opponent was tonight. The challengers were all usually variations of the same: desperate men who owed more than they could repay to Falcone. Fools willing to risk their lives for a chance to lift their debts by taking on one of his Leopards in the ring. The prize: never having to look over their shoulders for a waiting shadow. The cost of failing: having their asses handed to them—and the debts remained. Usually with the promise of a one-way ticket to the bottom of the Sprang River. The odds of winning: slim to none.

Regardless of whatever sad sack she'd be battling tonight, Selina prayed Falcone would give her the nod faster than last time. That fight . . . He'd made her keep that particularly brutal match going. The crowd had been too excited, too ready to spend money on the cheap alcohol and everything else for sale in the subterranean warren. She'd taken home more bruises than usual, and the man she'd beaten to unconsciousness . . .

Not her problem, she told herself again and again. Even when she saw her adversaries' bloodied faces in her dreams, both asleep and waking. What Falcone did with them after the fight was not her problem. She left her opponents breathing. At least she had that.

And at least she wasn't dumb enough to push back outright, like some of the other Leopards. The ones who were too proud or too stupid or too young to get how the game was played. No, her small rebellions against Carmine Falcone were subtler. He wanted men dead—she left them unconscious, but did it so well that not one person in the crowd objected.

A fine line to walk, especially with her sister's life hanging in the balance. Push back too much, and Falcone might ask questions, start wondering who meant the most to her. Where to strike hardest. She'd never allow it to get to that point. Never risk Maggie's safety like that—even if these fights were all for her. Every one of them.

It had been three years since Selina had joined the Leopards, and nearly two and a half since she'd proved herself against the other girl gangs well enough that Mika, her Alpha, had introduced her to Falcone. Selina hadn't dared miss that meeting.

Order in the girl gangs was simple: The Alpha of each gang ruled and protected, laid down punishment and reward. The Alphas' commands were law. And the enforcers of those commands were their Seconds and Thirds. From there, the pecking order turned murkier. Fighting offered a way to rise in the ranks—or you could fall, depending on how badly a match went. Even an Alpha might be challenged if you were stupid or brave enough to do so.

But the thought of ascending the ranks had been far from Selina's mind when Mika had brought Falcone over to watch her take on the Second of the Wolf Pack and leave the girl leaking blood onto the concrete of the alley. Before that fight, only four leopard spots had been inked onto Selina's left arm, each a trophy of a fight won.

Selina adjusted the hem of her white tank. At seventeen, she now had twenty-seven spots inked across both arms.

Undefeated.

That's what the match emcee was declaring down the hall. Selina could just make out the croon of words: *The undefeated champion, the fiercest of Leopards . . .*

A thump on the metal door was her signal to go. Selina checked her shirt, her black spandex pants, the green sneakers that matched her eyes—though no one had ever commented on it. She flexed her fingers within their wrappings. All good.

Or as good as could be.

The rusty door groaned as she opened it. Mika was tending to the new girl in the hall beyond, the flickering fluorescent lights draining the Alpha's golden-brown skin of its usual glow.

Mika threw Selina an assessing look over her narrow shoulder, her tight braid shifting with the movement. The new girl sniffling in front of her gingerly wiped away the blood streaming from her swollen nose. One of the kitten's eyes was already puffy and red, the other swimming with unshed tears.

No wonder the crowd was riled. If a Leopard had taken that bad a beating, it must have been one hell of a fight. Brutal enough that Mika put a hand on the girl's pale arm to keep her from swaying.

Down the shadowy hall that led into the arena, one of Falcone's bouncers beckoned. Selina shut the door behind her. She'd left no valuables behind. She had nothing worth stealing, anyway.

"Be careful," Mika said as she passed, her voice low and soft. "He's got a worse batch than usual tonight." The kitten hissed, yanking her head away as Mika dabbed her split lip with a disinfectant wipe. Mika snarled a warning at her, and the kitten wisely fell still, trembling a bit as the Alpha cleaned out the cut. Mika added without glancing back, "He saved the best for you. Sorry."

"He always does," Selina said coolly, even as her stomach roiled. "I can handle it."

She didn't have any other choice. Losing would leave Maggie with no one to look after her. And refusing to fight? Not an option, either.

In the three years that Selina had known Mika, the Alpha had never suggested ending their arrangement with Carmine Falcone. Not when having Falcone back the Leopards made the other East End gangs think twice about pushing in on their territory. Even if it meant doing these fights and offering up Leopards for the crowd's enjoyment.

Falcone turned it into a weekly spectacle—a veritable Roman circus to make the underbelly of Gotham City love *and* fear him. It certainly helped that many of the other notorious lowlifes had been imprisoned thanks to a certain do-gooder running around the city in a cape.

Mika eased the kitten to the prep room, giving Selina a jerk of the chin—an order to go.

But Selina paused to scan the hall, the exits. Even down here, in the heart of Falcone's territory, it was a death wish to be defenseless in the open. Especially if you were an Alpha with as many enemies as Mika had.

Three figures slipped in from a door at the opposite end of the hall, and Selina's shoulders loosened a bit. Ani, Mika's Second, with two other Leopards flanking her.

Good. They'd guard the exit while their Alpha tended to their own.

The crowd's cheering rumbled through the concrete floor, rattling the loose ceramic tiles on the walls, echoing along Selina's bones and breath as she neared the dented metal door to the arena. The bouncer gestured for her to hurry the hell up, but she kept her strides even. Stalking.

The Leopards, these fights . . . they were her job. And it paid well. With her mother gone and her sister sick, no legit job could pay as much or as quickly.

The bouncer opened the door, the unfiltered roar of the crowd bursting down the hall like a pack of rabid wolves.

Selina Kyle blew out a long breath as she lifted her chin and stepped into the sound and the light and the wrath.

Let the bloodying begin.

DAUGHTER OF IMMORTALS.

DAUGHTER OF DEATH.

THEIR FRIENDSHIP

WILL CHANGE THE WORLD.

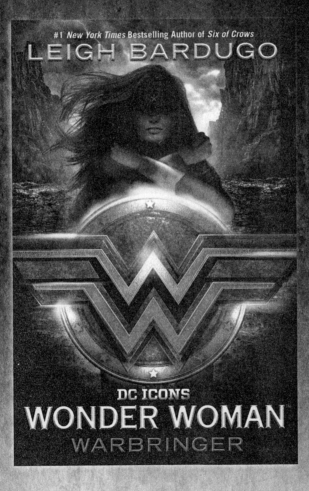

TURN THE PAGE TO SEE HOW

DIANA'S BATTLE BEGINS

IN THE NEXT DC ICONS STORY!

CHAPTER 1

You do not enter a race to lose.

Diana bounced lightly on her toes at the starting line, her calves taut as bowstrings, her mother's words reverberating in her ears. A noisy crowd had gathered for the wrestling matches and javelin throws that would mark the start of the Nemeseian Games, but the real event was the footrace, and now the stands were buzzing with word that the queen's daughter had entered the competition.

When Hippolyta had seen Diana amid the runners clustered on the arena sands, she'd displayed no surprise. As was tradition, she'd descended from her viewing platform to wish the athletes luck in their endeavors, sharing a joke here, offering a kind word of encouragement there. She had nodded briefly to Diana, showing her no special favor, but she'd whispered, so low that only her daughter could hear, "You do not enter a race to lose."

Amazons lined the path that led out of the arena, already stamping their feet and chanting for the games to begin.

On Diana's right, Rani flashed her a radiant smile. "Good luck today." She was always kind, always gracious, and, of course, always victorious.

To Diana's left, Thyra snorted and shook her head. "She's going to need it."

Diana ignored her. She'd been looking forward to this race for weeks—a trek across the island to retrieve one of the red flags hung beneath the great dome in Bana-Mighdall. In a flat-out sprint, she didn't have a chance. She still hadn't come into the fullness of her Amazon strength. *You will in time*, her mother had promised. But her mother promised a lot of things.

This race was different. It required strategy, and Diana was ready. She'd been training in secret, running sprints with Maeve, and plotting a route that had rougher terrain but was definitely a straighter shot to the western tip of the island. She'd even— well, she hadn't exactly *spied*. . . . She'd gathered intelligence on the other Amazons in the race. She was still the smallest, and of course the youngest, but she'd shot up in the last year, and she was nearly as tall as Thyra now.

I don't need luck, she told herself. *I have a plan.* She glanced down the row of Amazons gathered at the starting line like troops readying for war and amended, *But a little luck wouldn't hurt, either.* She wanted that laurel crown. It was better than any royal circlet or tiara—an honor that couldn't be given, that had to be earned.

She found Maeve's red hair and freckled face in the crowd and grinned, trying to project confidence. Maeve returned the smile and gestured with both hands as if she were tamping down the air. She mouthed the words, "Steady on."

Diana rolled her eyes but nodded and tried to slow her breathing. She had a bad habit of coming out too fast and wasting her speed too early.

Now she cleared her mind and forced herself to concentrate on the course as Tekmessa walked the line, surveying the runners, jewels glinting in her thick corona of curls, silver bands flashing on her brown arms. She was Hippolyta's closest advisor, second in rank only to the queen, and she carried herself as if her belted indigo shift were battle armor.

"Take it easy, Pyxis," Tek murmured to Diana as she passed. "Wouldn't want to see you crack." Diana heard Thyra snort again, but she refused to flinch at the nickname. *You won't be smirking when I'm on the victors' podium*, she promised.

Tek raised her hands for silence and bowed to Hippolyta, who sat between two other members of the Amazon Council in the royal loge—a high platform shaded by a silken overhang dyed in the vibrant red and blue of the queen's colors. Diana knew that was where her mother wanted her right now, seated beside her, waiting for the start of the games instead of competing. None of that would matter when she won.

Hippolyta dipped her chin the barest amount, elegant in her white tunic and riding trousers, a simple circlet resting against her forehead. She looked relaxed, at her ease, as if she might decide to leap down and join the competition at any time, but still every inch the queen.

Tek addressed the athletes gathered on the arena sands. "In whose honor do you compete?"

"For the glory of the Amazons," they replied in unison. "For the glory of our queen." Diana felt her heart beat harder. She'd never said the words before, not as a competitor.

"To whom do we give praise each day?" Tek trumpeted.

"Hera," they chorused. "Athena, Demeter, Hestia, Aphrodite, Artemis." The goddesses who had created Themyscira and gifted it to Hippolyta as a place of refuge.

Tek paused, and along the line, Diana heard the whispers of other names: Oya, Durga, Freyja, Mary, Yael. Names once cried out in death, the last prayers of female warriors fallen in battle, the words that had brought them to this island and given them new life as Amazons. Beside Diana, Rani murmured the names of the demon-fighting Matri, the seven mothers, and pressed the rectangular amulet she always wore to her lips.

Tek raised a blood-red flag identical to those that would be waiting for the runners in Bana-Mighdall.

"May the island guide you to just victory!" she shouted.

She dropped the red silk. The crowd roared. The runners surged toward the eastern arch. Like that, the race had begun.

Diana and Maeve had anticipated a bottleneck, but Diana still felt a pang of frustration as runners clogged the stone throat of the tunnel, a tangle of white tunics and muscled limbs, footsteps echoing off the stone, all of them trying to get clear of the arena at once. Then they were on the road, sprinting across the island, each runner choosing her own course.

You do not enter a race to lose.

Diana set her pace to the rhythm of those words, bare feet slapping the packed earth of the road that would lead her through the tangle of the Cybelian Woods to the island's northern coast.

Ordinarily, a miles-long trek through this forest would be a slow one, hampered by fallen trees and tangles of vines so thick they had to be hacked through with a blade you didn't mind dulling. But Diana had plotted her way well. An hour after she entered the woods, she burst from the trees onto the deserted coast road. The wind lifted her hair, and salt spray lashed her face. She breathed deep, checked the position of the sun. She was going to win—not just place but win.

She'd mapped out the course the week before with Maeve, and they'd run it twice in secret, in the gray-light hours of early morning, when their sisters were first rising from their beds, when the kitchen fires were still being kindled, and the only curious eyes they'd had to worry about belonged to anyone up early to hunt game or cast nets for the day's catch. But hunters kept to the woods and meadows farther south, and no one fished off this part of the coast; there was no good place to launch a boat, just the steep steel-colored cliffs plunging straight down to the sea, and a tiny, unwelcoming cove that could only be reached by a path so narrow you had to shuffle down sideways, back pressed to the rock.

The northern shore was gray, grim, and inhospitable, and Diana knew every inch of its secret landscape, its crags and caves, its tide pools teeming with limpets and anemones. It was a good place to be alone. *The island seeks to please,* her mother had told her. It was why Themyscira was forested by redwoods in some places and rubber trees in others; why you could spend an afternoon roaming the grasslands on a scoop-neck pony and the evening atop a camel, scaling a moonlit dragonback of sand dunes. They were all pieces of the lives the Amazons had led before they came to the island, little landscapes of the heart.

Diana sometimes wondered if Themyscira had called the northern coast into being just for her so that she could challenge herself climbing on the sheer drop of its cliffs, so that she could have a place to herself when the weight of being Hippolyta's daughter got to be too much.

You do not enter a race to lose.

Her mother had not been issuing a general warning. Diana's losses meant something different, and they both knew it—and not only because she was a princess.

Diana could almost feel Tek's knowing gaze on her, hear the mocking in her voice. *Take it easy, Pyxis.* That was the nickname Tek had given her. Pyxis. A little clay pot made to store jewels or a tincture of carmine for pinking the lips. The name was harmless, meant to tease, always said in love—or so Tek claimed. But it stung every time: a reminder that Diana was not like the other Amazons, and never would be. Her sisters were battle-proven warriors, steel forged from suffering and honed to greatness as they passed from life to immortality. All of them had earned their place on Themyscira. All but Diana, born of the island's soil and Hippolyta's longing for a child, fashioned from clay by her mother's hands—hollow and breakable. *Take it easy, Pyxis. Wouldn't want to see you crack.*

Diana steadied her breathing, kept her pace even. *Not today, Tek. This day the laurel belongs to me.*

She spared the briefest glance at the horizon, letting the sea breeze cool the sweat on her brow. Through the mists, she glimpsed the white shape of a ship. It had come close enough to the boundary that Diana could make out its sails. The craft was small—a schooner maybe? She had trouble remembering nautical details. Mainmast, mizzenmast, a thousand names for sails, and knots for rigging. It was one thing to be out on a boat, learning from Teuta, who had sailed with Illyrian pirates, but quite another to be stuck in the library at the Epheseum, staring glazed-eyed at diagrams of a brigantine or a caravel.

Sometimes Diana and Maeve made a game of trying to spot ships or planes, and once they'd even seen the fat blot of a cruise ship on the horizon. But most mortals knew to steer clear of their particular corner of the Aegean, where compasses spun and instruments suddenly refused to obey.

Today it looked like a storm was picking up past the mists of the boundary, and Diana was sorry she couldn't stop to watch it. The rains that came to Themyscira were tediously gentle and predictable, nothing like the threatening rumble of thunder, the shimmer of a far-off lightning strike.

"Do you ever miss storms?" Diana had asked one afternoon as she and Maeve lazed on the palace's sun-soaked rooftop terrace, listening to the distant roar and clatter of a tempest. Maeve had died in the Crossbarry Ambush, the last words on her lips a prayer to Saint Brigid of Kildare. She was new to the island by Amazon standards, and came from Cork, where storms were common.

"No," Maeve had said in her lilting voice. "I miss a good cup of tea, dancing, boys—definitely not rain."

"We dance," Diana protested.

Maeve had just laughed. "You dance differently when you know you won't live forever." Then she'd stretched, freckles like dense clouds of pollen on her white skin. "I think I was a cat in another life, because all I want is to lie around sleeping in the world's biggest sunbeam."

Steady on. Diana resisted the urge to speed forward. It was hard to remember to keep something in reserve with the early-morning sun on her shoulders and the wind at her back. She felt strong. But it was easy to feel strong when she was on her own.

A *boom* sounded over the waves, a hard metallic clap like a door slamming shut. Diana's steps faltered. On the blue horizon, a billowing column of smoke rose, flames licking at its base. The schooner was on fire, its prow blown to splinters and one of its masts smashed, the sail dragging over the rails.

Diana found herself slowing but forced her stride back on pace. There was nothing she could do for the schooner. Planes crashed. Ships were wrecked upon the rocks. That was the nature of the mortal world. It was a place where disaster could happen and often did. Human life was a tide of misery, one that never reached the island's shores. Diana focused her eyes on the path. Far, far ahead she could see sunlight gleaming gold off the great dome at Bana-Mighdall. First the red flag, then the laurel crown. That was the plan.

From somewhere on the wind, she heard a cry.

A gull, she told herself. *A girl*, some other voice within her insisted. *Impossible.* A human shout couldn't carry over such a great distance, could it?

It didn't matter. There was nothing she could do.

And yet her eyes strayed back to the horizon. *I just want to get a better view*, she told herself. *I have plenty of time. I'm ahead.*

There was no good reason to leave the ruts of the old cart track, no logic to veering out over the rocky point, but she did it anyway.

The waters near the shore were calm, clear, vibrant turquoise. The ocean beyond was something else—wild, deep-well blue, a sea gone almost black. The island might seek to please her and her sisters, but the world beyond the boundary didn't concern itself with the happiness or safety of its inhabitants.

Even from a distance, she could tell the schooner was sinking. But she saw no lifeboats, no distress flares, only pieces of the broken craft carried along by rolling waves. It was done. Diana rubbed her hands briskly over her arms, dispelling a sudden chill, and started making her way back to the cart track. That was the way of human life. She and Maeve had dived out by the boundary many times, swum the wrecks of airplanes and clipper ships and sleek motorboats. The salt water changed the wood, hardened it so it did not rot. Mortals were not the same. They were food for deep-sea fishes, for sharks—and for time that ate at them slowly, inevitably, whether they were on water or on land.

Diana checked the sun's position again. She could be at Bana-Mighdall in forty minutes, maybe less. She told her legs to move. She'd only lost a few moments. She could make up the time. Instead, she looked over her shoulder.

There were stories in all the old books about women who made the mistake of looking back. On the way out of burning cities. On the way out of hell. But Diana still turned her eyes to that ship sinking in the great waves, tilting like a bird's broken wing.

She measured the length of the cliff top. There were jagged rocks at the base. If she didn't leap with enough momentum, the impact would be ugly. Still, the fall wouldn't kill her. *That's true of a real Amazon*, she thought. *Is it true for you?* Well, she *hoped* the fall wouldn't kill her. Of course, if the fall didn't, her mother would.

Diana looked once more at the wreck and pushed off, running full out, arms pumping, stride long, picking up speed, closing the distance to the cliff's edge. *Stop stop stop*, her mind clamored. *This is madness.* Even if there were survivors, she could do nothing for them. To try to save them was to court exile, and there would be no exception to the rule—not even for a princess. *Stop.* She wasn't sure why she didn't obey. She wanted to believe it was because a hero's heart beat in her chest and demanded she answer that frightened call. But even as she launched herself off the cliff and into the empty sky, she knew part of what drew her on was the challenge of that great gray sea that did not care if she loved it.

Her body cut a smooth arc through the air, arms pointing like a compass needle, directing her course. She plummeted toward the water and broke the surface in a clean plunge, ears full of sudden silence, muscles tensed for the brutal impact of the rocks. None came. She shot upward, drew in a breath, and swam straight for the boundary, arms slicing through the warm water.

There was always a little thrill when she neared the boundary, when the temperature of the water began to change, the cold touching her fingertips first, then settling over her scalp and shoulders. Diana and Maeve liked to swim out from the southern beaches, daring themselves to go farther, farther. Once they'd glimpsed a ship passing in the mist, sailors standing at the stern. One of the men had lifted an arm, pointing in their direction. They'd plunged to safety, gesturing wildly to each other beneath the waves, laughing so hard that by the time they reached shore, they were both choking on salt water. *We could be sirens*, Maeve had shrieked as they'd flopped onto the warm sand, except neither of them could carry a tune. They'd spent the rest of the afternoon singing violently off-key Irish drinking songs and laughing themselves silly until Tek had found them. Then they'd shut up quick. Breaking the boundary was a minor infraction. Being seen by mortals anywhere near the island was cause for serious disciplinary action. And what Diana was doing now?

Stop. But she couldn't. Not when that high human cry still rang in her ears.

Diana felt the cold water beyond the boundary engulf her fully. The sea had her now, and it was not friendly. The current seized her legs, dragging her down, a massive, rolling force, the barest shrug of a god. *You have to fight it*, she realized, demanding that her muscles correct her course. She'd never had to work against the ocean.

She bobbed for a moment on the surface, trying to get her bearings as the waves crested around her. The water was full of debris, shards of wood, broken fiberglass, orange life jackets that the crew must not have had time to don. It was nearly impossible to see through the falling rain and the mists that shrouded the island.

What am I doing out here? she asked herself. *Ships come and go. Human lives are lost.* She dove again, peered through the rushing gray waters, but saw no one.

Diana surfaced, her own stupidity carving a growing ache in

her gut. She'd sacrificed the race. This was supposed to be the moment her sisters saw her truly, the chance to make her mother proud. Instead, she'd thrown away her lead, and for what? There was nothing here but destruction.

Out of the corner of her eye, she saw a flash of white, a big chunk of what might have been the ship's hull. It rose on a wave, vanished, rose again, and as it did, Diana glimpsed a slender brown arm holding tight to the side, fingers spread, knuckles bent. Then it was gone.

Another wave rose, a great gray mountain. Diana dove beneath it, kicking hard, then surfaced, searching, bits of lumber and fiber-glass everywhere, impossible to sort one piece of flotsam from another.

There it was again—an arm, two arms, a body, bowed head and hunched shoulders, lemon-colored shirt, a tangle of dark hair. A girl—she lifted her head, gasped for breath, dark eyes wild with fear. A wave crashed over her in a spray of white water. The chunk of hull surfaced. The girl was gone.

Down again. Diana aimed for the place she'd seen the girl go under. She glimpsed a flash of yellow and lunged for it, seizing the fabric and using it to reel her in. A ghost's face loomed out at her from the cloudy water—golden hair, blue gaze wide and lifeless. She'd never seen a corpse up close before. She'd never seen a boy up close before. She recoiled, hand releasing his shirt, but even as she watched him disappear, she marked the differences—hard jaw, broad brow, just like the pictures in books.

She resurfaced, but she'd lost all sense of direction now—the waves, the wreck, the bare shadow of the island in the mists. If she drifted out much farther, she might not be able to find her way back.

Diana could not stop seeing the image of that slender arm, the ferocity in those fingers, clinging hard to life. *Once more*, she told herself. She dove, the chill of the water fastening tight around her bones now, burrowing deeper.

One moment the world was gray current and cloudy sea, and

the next the girl was there in her lemon-colored shirt, facedown, arms and legs outstretched like a star. Her eyes were closed.

Diana grabbed her around the waist and launched them toward the surface. For a terrifying second, she could not find the shape of the island, and then the mists parted. She kicked forward, wrapping the girl awkwardly against her chest with one arm, fingers questing for a pulse with the other. *There*—beneath the jaw, thready, indistinct, but there. Though the girl wasn't breathing, her heart still beat.

Diana hesitated. She could see the outlines of Filos and Ecthros, the rocks that marked the rough beginnings of the boundary. The rules were clear. You could not stop the mortal tide of life and death, and the island must never be touched by it. There were no exceptions. No human could be brought to Themyscira, even if it meant saving a life. Breaking that rule meant only one thing: exile.

Exile. The word was a stone, unwanted ballast, the weight unbearable. It was one thing to breach the boundary, but what she did next might untether her from the island, her sisters, her mother forever. The world seemed too large, the sea too deep. *Let go.* It was that simple. Let this girl slip from her grasp and it would be as if Diana had never leapt from those cliffs. She would be light again, free of this burden.

Diana thought of the girl's hand, the ferocious grip of her knuckles, the steel-blade determination in her eyes before the wave took her under. She felt the ragged rhythm of the girl's pulse, a distant drum, the sound of an army marching—one that had fought well but could not fight on much longer.

She swam for shore.

As she passed through the boundary with the girl clutched to her, the mists dissolved and the rain abated. Warmth flooded her body. The calm water felt oddly lifeless after the thrashing of the sea, but Diana wasn't about to complain.

When her feet touched the sandy bottom, she shoved up, shifting her grip to carry the girl from the shallows. She was eerily light, almost insubstantial. It was like holding a sparrow's body between her cupped hands. No wonder the sea had made such easy sport of this creature and her crewmates; she felt temporary, an artist's cast of a body rendered in plaster.

Diana laid her gently on the sand and checked her pulse again. No heartbeat now. She knew she needed to get the girl's heart going, get the water out of her lungs, but her memory on just how to do that was a bit hazy. Diana had studied the basics of reviving a drowning victim, but she hadn't ever had to put it into practice outside the classroom. It was also possible she hadn't paid close attention at the time. How likely was it that an Amazon was going to drown, especially in the calm waters off Themyscira? And now her daydreaming might cost this girl her life.

Do something, she told herself, trying to think past her panic. *Why did you drag her out of the water if you're only going to sit staring at her like a frightened rabbit?*

Diana placed two fingers on the girl's sternum, then tracked lower to what she hoped was the right spot. She locked her hands together and pressed. The girl's bones bent beneath her palms. Hurriedly, Diana drew back. What was this girl made of, anyway? Balsa wood? She felt about as solid as the little models of world monuments Diana had been forced to build for class. Gently, she pressed down again, then again. She shut the girl's nose with her fingers, closed her mouth over cooling mortal lips, and breathed.

The gust drove into the girl's chest, and Diana saw it rise, but this time the extra force seemed to be a good thing. Suddenly, the girl was coughing, her body convulsing as she spat up salt water. Diana sat back on her knees and released a short laugh. She'd done it. The girl was alive.

The reality of what she'd just dared struck her. All the hounds of Hades: *She'd done it. The girl was alive.*

And trying to sit up.

"Here," Diana said, bracing the girl's back with her arm. She couldn't simply kneel there, watching her flop around on the sand like a fish, and it wasn't as if she could put her back in the ocean. Could she? No. Mortals were clearly too good at drowning.

The girl clutched her chest, taking huge, sputtering gulps of air. "The others," she gasped. Her eyes were so wide Diana could see white ringing her irises all the way around. She was trembling, but Diana wasn't sure if it was because she was cold or going into shock. "We have to help them—"

Diana shook her head. If there had been any other signs of life in the wreck, she hadn't seen them. Besides, time passed more quickly in the mortal world. Even if she swam back out, the storm would have long since had its way with any bodies or debris.

"They're gone," said Diana, then wished she'd chosen her words more carefully. The girl's mouth opened, closed. Her body was shaking so hard Diana thought it might break apart. That couldn't actually happen, could it?

Diana scanned the cliffs above the beach. Someone might have seen her swim out. She felt confident no other runner had chosen this course, but anyone could have seen the explosion and come to investigate.

"I need to get you off the beach. Can you walk?" The girl nodded, but her teeth were chattering, and she made no move to stand. Diana's eyes scoured the cliffs again. "Seriously, I need you to get up."

"I'm trying."

She didn't look like she was trying. Diana searched her memory for everything she'd been told about mortals, the soft stuff—eating habits, body temperature, cultural norms. Unfortunately, her mother and her tutors were more focused on what Diana referred to as the Dire Warnings: War. Torture. Genocide. Pollution. Bad Grammar.

The girl shivering before her on the sand didn't seem to qualify for inclusion in the Dire Warnings category. She looked about the same age as Diana, brown-skinned, her hair a tangle of long, tiny braids covered in sand. She was clearly too weak to hurt anyone but herself. Even so, she could be plenty dangerous to Diana. Exile dangerous. Banished-forever dangerous. Better not to think about that. Instead, she thought back to her classes with Teuta. *Make a plan. Battles are often lost because people don't know which war they're fighting.* All right. The girl couldn't walk any great distance in her condition. Maybe that was a good thing, given that Diana had nowhere to take her.

She rested what she hoped was a comforting hand on the girl's shoulder. "Listen, I know you're feeling weak, but we should try to get off the beach."

"Why?"

Diana hesitated, then opted for an answer that was technically true if not wholly accurate. "High tide."

It seemed to do the trick, because the girl nodded. Diana stood and offered her a hand.

"I'm fine," the girl said, shoving to her knees and then pushing up to her feet.

"You're stubborn," Diana said with some measure of respect. The girl had almost drowned and seemed to be about as solid as driftwood and down, but she wasn't eager to accept help—and she definitely wasn't going to like what Diana suggested next. "I need you to climb on my back."

A crease appeared between the girl's brows. "Why?"

"Because I don't think you can make it up the cliffs."

"Is there a path?"

"No," said Diana. That was definitely a lie. Instead of arguing, Diana turned her back. A minute later, she felt a pair of arms around her neck. The girl hopped on, and Diana reached back to take hold of her thighs and hitch her into position. "Hold on tight."

The girl's arms clamped around her windpipe. "Not that tight!" Diana choked out.

"Sorry!" She loosened her hold.

Diana took off at a jog.

The girl groaned. "Slow down. I think I'm going to vomit."

"Vomit?" Diana scanned her knowledge of mortal bodily functions and immediately smoothed her gait. "Do *not* do that."

"Just don't drop me."

"You weigh about as much as a heavy pair of boots." Diana

picked her way through the big boulders wedged against the base of the cliff. "I need my arms to climb, so you're going to have to hold on with your legs, too."

"Climb?"

"The cliff."

"You're taking me *up the side of the cliff*? Are you out of your mind?"

"Just hold on and try not to strangle me." Diana dug her fingers into the rock and started putting distance between them and the ground before the girl could think too much more about it.

She moved quickly. This was familiar territory. Diana had scaled these cliffs countless times since she'd started visiting the north shore, and when she was twelve, she'd discovered the cave where they were headed. There were other caves, lower on the cliff face, but they filled when the tide came in. Besides, they were too easy to crawl out of if someone got curious.

The girl groaned again.

"Almost there," Diana said encouragingly.

"I'm not opening my eyes."

"Probably for the best. Just don't . . . you know."

"Puke all over you?"

"Yes," said Diana. "That." Amazons didn't get sick, but vomiting appeared in any number of novels and featured in a particularly vivid description from her anatomy book. Blessedly, there were no illustrations.

At last, Diana hauled them up into the divot in the rock that marked the cave's entrance. The girl rolled off and heaved a long breath. The cave was tall, narrow, and surprisingly deep, as if someone had taken a cleaver to the center of the cliff. Its gleaming black rock sides were perpetually damp with sea spray. When she was younger, Diana had liked to pretend that if she kept walking, the cave would lead straight through the cliff and open onto some other land entirely. It didn't. It was just a cave, and remained a cave no matter how hard she wished.

Diana waited for her eyes to adjust, then shuffled farther

inside. The old horse blanket was still there—wrapped in oilcloth and mostly dry, if a bit musty—as well as her tin box of supplies.

She wrapped the blanket around the girl's shoulders.

"We aren't going to the top?" asked the girl.

"Not yet." Diana had to get back to the arena. The race must be close to over by now, and she didn't want people wondering where she'd gotten to. "Are you hungry?"

The girl shook her head. "We need to call the police, search and rescue."

"That isn't possible."

"I don't know what happened," the girl said, starting to shake again. "Jasmine and Ray were arguing with Dr. Ellis and then—"

"There was an explosion. I saw it from shore."

"It's my fault," the girl said as tears spilled over her cheeks. "They're dead and it's my fault."

"Don't," Diana said gently, feeling a surge of panic. "It was the storm." She laid her hand on the girl's shoulder. "What's your name?"

"Alia," the girl said, burying her head in her arms.

"Alia, I need to go, but—"

"No!" Alia said sharply. "Don't leave me here."

"I have to. I . . . need to get help." What Diana needed was to get back to Ephesus and figure out how to get this girl off the island before anyone found out about her.

Alia grabbed hold of her arm, and again Diana remembered the way she'd clung to that piece of hull. "Please," Alia said. "Hurry. Maybe they can send a helicopter. There could be survivors."

"I'll be back as soon as I can," Diana promised. She slid the tin box toward the girl. "There are dried peaches and pili seeds and a little fresh water inside. Don't drink it all at once."

Alia's eyelids stuttered. "All at once? How long will you be gone?"

"Maybe a few hours. I'll be back as fast as I can. Just stay warm and rest." Diana rose. "And don't leave the cave."

Alia looked up at her. Her eyes were deep brown and heavily

lashed, her gaze fearful but steady. For the first time since Diana had pulled her from the water, Alia seemed to be truly seeing her. "Where are we?" she asked. "What is this place?"

Diana wasn't quite sure how to answer, so all she said was "This is my home."

She hooked her hands back into the rock and ducked out of the cave before Alia could ask anything else.

DC ICONS

CLARK